THE DARK
CAULDRON

With special thanks to Elizabeth Galloway

For Jo Hoyle, with much love

www.beastquest.co.uk

ORCHARD BOOKS
338 Euston Road, London NW1 3BH
Orchard Books Australia
Level 17/207 Kent St, Sydney, NSW 2000

A Paperback Original
First published in Great Britain in 2010

Beast Quest is a registered trademark of Beast Quest Limited
Series created by Beast Quest Limited, London

A CIP catalogue record for this book is available from
the British Library.

ISBN 978 1 40830 943 8

7 9 10 8

Printed in Great Britain by CPI Group (UK) Ltd, Croydon, CR0 4YY

The paper and board used in this paperback are natural recyclable
products made from wood grown in sustainable forests. The
manufacturing processes conform to the environmental regulations
of the country of origin.

Orchard Books is a division of Hachette Children's Books,
an Hachette UK company.

www.hachette.co.uk

MASTER YOUR DESTINY

THE DARK
CAULDRON

BY ADAM BLADE

ORCHARD BOOKS

CAUSEWAY

THE FOREST
OF FEAR

RIVER OF LAVA

SEXTON

CAVES

GRASSY
PLAINS

RAPIDS

THE WINDING RIVER

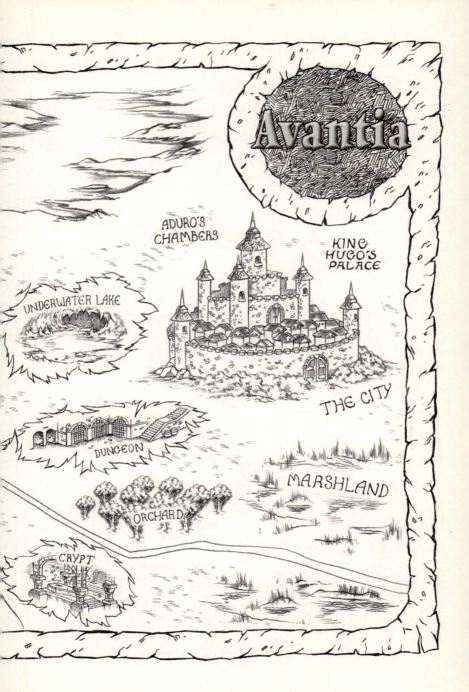

Avantia is doomed!

I have stolen Wizard Aduro's magic cauldron, and soon I will use its power to destroy the kingdom. The cauldron is guarded by two terrifying Beasts – Aldroim the Shape Shifter and Cornix the Deadly Trickster. Anyone who tries to take it from me must battle Aldroim's slashing talons and Cornix's clawed wings.

But what's this? Tom and Elenna have long fought against my Beasts, and now they have a new companion on their Quest – YOU.

Do you have the strength and courage to defeat Aldroim and Cornix? Can you reclaim the cauldron before I destroy Avantia forever?

Have your sword ready...

Malvel

1

"On guard!" shouts Tom.

You charge, your wooden practice swords clattering together. Tom's sword goes spinning out of his hand.

Taladon, Avantia's Master of the Beasts, suggested you take weaponry practice with Tom and Elenna, as part of your training to be a knight.

"You've won," Tom laughs. "Maybe you should go on the Beast Quests instead of me!"

But the sky suddenly darkens. Black angry clouds swirl overhead.

Elenna stops firing arrows into a straw target. "What's happening?" she cries.

A mocking cackle echoes around you, seeming to wind its way round the palace turrets.

"Malvel," says Tom grimly. The Dark Wizard of Avantia is up to something.

A spear of jagged lightning strikes the palace's tallest tower, where the Good Wizard, Aduro, has his chambers. Smoke billows from its windows. You all cast aside your practice swords and arrows, grab your real weapons, and race up the tower's spiral steps.

Aduro is lying, shaken, on the floor of his spell room. You rush to his side. The Good Wizard points to the empty space in the corner of the room.

"My magic cauldron," he says. "Malvel has stolen it! He has created two terrible new Beasts to guard it: Aldroim the Shape Shifter and Corvix the Deadly Trickster." Aduro grows pale. "With the cauldron, Malvel will have enough power to destroy the kingdom."

You pull back your shoulders, hand on the hilt of your sword. "Then it's up to us to get it back. Which way did the Beasts go?"

⟞⟢ *Choose your destiny* ⟞⟢

To search the castle's dungeons with Tom, turn to
47.

To scour the lands surrounding the castle with Elenna, turn to **26**.

2

"That cauldron belongs to Aduro!" you yell. Your swords raised, you and Tom charge at Malvel.

But the Dark Wizard knocks you both aside with another blast of magic. You peel yourself off the ground, only for Malvel to knock you back down again. Warm blood trickles down your face. You hear Elenna scream as Aldroim sinks his jaws into her neck. Then her limp body falls to the ground.

You struggle to kneel but Malvel grins down at you, aiming his staff to deliver the final blow.

Your Quest has failed. And now Avantia is doomed...

3

"I don't trust that light," you say.

As you, Elenna, Lightning, Storm and Silver back away, the cave ceiling groans.

"It's a rockfall," you yell. "Run!"

"Don't leave me here," begs a voice.

You see that the light's being held by a woman wearing a red velvet cloak, with long hair tumbling over her face.

"Come with us," you call.

She approaches – and then throws aside her cloak, revealing the feathery body of a crow. Her wings are clawed and her face is a terrifying human skull. Cornix the Deadly Trickster!

Cornix seizes Elenna, smothering her with her cloak. You strike at her, but she swipes your blade aside. You need to get the Beast away from Elenna – fast!

"Come on," you challenge Cornix, throwing aside your weapons. "I'm unarmed!"

The Beast's face twists into a gruesome grin. As Cornix springs from Elenna

towards you, the falling rocks knock her to the ground. You seize your sword and run her through. The Beast melts away - and in her place is Aduro's cauldron!

As the caves collapse, you race out to the Winding River. A rickety bridge sways over the swirling rapids. It's the quickest way to the palace – but is it safe?

 *Choose your destiny*

*To go over the bridge, turn to **7**.*

*To go upriver and try to find a safer crossing, turn to **30**.*

4

You lead Lightning, Elenna and Silver into the caves. The light soon fades.

"Anything could attack us in here," mutters Elenna, as you stumble along.

But after a while you see an orb of light glowing ahead.

You all run towards it – then Elenna screams. She's fallen through the cave floor!

You drop to your hands and knees, crawling along until you reach a hole where Elenna's clinging to the edge. At the bottom you can see hundreds of glinting eyes. It's a snake pit! You haul Elenna to safety, your muscles shaking.

The orb of light flickers. You wonder if it lured you to the snake pit...or if it's your only hope of finding your way in the dark.

Choose your destiny

To ignore the light, turn to ***3****.*

To follow the light, turn to ***19****.*

5

As you leave the green portal, you rub
your eyes, hardly believing the wonderful
scene before you. You, Tom and Elenna are
in King Hugo's Banqueting Hall. Taladon
smiles at you from across a table groaning
with delicious food.

Tom gets to his feet, raising his goblet for
a toast. He grins at you. "You're a true
knight of Avantia! Will you join me and
Elenna on our next Beast Quest?"

The End

6

"Charge!" you yell. You all rush at Aldroim.

The Beast springs at Silver. You wrestle Aldroim away, but he fires a blast of oil at you and crouches, ready to spring again.

"Attack!" you cry, and you all charge at the Beast again – but he turns into thousands of droplets of oil. On the ground is the cauldron!

You hear Aldroim's snarls – the Beast isn't yet defeated. Should you stay and fight him, or take the cauldron back to Aduro?

Choose your destiny

To ride to the palace, turn to **8**.

To fight Aldroim, turn to **13**.

7

"Come on, Lightning," you say. "We must cross the bridge!"

Your mare whinnies with fear, so you dismount and lead her forwards. Elenna, Storm and Silver follow.

Crash! The bridge splits, and you all plunge into the rapids.

Water fills your nose and mouth, but you kick upwards. With a gasp, you emerge above the surface. You and Elenna manage to steer the animals to shore.

Suddenly, a cloud of Malvel's evil bats appear, clawing your faces. Silver snaps at them as they try to seize the cauldron.

Elenna casts you a desperate glance. "If we can't shake off these bats, we'll never get to the palace."

Choose your destiny

To stay together and head for the palace,
turn to 10.

To send Elenna on ahead with the cauldron
while you fight the bats, turn to 21.

8

"To the palace!" you yell and ride off on Lightning. Tom and Elenna follow behind on Storm, and Silver runs alongside them. You glance over your shoulder at the lake. Aldroim glimmers on the surface in the form of an oil slick. But when you look back a second time, the oil slick has gone...

A huge shadow falls over you. Aldroim – in cat-form – has leapt into the air, heading straight for you. The Beast's front claws rake Lightning's back, and your terrified horse bucks, throwing you to the ground. She gallops off into the forest, screaming in terror and pain.

You immediately leap to your feet and circle the snarling Beast. When you swing your sword at him, he lunges aside and leaps at you. You spin away just in time.

"We need to surround him," shouts Tom, with Elenna by his side. "If we fight together, we'll be strong enough to defeat him."

But you know that Aldroim is immensely powerful and cunning. After all, he almost killed you with a sneaky attack. In order to save the others, should you try to defeat this Beast alone?

Choose your destiny

To take Tom's advice, turn to **39**.

To attack Aldroim alone, turn to **14**.

9

"Let her go!" you yell, charging at Aldroim.

You slash the Beast's coat with your
sword, and he gives a roar of fury. He
shoots jets of oil from between his jaws
and you duck and weave to avoid them.
Furious, the Beast leaps at you and you
just have time to raise your shield to
defend yourself.

You're knocked onto the ground,
Aldroim standing over you. It's over...

But an arrow plunges into the Beast's
shoulder. Elenna! She must have wriggled
free when the Beast leapt at you. She fires
more arrows at Aldroim, and you roll
aside. Defeated for now, the Beast leaps
into the lake and once more turns into an
oil slick.

Tom and Malvel are battling further
down the lake shore. Tom seems exhausted
– rather than attacking Malvel, he's forced
to deflect bolts of magic with his shield.

Malvel raises his hand and blasts Tom so
powerfully that he falls to the ground. The

wizard raises his staff – he's about to strike the killing blow. You need to act now! But the wrong decision will cost Tom's life.

Choose your destiny

To attack Malvel with the dagger you found,
turn to **17**.
To deflect Malvel's blow with your shield,
turn to **32**.

"We'll make it to the palace if we stick together," you tell Elenna.

Through the evil squeaking of the vicious bats, you hear mocking laughter.

The bats carry the cauldron over to the Dark Wizard.

You see Malvel chanting a spell. Green smoke billows from the cauldron. It wraps around the plants and trees, making them wither and die.

Malvel is poisoning the kingdom.

Your Quest has failed. And now Avantia is doomed...

11

You close your eyes as you all step through the blue portal. Any moment now you'll be in the palace, with King Hugo, Aduro and Taladon congratulating you on completing a dangerous Quest.

You've never been in a portal before; you're surprised it's so hot. You open your eyes, and see that Tom and Elenna are looking worried.

"This doesn't feel right," you say. "We should turn back."

But the portal entrance is closed. There is no way back.

You give a cry of terror as the walls and ground below you turns to fire. Flames lick and whip at you.

The last thing you hear is the sound of Malvel's mocking laughter as he says: "I win."

Your Quest has failed. And now Avantia is doomed...

12

"Now!" you yell, and powerfully strike your blade against Tom's. Sparks fly from the metal, falling onto the Beast. Aldroim's hide smokes, starts to melt, then explodes into a fireball. You, Tom and Elenna are blasted aside. With a terrible cry, the Beast vanishes.

"Yes!" you shout. "We did it! Now we just need to take the cauldron back to the palace."

The air in front of you shimmers and Aduro magically appears. "You are true servants of Avantia," he says, as you pass him the cauldron. "It looks like Tom and Elenna have a new companion for their Quests!" But then the wizard becomes serious. "You still have one more choice to make," he says. "And this may be your most important decision to date."

Your heart sinks. "Has Malvel conjured up more evil Beasts?"

Aduro's wise face creases into a smile. "I have a happier choice for you than that," he laughs. "You must decide how to celebrate your success, following this perilous Quest. Now, would you like a victory parade through the streets or a delicious feast at the palace?"

Choose your destiny

To celebrate with a parade through the City, turn to **27**.

To celebrate with a banquet at King Hugo's palace, turn to **5**.

13

You, Tom and Elenna stand braced for battle. Aldroim gleams on the lake in the form of an oil slick. Then the oil foams and rises to form the ferocious shape of the Beast. Aldroim leaps from the water, his ferocious claws slashing the air.

He fires jets of oil at you, which you just manage to deflect with your shield. You strike the Beast's hide with your sword. Tom does the same, while Elenna's arrows find their mark.

As you fight, your sword accidentally jars against Tom's, and a spark flies from the clashing metal. Aldroim leaps back with a yelp of fear.

"That's it," yells Elenna. "Oil catches fire easily. Clash swords again – the sparks could destroy the Beast!"

Aldroim lunges forward and you knock the Beast back with a blow from your shield. You could do as Elenna suggests... Or should you seek the glory of defeating the Beast alone?

⊷═══┥ *Choose your destiny* ┝═══⊶
To strike swords with Tom, so you can try to destroy Aldroim with fire, turn to **12**.
To try to defeat the Beast without help from Tom or Elenna, turn to **14**.

14

"Keep away, Tom," you shout. "This Beast is mine!"

You thrust at Aldroim with your sword, but the Beast's tail sweeps round and knocks you flying.

"No!" yells Tom, and lands a blow on the Beast's side. Oily blood pours from the wound. You get to your feet, but Aldroim shoots a jet of oil into your face. You're blind!

The pain is agonising. You stagger away from the battle, the air ringing with Tom and Elenna's shouts as they continue fighting. Lightning nuzzles you, trying to offer comfort. But you push him away and keep moving. Your legs are wet and you realise you've stumbled into the lake. Water... Maybe it'll soothe the pain.

You fall into it, but the water floods your nose and lungs. You drift into oblivion...

Your Quest has failed. And now Avantia is doomed...

15

"You're right," you say to Elenna, fighting back a swell of homesickness.

You, Elenna, Lightning and Silver enter the forest. The trees are so dense that it's as dark as night. Branches and trunks loom in the gloom and Silver whines anxiously.

"What's wrong?" Elenna asks her wolf.

Silver gives a howl and races off among the trees. Elenna leaps from Lightning's back and races after the wolf.

A swirling mist descends and you dismount Lightning. She whinnies nervously as you lead her among the trees, gripping your sword tightly. You jump as eerie lights dance about you. The Beast must be nearby...

"Who's there?" you call. "Show yourself!"

"I'm right here," says a voice behind you. Elenna?

When you spin round you see a woman in a velvet cloak. Her face is covered by a hood.

"There's a Beast in this forest," you warn her. "You need to get out of here."

But the woman stays fixed to the spot. Doesn't she understand? As you push through the trees towards her, she throws aside her cloak to reveal the body of a crow and a skull instead of a face.

"Cornix!" you yell.

The Beast swoops over you, her cloak wrapping around your limbs. You fall to the ground. If you don't act quickly, you'll be killed...

Choose your destiny

To dig your fingers into Cornix's skull eyes,
turn to **18**.

To use the lantern to set Cornix's cloak alight,
turn to **35**.

16

You and Tom strain against the ropes of
animal skin that tie you to the pillar. You
can feel it loosening slightly and you're
able to slip lower down. You stretch out
one of your feet – and manage to hook the
handle of Tom's shield! You drag it towards
the pillar and Tom rubs the dragon scale.

Up in the sky, Ferno immediately turns
in the air. The Fire Dragon swoops towards
you. He slices through your bonds with
his teeth.

"We're free!" you cry, rubbing your sore wrists.

You and Tom climb onto Ferno's back and he takes off.

You spot a group of figures walking alongside a lake, far below you. As you near them, you realise it's Elenna, Lightning, Storm and Silver. Ferno alights next to them, then roars a goodbye.

Silver is behaving strangely, growling at the lake. "I can't get him to calm down," says Elenna, frowning.

Then you realise why Silver's so agitated. The sheen on the lake's surface rises into the shape of a massive leopard. Oil drips from its flanks. Aldroim!

You have the Beast surrounded – but what's the best way to attack?

Choose your destiny

*To all charge Aldroim, turn to **6**.*
To separate the group so you can attack
*and provide cover, turn to **28**.*

The black and red gems on the dagger glow as you draw it from your belt. You know this is your last chance to defeat the Evil Wizard. As he turns, you throw the dagger at him with all your strength. "For Avantia!" you yell.

Malvel gives a terrible cry as the dagger pierces his shoulder. He staggers back, dark smoke pouring from the wound. Then, in a shower of red sparks, he vanishes. The cauldron clatters to the ground and Elenna darts forward to seize it.

"We've completed the Quest!" you say, feeling dizzy with relief. It's time to take the cauldron back to Aduro.

Storm, Lightning and Silver trot up to you. But as you prepare to mount Lightning, an oily slick on the lake shimmers. Aldroim remains undefeated...

Choose your destiny

To ride back to the palace, turn to **8**.
To stay and battle with the Beast, turn to **13**.

18

"You won't defeat me!" you shout, grabbing Cornix's freezing cold skull. You dig the heels of your palms into her eye-sockets.

But as she screams in agony, you feel the flesh of your hands freeze over. She's freezing you to the spot! You try to wrestle free, but it's no good – your body is stiffening.

"I need heat," you mutter. Looking around desperately, you spot a gap in the trees, through which the sun shines onto a lake. You manage to drag Cornix and yourself over to the water, heaving your bodies into it. Immediately you feel the freezing spell break.

Cornix shrieks with fury. Her skull face and feathery body contort and crumple into dust, which is whipped away on the wind, and her red velvet cloak melts into the lake. Floating in her place is the cauldron.

There's a crash and Elenna, Lightning

and Silver burst through the trees.

"The Beast is defeated!" you call.

But your friends are being chased by a darting cloud of bats. They scratch your faces and the animals' flanks, and try to snatch the cauldron.

"They've been sent by Malvel," you cry. "To the palace!" You leap into Lightning's saddle, dragging Elenna up behind you, and gallop through the forest. The bats follow.

You emerge beside the Winding River. There's a rickety old bridge that will take you back to the palace – but is it strong enough?

⊰⊱ *Choose your destiny* ⊰⊱

*To take a chance and cross the rickety bridge, turn to **7**.*

*To gallop down-river, searching for a safer crossing point, turn to **30**.*

19

"We'll be safer if we stay with the light,"
you say. You, Elenna, Lightning and Silver
follow it through the caves. It comes to rest
in a large cavern with spear-like pillars of
glittering gems jutting from the walls.

You approach the light, and see that it's a
lantern being held by a woman in a red
velvet cloak, dark hair falling about her
shoulders.

"Who are you?" you ask.

She sweeps aside her cloak, revealing the
foul body of a massive crow. Claws line her
wings and her face is a gruesome human
skull. It's Cornix the Deadly Trickster!

"Charge!" you shout. You and Elenna
draw your weapons and lunge at the Beast.
A desperate struggle ensues as Cornix tries
to engulf you with her cloak.

"Force her back against the cave wall,"
you say to Elenna.

You swing at the Beast with your blade,
and she falls – skewering herself on one of
the gemstone pillars. With a dreadful cry,

Cornix disappears. In her place is the cauldron.

"We did it!" Elenna says.

You grab the cauldron, race from the caves and emerge by the Winding River. You need to cross it to take the cauldron back to the palace as quickly as possible. But the river swirls with dangerous rapids and the rickety bridge doesn't look safe...

Choose your destiny

*To take a chance and cross the bridge, turn to **7**.*

*To move further downriver and try to find a safer crossing point, turn to **30**.*

20

A lightning bolt strikes your chest and you spin through the air. Flashing stars wheel overhead. What's happening? you think, before blackness descends.

You open your eyes to find yourself in a dimly lit room, sitting in an upright chair. When you try to move, you realise your hands are tied behind you. You look around wildly. The walls are lined with ancient books, dead creatures preserved in jars - and live spiders spinning webs.

Malvel's spell room, you realise, your heart pounding.

"So," says Malvel, emerging from the shadows. "You've decided to fight dirty. What would Taladon say?"

You feel a rush of shame.

Malvel cackles. "When I've found your friends, I'll be back to deal with you..." He vanishes in a puff of purple smoke.

You don't have long – you need to escape! Is there anything in the spell room you can use to cut your bonds?

Your sword and shield are on a shelf, but then you see that one of the pickled creatures is a fish with razor-sharp teeth...

You rock the chair back and forth, moving it across the floor, then tilt it to smash the jar holding the fish. You lean the chair over so you can rub the rope against the fish's teeth. The ropes give, and you're free!

Now, where's the way out? The door's bolted, but you see a gap in the wall. Can

you escape through there? You notice a crack of light under one of the bookcases, too – maybe there's a passageway behind it.

⚔ *Choose your destiny* ⚔

To try to escape through the gap in the wall,
turn to **53**.

To try to escape behind the bookcase,
turn to **43**.

"Go, Elenna," you say. "Take the cauldron and ride Lightning back to the palace. I'll stay and fight the bats."

Elenna looks worried, but she does as you suggest.

The bats swoop at you but you stand your ground, felling as many as you can with your sword. You whirl round, your blade flashing, and then a lightning bolt splits the sky. Malvel appears before you.

"You've been brave to stay," sneers the Dark Wizard. "Brave but foolish! Prepare to meet your end..."

You stand with your sword raised. I'm not going to be killed without a fight, you think.

But the waters of the Winding River churn and swell, and Sepron rises from them! He lunges at Malvel with a furious roar. The Dark Wizard howls in anger as Sepron wraps him in his scaly coils, forcing him to use his magic to disappear. You're safe!

"Thanks, Sepron," you say, rubbing his great head.

The air in front of you shimmers and Aduro appears in front of you, with Elenna by his side and the cauldron at his feet.

"Congratulations!" says the Good Wizard, his eyes twinkling. "You've completed your Quest. Now, how would you like a ride back to the palace?"

To your delight, Ferno swoops down from the sky above and lands next to Sepron.

"Come on," urges Elenna in the apparition. "It's time to celebrate!"

*Turn to **27**.*

22

You run to the edge of the lava and leap, arms wheeling and legs kicking. Then you feel solid ground beneath your feet. You've made it to the other side!

But Tom still needs to cross. The stream of lava starts to leap up in fiery fountains.

"Don't jump – it's too dangerous," you yell to Tom. "I'll go after Aldroim!"

Tom agrees. "I'll catch you up."

While he goes to find another way, you set off after the Beast. You move cautiously along the tunnels. A shaft of daylight streams through a gap in the tunnel wall, and you see oil smeared on the rock.

Aldroim.

You scramble out, emerging above ground – and hear footsteps behind you. You spin round, raising your sword.

"It's just us!" laughs Elenna. With her wolf, Silver, and your horse, Lightning, the two of you set off across the plains.

But instinct tells you something is wrong. You turn and see a bolt of black lightning,

heading right for your heart. Malvel!

"Meddling with my affairs?" he sneers.

You use your sword to deflect his evil
magic and it strikes Malvel's arm, knocking
the sword out of his grasp.

Malvel is unarmed. And at your mercy!

Choose your destiny

To refuse to strike Malvel while he's unarmed,
*turn to **45**.*

To seize your opportunity to destroy Malvel,
*turn to **20**.*

23

"You'll regret this!" snarls the prisoner, shaking the cell bars and cursing as you and Tom continue through the dungeon. You each take one of the torches lining the walls, and decide to follow the left fork.

The tunnel narrows and you are forced to walk single-file. Then it comes to an abrupt end, and you see a wooden door sunk into the stone wall. Writing is carved into it.

"Sealed by the Order of the First Master of the Beasts," you read. "Not to be re-opened."

"There might be a clue inside," says Tom.

You use the tip of your sword to prise away the bolts from the wall. The door falls to the ground, and you and Tom step into a crypt. Ancient tombs stand in rows. Everywhere is thick with dust. It's clear no one has been here for centuries. Except...

"Look." Tom points to a disturbance in the dust round one of the tombs.

You stand either side of it, then slide off

the stone lid. Lying inside is what looks like
the rotting carcasses of hundreds of
woodland creatures. But then the carcasses
merge, and you see the tell-tale glisten of
oil over fur.

"Aldroim!" you yell.

The Beast leaps onto its four paws,
pushing the stone lid so it sends Tom
flying.

Choose your destiny

*To attack the Beast with your sword, turn to **24**.*

To lunge at the Beast with your burning torch,

*turn to **33**.*

24

"I'm not afraid of you," you tell the snarling Beast, swinging your sword. But Aldroim springs aside and your blade strikes the stone tomb instead.

"Tom!" you cry. There's a gaping hole where he's been flung through the crypt walls.

"I'm alright," he shouts back, emerging from a pile of rubble and running to join you.

You try striking at Aldroim with your sword again but the Beast bounds away through the hole made by Tom. You run quickly after him and find yourself in a much larger cave, with a stream of burning, orange lava running through it.

Leading over the stream is a narrow stone bridge. Aldroim goes across it, but there's a loud creak and you realise that the huge weight of the Beast will soon make the bridge collapse. There's no way that you and Tom can risk crossing it and losing your lives.

"Look out!" You pull Tom back to safety as the lava starts to angrily bubble and froth before you.

Choose your destiny

To try to leap over the lava stream, turn to **22**.

To avoid the lava and let the Beast escape for now, turn to **40**.

25

You pull the collar of your jerkin over
your mouth and nose and keep charging.

But the fumes are so thick that you lose
your footing and topple into the lake.

Suddenly you see an enormous, winding
shape swimming towards you. It's Sepron!

The sea serpent lifts you above the
water's surface. Aldroim melts into the
water and floats down one of the tunnels.

You and Tom rush over to the prisoner.
"He's dead," says Tom grimly.

You both climb onto Sepron's back and the Good Beast races after Aldroim.

Malvel's cackle fills the cavern and the water rises. You and Tom have to hold your breath and cling fast to Sepron.

You see a dagger glinting in the cavern wall ahead. Should you grab it – or will this cause you to fall from Sepron's back?

⊱ *Choose your destiny* ⊰

To reach out and grab the dagger, turn to **41**.

To hold on to Sepron, turn to **50**.

You saddle up Lightning, your faithful
white mare. Elenna jumps up behind you
and you canter out of the castle gates,
Silver bounding ahead.

"Elenna – look." You rein Lightning in
and leap to the ground, pointing out
strange slicks of oil on some of the leaves.

"Maybe one of the Beasts came this
way," says Elenna.

You follow the oil patches into a foul-
smelling marsh overhung by slime-coated
trees. Lightning's hooves sink into the
mud, so sure-footed Silver tests the ground
for the most solid route. You lead your
horse across by her reins.

"Watch out!" yells Elenna.

You duck as a cloud of bats
swoops down on you. "Spies from
Malvel," you say grimly.

The bats' cries are so high-pitched that
Lightning whinnies with fright and
strays off the safe path – sinking into
the marsh. No!

Elenna soothes Lightning while you use your sword to hack down a tree branch. You put it in front of your horse, giving her a solid footing, and lean against her flank to push her to safety.

But in rescuing Lightning, you've sunk into the marsh yourself. The mud grips your ankles, sucking you down.

"Hold on," Elenna cries, stretching out her bow.

You grasp onto it but still you keep sinking. Your feet have gone straight through the layer of mud, and are hanging in space. And you realise you're pulling Elenna in, too. Should you just let go?

⚔ *Choose your destiny* ⚔

To try to scramble up to safety, turn to **37**.
To drop down through the mud into the emptiness below, turn to **44**.

27

You proudly ride Lightning through the City. The streets are lined with cheering crowds, waving banners that celebrate your success.

You turn to Tom and Elenna, riding Storm beside you. Silver bounds in front. "It looks like the whole kingdom's here," you smile.

King Hugo steps out before you. You bend your head in a bow, but the King stops you.

"I should bow to you," he says. "Thanks to you, the kingdom is safe from Malvel's evil."

He asks you to kneel. You dismount, and he takes out his sword, touching the tip to both of your shoulders.

"Arise," says King Hugo, "most Glorious Knight of Avantia!"

The End

28

"Cover me and Tom," you say to Elenna. She leads Lightning, Storm and Silver to the rocky outcrop. Then you see her fix an arrow to her bow, training it on Aldroim.

You and Tom circle the Beast, your swords drawn. Whenever Aldroim attacks you or Tom, Elenna fires off an arrow to stop him.

Finally, you and Tom force Aldroim to the ground. But as you're about to deliver the fatal blow, the Beast turns to oil and melts into the ground.

"The cauldron!" you say, snatching it up from the grass.

But the oil trickles down towards the lake. Aldroim is undefeated, and waiting to attack...

⊨⊶ *Choose your destiny* ⊷⊨

To ride to the palace, so you can take the
cauldron to Aduro, turn to **8**.
To fight Aldroim, turn to **13**.

29

You, Elenna, Lightning and Silver step
inside the murky forest. A dim light swings
between the trees and you spot a woman
in a cloak. But as she approaches, you see
that underneath the cloak she has a
hideous, feathery crow's body and an
evil, skull-like face!

"Cornix!" you shout, drawing your
sword and leaping forward to do battle.

The Beast's skeleton face laughs mockingly. She darts aside and you find yourself swiping your sword uselessly through thin air.

Thinking quickly, you leap into a tree and climb the branches until you're higher than Cornix, who hovers in the air, easily avoiding the arrows that Elenna shoots at her. Cornix swoops to attack Silver, who howls and scampers out of the way. Elenna races after her pet, abandoning her attack. As she kneels beside Silver, reassuring him, you see that Cornix is preparing to attack them both.

"No!" you shout, leaping out of the tree and landing on Cornix's back. You slip and land badly in the dust, rolling over. Cornix leaps up and stands over you, ready to strike a deadly blow. How will you defend yourself?

⟐ *Choose your destiny* ⟐

To seize the Beast by her skull, turn to **18**.
To smash her lantern against her, turn to **35**.

30

"There must be a safer crossing than this bridge," you say. You swipe away a couple of bats tugging at Lightning's mane and ears, making her whinny in distress. "Malvel's magic," you mutter.

More bats appear and drag Lightning to the ground, flinging you and Elenna from the saddle.

"No!" you cry as the bats smother Elenna. She screams and writhes, but they scratch and bite her until she lies still.

Then a group of screeching bats pluck you into the air. They lift you higher and higher, their claws piercing your flesh, until they drop you. You hear their wicked hisses of delight as you plummet towards the ground.

Your Quest has failed. And now Avantia is doomed...

"Come on!" you say, trying to pull Silver away from Elenna. But he curls up beside his mistress, nuzzling her pale face. You turn to Lightning, but your horse hangs her head, refusing to budge. "I'll have to hide alone," you realise.

You dash through the orchard, crashing past branches. "Ow! What's that?" You feel a sharp pain on the back of your neck – then others on your arms and legs. It's the wasps from the apple trees.

You cry out in panic as a swarm of the vicious insects chase you through the trees, stinging you over and over. It's almost a relief when the ground gives way and you fall into an animal trap, your body crumpling onto the stakes at its bottom.

Your Quest has failed. And now Avantia is doomed...

"No!" you yell. With a cry of determination you leap forward, deflecting Malvel's blow with your shield.

The evil wizard roars furiously, throwing out a hand to send a jet of red light that knocks you backwards. Your sword goes flying, so you leap to your feet and launch yourself at Malvel – but he fires a blast of magic that makes you pass straight through his body.

How can I fight such an evil wizard? you think.

"Catch!" shouts Tom, and throws you his sword.

Hanging vines droop over the lake. You leap into the air and hurl Tom's blade, slicing clean through them. They fall over Malvel, who becomes knotted up in their twisting tendrils.

"You'll pay for this," the Dark Wizard snarls as he struggles.

You throw yourself on top of him, and Elenna shoots off arrows to pin the net of vines to the ground. For now, Malvel's trapped.

Tom runs over to grab his sword. "I can see an oil slick on the water," he says. "Aldroim's waiting!"

You turn back to Malvel, but he's disappeared. Smoke drifts across a rickety old bridge, then winds downriver.

That's where Malvel's gone, you realise. Should I follow him, or stay and fight Aldroim?

Choose your destiny

*To follow Malvel downriver, turn to **30**.*
To join Tom and Elenna in fighting Aldroim,
*turn to **13**.*

"Take that!" you yell, lunging at Aldroim with your torch. But the Beast blasts it away with a huge jet of oil, turning it into a fireball.

Aldroim gives a ferocious roar, and his mighty jaws let out a cloud of noxious fumes.

"I can't breathe," chokes Tom, struggling to free himself from underneath the heavy tomb lid.

As you fall to the ground, your lungs full of the foul air, the Beast sniffs the air, gives a huge roar which reverberates all around, and then bounds out of the crypt.

When the fumes clear, you help free Tom, light your torches, and race after Aldroim. You pass through rooms of dusty tombs and ancient burial chambers, until you reach a huge cavern with an underground stream, filled with boiling hot lava. The huge Beast bounds easily over it, then turns around and blasts oil on the lava. It erupts into gigantic fiery fountains, which reach high into the air.

You turn to Tom. "Can we risk jumping across, or do you think the flames are too high?"

▶─── *Choose your destiny* ───◀

To try to leap over the stream, turn to **22**.

To find another way to reach the Beast,

turn to **40**.

34

Your heart pounding, you strike out for shore, in the direction the voices are coming from, and duck down at the edge of the water. Two figures emerge, a man with wickedly flashing eyes – and Tom.

"Hey!" you shout happily.

Tom grins back – but then his smile

fades. "Get out of the water!" he yells.

Over your shoulder you see the oil rise from the surface of the lake, forming a massive, leopard-shaped Beast. Oil drips and its eyes glow red. Aldroim!

"I've led you to the Beast," says the man. "Now I take my freedom!"

He starts running. But Aldroim gives a roar and leaps from the water, knocking the man to the ground. He may be an enemy of Avantia, you decide, but no one deserves such a fate.

You draw your sword to charge at Aldroim, just as the air around him is filled with noxious gases. You want to call on a Good Beast to help – but the prisoner could be dead before it arrives.

⟨══⟩⊱ *Choose your destiny* ⊰⟨══⟩

To charge at Aldroim, turn to 25.
To summon a Good Beast, turn to 52.

You grab Cornix's lantern and smash it onto her cloak.

The Beast gives a shriek of rage as the red velvet bursts into flames. She grabs at you with a clawed wing, but an arrow strikes her. Elenna has returned with Silver.

Cornix flaps her ruined wings and just manages to take to the air.

But as the Beast jaggedly flies away from the forest, Ferno appears on the horizon, breathing flames. He chases after Cornix, bringing her to the ground. Fire envelops her body until it dissolves to nothing.

"Thank you, Ferno," you say. The fire dragon dips his giant head then takes off.

The cauldron lies among Cornix's ashes. You've done it! But the sky darkens. A cloud of bats, armed with vicious fangs, swoop down on you, trying to seize the cauldron. A mocking laugh fills the air.

"These are Malvel's bats," you say grimly. "We'll have to outrun them!"

You and Elenna leap onto Lightning's

back and Silver sprints alongside as you race to the palace.

The chase brings you to a bridge that crosses a section of rapids in the Winding River. Lightning rears up, refusing to go any further; the wooden planks are rotten.

Elenna turns pale. "We're caught between Malvel's bats and the rapids!"

━━◆ *Choose your destiny* ◆━━

*To take your chances on the bridge, turn to **7**.*
*To gallop further up the river and look for another place to cross, turn to **30**.*

36

"No," you say to Malvel. "I won't play along with your evil games."

Malvel throws back his head and cackles. "You don't have a choice."

With his free hand, the Dark Wizard shoots bolts of black fire at Lightning. You dive to parry them with your sword, the force jarring your arm and causing you to wince in pain.

Malvel laughs, and aims more bolts at Elenna and Silver. You lunge again, and only just manage to block them. As you catch your breath, you realise Malvel is trying to goad you into fighting him. He's up to something, you think. But what is it?

To your amazement, Malvel tosses aside his sword. "Look," he says. "I'm unarmed! Are you so pathetic and cowardly that you'll still refuse to fight me?"

"Don't do it," calls Elenna. "It's a trick."

I wouldn't attack an unarmed man, you think. But this is Malvel, the most evil wizard in all of Avantia!

If you refuse to fight, will you be throwing away the best chance you'll ever have of defeating the Dark Wizard for good?

Choose your destiny

To follow Elenna's warning, turn to **45**.

To attack Malvel, turn to **20**.

37

"Don't let go," says Elenna. She gives a cry of dermination and pulls you free of the mud's sucking grip.

You, Elenna, Lightning and Silver follow Malvel's cloud of bats, still visible on the horizon, hoping they'll lead you to the missing cauldron. Soon you enter an orchard groaning with apples. Wasps buzz round the fruit.

"I'm starving!" grins Elenna. She pulls an apple from a branch.

But there's something not right about the apples. They're unnaturally red and shiny...

Elenna crunches into the apple and falls to the ground. Silver whines in distress, then darts to the edge of the orchard, his hackles raised. Something's coming!

Choose your destiny

To stay with Elenna and try to save her, turn to ***51****.*

To flee from the intruder, turn to ***31****.*

38

You put down the piece of flint you've found.

"We've trusted the prisoner so far," you say. "We should let him lead us a little further."

"Flame and oil," mutters the prisoner, shaking his head. "It would have blown us all up."

You feel a chill creep down your spine as you realise how close you came to dying.

You stagger on in the dark. The tunnel widens, and it becomes lighter, finally opening up into an underground lake.

Hundreds of stalactites hang down from the cavern roof, making an intricate labyrinth of arches and tunnels. The water is coated with a glistening sheen of oil.

"Aldroim's passed this way," says Tom.

The prisoner backs away. "I've shown you the right tunnel," he says, "Now release me!"

But the surface of the water bubbles and darkens.

A four-legged Beast rises up from the depths. "Aldroim," you murmur. He's the shape of a massive leopard, but his skin drips with oil and his eyes glow a deep red. He gives a ferocious roar – leaping from the water and onto the prisoner!

You and Tom draw your swords and, with a battle cry, charge the Beast. It turns to breathe noxious fumes at you.

⟩⟩⟨⟨ *Choose your destiny* ⟩⟩⟨⟨

*To keep charging at the beast, turn to **25**.*

*To use the token on Tom's shield to summon Sepron, turn to **52**.*

39

You, Tom and Elenna form a triangle around the Beast. A thrill of excitement courses through you – you can sense that victory is near!

Elenna fires an arrow into the Beast's side. It swings round to her, and now you can attack without being seen. You bound forward and stab your sword into Aldroim's shoulder. The Beasts growls in anger and tries to counter-attack, but Tom has lunged forward to deliver another blow.

You pull your sword free and drive it into the evil Beast's throat. It slumps to the ground, turning into oil, and disappears.

You wipe the sweat from your face. "We've defeated Aldroim!"

As the three of you cheer, the air lights up and a green portal appears.

"Aduro must have created it to take us home," says Tom.

You walk towards it. But the air lights up a second time, and a blue portal appears beside the green one. You stare at each other uncertainly.

"One of these could be from Malvel," you say slowly. "So which one do we walk through?"

━━━━⊱✦ *Choose your destiny* ✦⊰━━━━

*To walk through the green portal, go to **5**.*
*To walk through the blue portal, go to **11**.*

Aldroim bounds away on the other side of the burning stream. Feeling disappointed, you and Tom follow the stream downhill. You soon see that the boiling lava flows into a wide river, where it cools.

Something is moored against the shore, bobbing in the water.

"A boat," you realise excitedly.

You jump in, taking an oar each, and paddle downriver.

Tom stiffens. "What's that noise?" he asks.

You hear rushing water... It's a waterfall!

You desperately paddle backwards, but it's no good – the boat tips closer to the edge and then over. The boat falls...onto the scaly back of Sepron! The Good Beast roars in greeting as he carries you safely along the underground river. Through the foaming water you spot something lodged in the wall, above a ledge – a dagger!

Choose your destiny

To try to reach the dagger from Sepron's back,
turn to **41**.

To try to roll onto the ledge and get the dagger,
turn to **50**.

Leaning as far as you dare, your fingers brush the red and black jewels on the dagger's hilt. Almost there...

"I've got you," says Tom, gripping your arm. You pull the dagger from the wall.

Sepron races on. You blink as you emerge into daylight, in a lake far outside the castle.

With a roar of fury, Sepron rears up, flinging you and Tom onto the shore. Then you see what's made him so angry – Malvel.

"Well, well," sneers the wizard from across the lake. Aduro's cauldron is slung over his staff. "Aldroim has done well. Your Quest is over!"

"Not while there's blood in our veins," declares Tom.

You both draw your swords and charge, and Sepron lunges at the Dark Wizard. But Malvel fires a blast of evil magic that knocks you all backwards. An oily jet shoots at Sepron from further up the lake, temporarily blinding him. He thrashes helplessly in the water.

You realise where the jet of oil came from. On the lake shore, Aldroim snarls at you, his red eyes glowing. Malvel triumphantly rattles the cauldron with his staff, and to your horror you see that the Beast's tail is wrapped round something... it's Elenna!

⟐ Choose your destiny ⟐

To take the cauldron from Malvel, turn to 2.

To try to save Elenna from Aldroim, turn to 9.

42

"I'll fight you," you say, drawing your sword. Elenna leads Lightning and Silver away, and fits an arrow to her bow. You know your friend will be ready if you need her.

"Prepare to die," sneers Malvel. He fixes you with a cruel grin and lunges foward, his blade flashing. You just manage to deflect his blow and dodge aside, your heart pounding.

Malvel strikes again, but now you're ready for him. You crash your shield into his, making the Dark Wizard stumble.

"Yes!" shouts Elenna.

You circle Malvel, and when he swings his blade at you in a deadly arc, you leap over it. Malvel gives a snarl of surprise and you take your chance, putting your sword under his and bringing your arm up. Malvel's weapon flies from his hand.

The Dark Wizard sinks to his knees and you stand over him triumphantly, your blade to his throat.

"Do it," urges Malvel, his eyes glinting. "Go on – kill me."

You pause. He may be the Dark Wizard, but should you harm an unarmed man? Taladon's words replay in your mind: A true knight never uses an unfair advantage.

Choose your destiny

To drive your blade into Malvel's throat, turn to **20**.

To allow Malvel to pick up his sword, turn to **45**.

43

You lean against the bookcase, which moves aside with a groaning noise to reveal a dark spiral stone stairway. You grab your sword and shield from the shelf, and then notice something glinting on the bookcase. A dagger! The hilt is encrusted with red and black jewels. You tuck it into your belt and head down the stairs.

You hold your sword out ahead of you, feeling your way in the dark.

What's that? you think, as a darting

shadow makes you jump. Luckily it's just one of the large spiders you saw in the spell chamber.

You emerge blinking in the daylight to the sound of shouts. You see green flames shoot into the air behind a rocky outcrop. Could that be Malvel's evil magic you wonder? Has he found your friends?

You see a lake and run torwards it. First you spot Lightning and Silver, tethered by some trees, and then Elenna, ducking behind some rocks.

"Tom's fighting Malvel," she whispers.

You peer over the rocks to see the duel. It's clear Tom's struggling. One of Malvel's blows makes him stumble to the ground, and the Dark Wizard raises his staff. He's going to kill Tom! How can you save him?

―✦ *Choose your destiny* ✦―

To attack Malvel with the dagger you found,
turn to **17**.

To deflect the blow with your shield, turn to **32**.

44

"It's alright," you tell Elenna, and let go of the bow. You slip down through the oozing, burbling mud, and for a few awful moments you can't breathe. But your legs slide out into the emptiness beneath, and you use your arms to push yourself clear.

You drop with a splash into an underwater lake inside a vast cavern. Low-hanging stalctites form a maze of arches and tunnels and there's a glistening sheen on the water. Is it oil left by the Beast?

You can hear voices on the shore. They sound like they're arguing. Treading water, you look around. One of the stalactites is hollowed out, making an upward-travelling tunnel. Light glimmers through it. Should you stay – or go?

⊰⊹⊱ *Choose your destiny* ⊰⊹⊱

*To see who the voices belong to, turn to **34**.*

*To climb up the stalactite, turn to **55**.*

45

"No," you say, lowering your blade. You won't attack an unarmed man – not even Malvel.

"You're as spineless as Taladon," mocks Malvel. "Who needs a sword when they have magic?"

He raises his hands to cast a deadly spell, and you throw up your arms to protect yourself. But the sky darkens and an angry roar fills the air.

"Ferno!" shouts Elenna from where she, Lightning and Silver are sheltering. The Fire Dragon has come to your rescue!

Ferno swoops down at Malvel, his huge wings beating the air and his red and black scales glittering. His massive jaws let out a blast of flame, forcing Malvel to disappear in a puff of black smoke that winds across the sky.

"Thank you, Ferno!" you yell. The Good Beast dips his great head in acknowledgement, then flies away.

"Maybe we should follow Malvel's

smoke," suggests Elenna. "It might lead us to the cauldron."

You gaze out over the plains and watch the black coil drift towards a forest – passing somewhere you know well.

"It's right by Sexton," you say excitedly. "My home village."

"Where your brothers are," adds Elenna. She puts a hand on your shoulder. "Tom and I will understand if you want to go home."

But a different thought occurs to you. "My brothers could help!" Surely more eyes and ears mean a higher chance of finding the cauldron?

Elenna shakes her head. "The fewer Questers there are, the more quickly we can travel."

Choose your destiny

*To ask your brothers to join in the Quest, turn to **48**.*

*To take Elenna's advice and carry on without them, turn to **15**.*

46

You give a cry of triumph as you feel the stones – you recognise one of them as cool, smooth flint.

"No!" snarls the prisoner, clawing and grappling with you.

Tom draws his blade. "Keep away," he warns. You hear the prisoner moving down the tunnel, whimpering.

You rip a strip of cloth from your jerkin, place it on a large stone and strike the stone with the flint. A spark leaps from the stone and the cloth catches.

In the sudden glow you see Tom's face. The prisoner turns, his features twisted with terror. You look at the cloth and see that it's draped over one of the oil puddles.

Horror fills you. "Mixing oil and fire makes an—"

The explosion blasts you against the wall. Then everything goes black.

Your Quest has failed. And now Avantia is doomed...

47

While Elenna races outside, you and Tom take the winding stone steps down to the dungeon, deep beneath the castle.

"That's strange," you say, pointing at the flagstones. "Patches of oil. Could they be from one of the Beasts?"

The slick pools lead to the entrance of the dungeon – where you both gasp with shock. The iron portcullis has been ripped off its hinges. Passed out on the ground, covered in oil, is Groanus, the dungeon guard.

You wipe the liquid from Groanus's face, and he splutters as he comes round.

"What happened?" asks Tom, kneeling beside him.

Groanus shivers. "A monster... I saw a face like a cat's, and eyes like burning coals..."

You and Tom run through the broken portcullis, into the dark dungeon. The damp tunnel is lined with cells holding those who have tried to harm Avantia. But then the tunnel forks.

"Which way now?" says Tom, looking around.

"I could tell you which way the Beast went," sneers a voice from one of the cells. "But it'll cost you."

You turn to see a prisoner smirking at you through his cell's bars. The candles mounted on the walls light up a placard detailing his crime: murder.

"What's your price?" you ask warily.

"Release me," he says, spitting on the ground.

You stare at Tom. Can you risk putting yourselves at the mercy of a murderer? And if you don't, will you ever reach the Beast in time?

Choose your destiny

*To release the prisoner, turn to **49**.*

*To go on without the prisoner, turn to **23**.*

48

"Welcome to Sexton!" you say, grinning as you, Elenna, Lightning and Silver step through the gate into your home village.

A voice shouts. "Look who's here!" You turn to see your eldest brother, Luke, running towards you in his carpenter's apron. Luke pulls you into a bear hug as your youngest brother, Sam, arrives, splattered with mud from the family farm.

They both leap at the chance to come on the Quest, but Elenna takes you aside.

"Are you sure about this?" she whispers. "Carpenters and farmers won't be any use against a Beast."

But you've made your decision and you all set off into the forest. A mist quickly descends, and you stumble over tree roots, unable to see properly. A chill creeps over your flesh as eerie lights dance through the trees.

"It's the Beast," you say, drawing your sword.

But Sam is quaking with terror. Too late,

you realise you can't ask your little brother to face a deadly battle – you must flee.

As you run, the lights grow nearer. "Stop," cries a female voice. You can see the shadowy outline of a cloaked woman carrying a lantern.

"Don't listen to her!" Elenna urges.

But the woman has caught up with you. She casts aside her red velvet cloak to reveal a crow's body and skull's face. Cornix! With deadly speed she pounces on Luke, covering him with her cloak. His lifeless body falls to the ground.

"No!" you cry. Cornix fixes you with her bony stare, and you know you're her next victim. "Elenna – save Sam!"

She pulls your little brother onto Lightning, and gallops off through the forest, Silver sprinting behind. Then Cornix's teeth rip your flesh.

Your Quest has failed. And now Avantia is doomed...

"Don't try anything," you warn the prisoner. Tom stands guard while you use the tip of your blade to unlock the cell door. The prisoner leaps out and you raise your shield – but he just laughs ghoulishly.

"This way," he sneers, heading down the right-hand tunnel.

"We need to keep a close eye on him," Tom mutters.

The line of candles along the wall ends and the tunnel is plunged into darkness. At least the increasing amount of oily slime on the walls and floor lets you know you're being led in the right direction.

Unable to see properly, you slip across one of these oil puddles and stagger through some rubble, your sword clattering against the stone. This gives you an idea.

"Tom! We can strike these stones together to get a light, then make a torch from a strip of our clothes."

Tom agrees, but as you feel around in the dark for suitable stones, clammy hands clutch at you.

"No!" the prisoner shrieks. "You'll kill us all!"

Is he right? Or does he want to murder you in the dark?

Choose your destiny

*To take your chances in the dark, turn to **38**.*

*To ignore the prisoner and continue trying to light your way, turn to **46**.*

"No!" you yell as your fingers loosen and you slide from Sepron's back, into the foaming water. The force of the current drags you along, until something seizes your ankle – Tom! He must have dived in after you.

The current washes you both up onto a stretch of shore. A passageway leads into the daylight. Relief fills you as you lead the way up the squelchy steps.

"We're coming out onto a hilltop," you call back to Tom. "I can see a stone pillar at the top."

But when you emerge from the tunnel a gag magically appears around your mouth and ropes made from stinking animal skin bind you to the pillar. Tom suffers the same fate.

The wind whips round the hilltop and you hear Malvel's mocking laughter carried on the wind.

In the distant sky you see a familiar outline. "Ferno!"

But how can you attract the Fire Dragon's attention? Tom's shield lies a few paces away – touching the dragon scale embedded in it would summon the Good Beast. But what if you can't reach it?

⬥═══ *Choose your destiny* ═══⬥
*To try to reach Tom's shield, turn to **16**.*
To try to shout to Ferno through your gag,
*turn to **54**.*

51

You thump Elenna's back and the piece of apple dislodges.

"Thanks," she splutters, the colour returning to her cheeks.

Silver snarls, and you see the intruders – a pack of wolves! One of the wolves leaps at Lightning's throat, but you despatch it with your sword. Silver grabs another in his jaws and the pack flee, tails down.

You continue through the trees – but the wolves are gathered at the edge of the wood, whining miserably.

"Something must have scared them," says Elenna.

A mocking cackle fills the air, and Malvel appears.

"Now," says the Dark Wizard. "Which of you two fools is going to fight me?"

⟨━━━⇾ *Choose your destiny* ⇽━━━⟩

*To accept Malvel's challenge, turn to **42**.*
To refuse to play the Dark Wizard's games,
*turn to **36**.*

Aldroim's noxious fumes burn your throat.
"We must summon Sepron," you splutter.

You use your sword to fend off Aldroim
while Tom rubs the serpent tooth
embedded in his shield.

The Beast sees the prisoner trying to
creep along the edge of the lake and lunges
at him, sinking his teeth into the man's
flesh. You and Tom rush to help, but Tom
grabs your arm.

"It's too late," he says, as Aldroim drops
the man's lifeless body to the ground.

The Beast snarls at you, his revolting
breath making you stagger back. Then he
jumps. There's only one escape route
available – the lake! You both leap in, the
stagnant water flooding your mouth.

"Sepron will be here soon," Tom gasps.

You look round for somewhere to hide
from Aldroim. "Let's climb one of the
stalactites," you suggest.

But as you and Tom climb up one of the
rocky pillars, Aldroim roars and leaps into

the water. The Beast momentarily becomes an oil slick, then reforms to swipe at you with deadly claws.

You hear the thunderous bellow of rushing water. Sepron arrives, sweeping through a tunnel into the cavern. Aldroim turns back into an oil slick and the sea serpent nudges both you and Tom onto his back then carries you safely out of the cavern. As the tunnel narrows, the water around you swirls so much it looks like it's boiling.

"Look," shouts Tom, pointing ahead to something glimmering in the wall. Should you grab it?

But the water's choking you even more than Aldroim's noxious fumes. There's a gap above you – you'll be able to breathe if you can reach it...

⊨— *Choose your destiny* —⊨

To hang on and try to grab the dagger,
turn to **41**.
To climb up through the gap above you,
turn to **56**.

You grab your weapons from the shelf and crouch down at the gap in the wall. The stone looks crumbly, and when you pull it comes away in your hand. You've soon ripped a space large enough to squeeze through.

The gap leads into damp, dark caves. You hold your sword ahead of you. Sticky cobwebs cling to your face. Then your sword clangs against a solid surface – a wall, blocking your path. You feel its surface, hoping you'll find a gap like you did in Malvel's spell room. There's one. You push your arm through, trying to make the gap bigger – when a hand grabs yours from the other side of the wall!

You give a shout of fear and pull back, then hear a familiar voice.

"It's me, Elenna! We've been looking for you."

Together, you pull away the stone work until you can join Elenna, Lightning, Storm and Silver on the other side of the wall.

You all stumble through the dark caves, the horses whickering unhappily, until Elenna gives a cry. "Over there – it's a light!"

You smile at her in the gloom. "Maybe it's the way out."

But your smile fades as the light disappears - then reappears in another part of the caves. Could it be Malvel's sorcery?

⟐ *Choose your destiny* ⟐

To ignore the light, turn to 3.

To try to follow the light, turn to 19.

54

"Ferno!" You and Tom shout through your gags, but your calls are muffled. You knock your head back against the pillar with frustration as Ferno flies further away. You've missed your chance.

Your head feels like it's bleeding. You strain round to look at the pillar, and see that it's covered with sharp-edged carvings. You can use them to cut through the ropes!

Your bonds soon fall away and you run down the hilltop to a causeway made up of columns of rock of all different heights. As you and Tom scramble through them, the columns become more spaced apart, and open onto a lake. You see a familiar figure ahead. "Elenna!"

Your friend waves and leads Storm and Lightning across the causeway towards you. Silver bounds from rock to rock.

You notice the water between the rocky columns has an oily sheen... It foams and rises to form Aldroim! The massive Beast charges at you and the other Questers.

"To the shore!" you yell. A desperate race ensues. Aldroim slices at Lightning with his claws, but you knock him away with your sword.

You make it to a rocky outcrop. Aldroim crouches down, ready to spring at you. How should you attack?

⊱═ Choose your destiny ═⊰

*To instruct Tom and Elenna to charge the Beast, turn to **6**.*

*To split up into two groups, one covering the other from behind the rocky outcrop, turn to **28**.*

55

You squeeze inside the stalactite and slowly clamber your way towards daylight.

"Let me help!" says a kindly voice, and a hand stretches down into the stalactite.

"Thanks," you say, gripping it gratefully. It's not until your helper pulls you out of the stalactite with supernatural strength that you realise anything is wrong.

"Malvel!" you shout as you fall to the ground. Elenna's there, too, and runs to pull you to your feet.

Lightning whinnies and Silver's hackles rise as Malvel draws a deadly looking sword.

"No more Quests for you two," the Dark Wizard snarls. "Now, which of you is brave enough to duel with me?"

Choose your destiny

*To accept Malvel's challenge and face the Dark Wizard in a duel, turn to **42**.*

*To refuse to play the Dark Wizard's games, turn to **36**.*

56

You reach up and grab a tree root hanging from the brightly lit hole above Sepron's back. The serpent races on his way and you hoist yourself up, heaving in lungfuls of air. You feel lightheaded with relief as you flop on the grass. You know Tom will be safe with Sepron.

Wait a minute... The grass is moving, even though there's no wind. It winds over your legs, wrapping around your neck and arms.

Malvel's enchanted the grass!

You struggle to your feet, but the blades just get longer. You jump for a tall tree branch and swing yourself up.

A familiar voice calls your name. Elenna! She's on the edge of the enchanted grass, with Silver and Lightning.

"Don't come closer!" you shout.

You look down from the tree branch and see that the grass is still. You have no option – you need to drop to the ground and run, hoping you're fast enough to make it. You swing your legs forward to give yourself a head start, and then race across the grass. You're almost at the edge when you feel thick coils of grass trip you and pull you back.

My Quest is over, you think.

But wait. You feel something else wrap around your wrist. It's Elenna! She uses an arrow like a scythe to cut through the grass while she pulls you to safety.

You're at the edge of a forest, with a cave beside it.

"Tom needs our help," you say. "But which will be the quickest way to reach him?"

Choose your destiny

*To enter the forest, turn to **29**.*

*To go inside the caves, turn to **4**.*

Fight the Beasts,
Fear the Magic

www.beastquest.co.uk

Have you checked out the Beast Quest website?
It's the place to go for games, downloads, activities,
sneak previews and lots of fun!

You can read all about your favourite beasts,
download free screensavers and desktop wallpapers
for your computer, and even challenge your friends
to a Beast Tournament.

Sign up to the newsletter at www.beastquest.co.uk
to receive exclusive extra content and the
opportunity to enter special members-only
competitions. We'll send you up-to-date info on all
the Beast Quest books, including the next exciting
series which features four brand-new Beasts!

Series 1-4
BEAST QUEST

☐ 1.	Ferno the Fire Dragon	978 1 84616 483 5	4.99
☐ 2.	Sepron the Sea Serpent	978 1 84616 482 8	4.99
☐ 3.	Arcta the Mountain Giant	978 1 84616 484 2	4.99
☐ 4.	Tagus the Horse-Man	978 1 84616 486 6	4.99
☐ 5.	Nanook the Snow Monster	978 1 84616 485 9	4.99
☐ 6.	Epos the Flame Bird	978 1 84616 487 3	4.99

Beast Quest: The Golden Armour

☐ 7.	Zepha the Monster Squid	978 1 84616 988 5	4.99
☐ 8.	Claw the Giant Monkey	978 1 84616 989 2	4.99
☐ 9.	Soltra the Stone Charmer	978 1 84616 990 8	4.99
☐ 10.	Vipero the Snake Man	978 1 84616 991 5	4.99
☐ 11.	Arachnid the King of Spiders	978 1 84616 992 2	4.99
☐ 12.	Trillion the Three-Headed Lion	978 1 84616 993 9	4.99

Beast Quest: The Dark Realm

☐ 13.	Torgor the Minotaur	978 1 84616 997 7	4.99
☐ 14.	Skor the Winged Stallion	978 1 84616 998 4	4.99
☐ 15.	Narga the Sea Monster	978 1 40830 000 8	4.99
☐ 16.	Kaymon the Gorgon Hound	978 1 40830 001 5	4.99
☐ 17.	Tusk the Mighty Mammoth	978 1 40830 002 2	4.99
☐ 18.	Sting the Scorpion Man	978 1 40830 003 9	4.99

Beast Quest: The Amulet of Avantia

☐ 19.	Nixa the Death Bringer	978 1 40830 376 4	4.99
☐ 20.	Equinus the Spirit Horse	978 1 40830 377 1	4.99
☐ 21.	Rashouk the Cave Troll	978 1 40830 378 8	4.99
☐ 22.	Luna the Moon Wolf	978 1 40830 379 5	4.99
☐ 23.	Blaze the Ice Dragon	978 1 40830 381 8	4.99
☐ 24.	Stealth the Ghost Panther	978 1 40830 380 1	4.99

FREE COLLECTOR CARDS INSIDE!

Series 5
⟩⟩ BEAST QUEST ⟨⟨

Tom must travel to Gwildor, Avantia's twin kingdom,
to free six new Beasts from an evil enchantment...

978 1 40830 437 2   978 1 40830 438 9   978 1 40830 439 6

978 1 40830 440 2   978 1 40830 441 9   978 1 40830 442 6

FREE COLLECTOR CARDS INSIDE!

Series 6
BEAST QUEST

Can Tom and his companions rescue his mother
from the clutches of evil Velmal...?

KOMODO
THE LIZARD KING

978 1 40830 723 6

MURO
THE RAT MONSTER

978 1 40830 724 3

FANG
THE BAT FIEND

978 1 40830 725 0

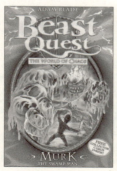

MURK
THE SWAMP MAN

978 1 40830 726 7

TERRA
CURSE OF THE FOREST

978 1 40830 727 4

VESPICK
THE WASP QUEEN

978 1 40830 728 1

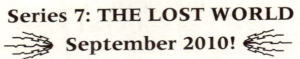

FREE COLLECTOR CARDS INSIDE!

Series 7: THE LOST WORLD
September 2010!

CONVOL
THE COLD-BLOODED BRUTE
978 1 40830 729 8

HELLION
THE FIERY FOE
978 1 40830 730 4

KRESTOR
THE CRUSHING TERROR
978 1 40830 731 1

MADARA
THE MIDNIGHT WARRIOR
978 1 40830 732 8

ELLIK
THE LIGHTNING HORROR
978 1 40830 733 5

CARNIVORA
THE WINGED SCAVENGER
978 1 40830 734 2

BEAST QUEST SPECIALS

978 1 84616 951 9

978 1 84616 994 6

978 1 40830 382 5

978 1 40830 436 5

978 1 40830 735 9

Join Tom and his brave companions for these
Beast Quest special bumper editions, with
two stories in one!

Veerle Poupeye
is a Jamaica-based art historian, critic
and curator. She was born in Belgium and studied there
at the Rijksuniversiteit Gent. She lectures on Caribbean art
history at the School of Visual Arts of the Edna Manley
College in Kingston and also directs the Visual Arts
programmes of the MultiCare Foundation, a non-profit-
making youth and community development organization.
She has published and lectured widely on Caribbean
art and culture.

WO

T
provid
range of illustrat
If you would
of titles
THA
30 Bloomsbu
In the Un
THAMI
500 Fifth Avenu

Pri

Veerle Poupeye

Caribbean Art

177 illustrations, 76 in color

THAMES AND HUDSON

For my father

For his encouragement and advice when I undertook this project, I would like to thank David Boxer (Jamaica), who has been a tremendous influence on my work over the years. I also appreciate the generosity of the many artists, collectors, art administrators and fellow art historians who willingly shared their knowledge, time and resources, particularly Gerald Alexis (Haiti), Mervyn Awon (Barbados), Marimar Benítez (Puerto Rico), Dominique Brebion (Martinique), Claire Broadbridge (Trinidad), Eddie Chambers (Britain), Christopher Cozier (Trinidad), Maud Duquella (Puerto Rico), Ruby Eckmeyer (Curaçao), Irina Leyva (Jamaica), Geoffrey MacLean (Trinidad), Jeannette Miller (Dominican Republic), Gerardo Mosquera (Cuba), Fredric Snitzer (USA), Marianne de Tolentino (Dominican Republic), Haydee Venegas (Puerto Rico), Cristina Vives (Cuba) and Denis Williams (Guyana). I am indebted to UNESCO (Jamaica), who provided a travel grant when it was most urgently needed; to the Honourable Aaron Matalon, O.J., and the MultiCare Foundation, for their support and understanding while I was preparing this book, and to my colleagues Nicholas Morris and Beti Campbell. Finally, my gratitude goes to Marc Rammelaere and my family and friends for their encouragement and assistance.

Designed by Liz Rudderham

First published in the United States of America in 1998 by Thames and Hudson Inc., 500 Fifth Avenue, New York, New York 10110

Library of Congress Catalog Card Number 97-60254
ISBN 0-500-20306-7

Printed and bound in Singapore

Contents

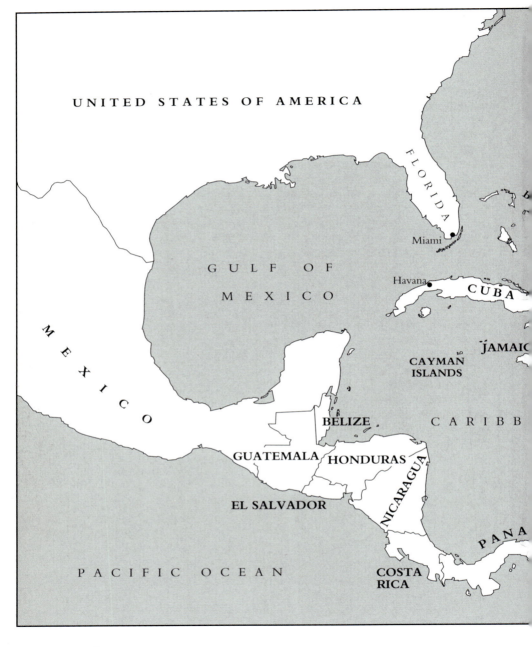

UNITED STATES OF AMERICA

FLORIDA

Miami

GULF OF
MEXICO

Havana

CUBA

MEXICO

JAMAIC

CAYMAN
ISLANDS

BELIZE

CARIBB

GUATEMALA

HONDURAS

NICARAGUA

EL SALVADOR

PANA

PACIFIC OCEAN

COSTA
RICA

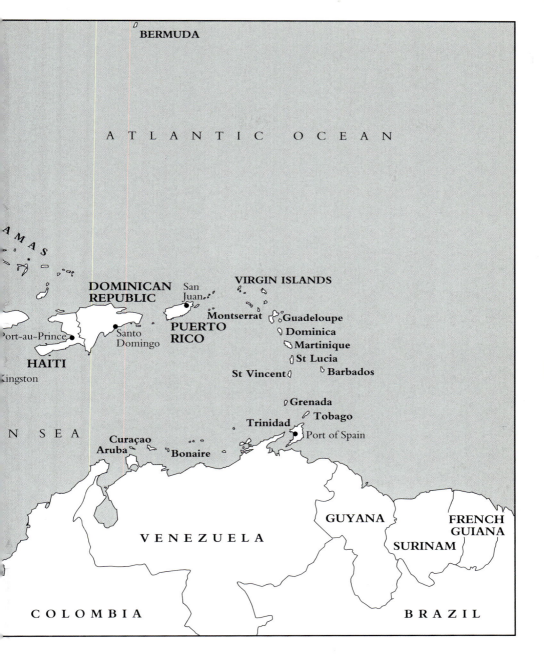

BERMUDA

A T L A N T I C   O C E A N

A M A S

DOMINICAN San
REPUBLIC Juan
VIRGIN ISLANDS

Montserrat
Guadeloupe
Port-au-Prince Santo
Domingo
PUERTO
RICO
Dominica
Martinique
St Lucia

HAITI
Kingston
St Vincent
Barbados

Grenada
Tobago
Trinidad
N   S E A
Curaçao
Aruba
Bonaire
Port of Spain

VENEZUELA
GUYANA
FRENCH
GUIANA
SURINAM

COLOMBIA
BRAZIL

7

1 Wifredo Lam *The Jungle* 1943

Introduction

The Cuban painter Wifredo Lam (1902–82) was the first Caribbean artist to be acknowledged in the West as an important figure in modern art history, well ahead of more recent interest in Latin American and Caribbean art. Although Lam's involvement with the European avant-garde accounts for his early recognition, the content of his mature work is assertively Afro-Caribbean, separating him from continental Latin and North American art, despite his affinity with the Chilean painter Matta (b. 1911).

Lam is often cited as the paradigmatic Caribbean artist. Like many Caribbeans, he was of mixed racial ancestry – his father was a Chinese immigrant and his mother was of African and European descent. He spent most of his adult life outside the Caribbean, something many modern Caribbean artists and intellectuals experience. Lam grew up in an environment where the Afro-Cuban Santería religion was commonly practised and returned to this heritage as a source for his mature work. Following a long Caribbean tradition of cultural dissidence, he used Afro-Caribbean culture as a vehicle for socio-political commentary and once described his art as 'an act of decolonization'. His most famous painting *The Jungle* (1943), which was painted in Cuba, has been described as the first visual manifesto of the Third World.

The use of Lam's art as a benchmark, however, illustrates how difficult it is to define Caribbean art without lapsing into dogmas or stereotypes. Writers, curators and cultural administrators often approach the subject in terms of what they feel art from the Caribbean should be, a problem that affects Caribbean art professionals and outsiders alike. Consequently, aspects of Caribbean art that do not match these preconceptions are often overlooked. It is doubtful, for instance, that a work such as the minimalist metal and fluorescent light sculpture *Avis Rara* (1981) by Bismarck 2 Victoria (b. 1952) would be considered for the average publication or exhibition of Caribbean art. Victoria, who is from the Dominican Republic, was studio assistant to Isamu Noguchi in New York for ten years, an experience that greatly influenced his purist artistic outlook, but the reason for excluding *Avis Rara* would probably not be that its maker has spent much of his adult life abroad (after all, so did Lam), but that its content and form are 'too Western' and not recognizably 'Caribbean'.

For this book, Caribbean art is therefore defined in its widest sense, both as art made in the Caribbean and as art made by artists of immediate Caribbean descent who live and work elsewhere. The term 'Caribbean art' is thus used generically and does not suggest that there is a cohesive school. What is described here as Caribbean art is in effect a loose grouping of national schools and individual expressions which have developed in relative isolation from each other. This sense of fragmentation is exacerbated by the island geography and the linguistic variety of the region, but in spite of this cultural 'balkanization', general developments have been remarkably similar throughout the Caribbean. Most national schools originated in the decolonization process, for instance, and the resulting quest for cultural identity has remained a unifying concern. Caribbean art is therefore usually in some way recognizably 'Caribbean', although the departures from this norm are nonetheless significant and provide a better understanding of the history of Caribbean art. The introduction of abstraction in the fifties and sixties, for example, also amounted to a universalist reaction against the indigenist canons of the early nationalist schools.

Caribbean art has developed in a polemical context and debate about its 'Caribbeanness' has played an integral part. It is a common notion, for instance, that authenticity in Caribbean art is measured by its independence from the Western artistic canons. This perception has been a factor in the international success of 'primitive' Caribbean art and has raised questions about cultural and even racial stereotyping. Caribbean intellectuals have also questioned the metropolitan Western influences in modern Caribbean art which many see as a product of cultural imperialism. Whereas some Caribbean art is indeed derivative and retardataire, these views fail to recognize the complexity and dialectic nature of the relationship between Caribbean and metropolitan Western culture.

Modern Caribbean art cannot be understood without considering its geographical, historical, intellectual and general cultural background in some detail. Geographically, the Caribbean is commonly defined as the chain of islands from Cuba and the Bahamas in the north, to Trinidad and Barbados in the south. Most definitions also include the Dutch islands of Curaçao, Aruba and Bonaire off the coast of Venezuela; the small island group of Bermuda in the Atlantic; Guyana, Surinam, French Guiana in South America; and Belize in Central America.

The Island Caribbean is often subdivided into the Greater and Lesser Antilles. The former consists of the larger islands of Cuba, Hispaniola

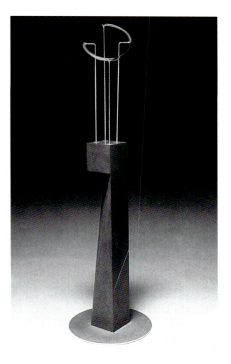

2 Bismarck Victoria *Avis Rara* 1981

(which is shared between Haiti and the Dominican Republic), Jamaica and Puerto Rico; the latter of the smaller islands in the eastern Caribbean. The term West Indies, which once applied to the entire region, is still used to describe the English-speaking part of the region, although the term Commonwealth Caribbean is gaining currency as a post-colonial alternative. The mainland territories of Guyana (formerly British Guiana), Surinam (formerly Dutch Guiana) and French Guiana are collectively called 'the Guianas'. Politically, economically and culturally, the fate of the Guianas has since Prehispanic times been tied to the Island Caribbean rather than South America. Because of the colonial history of the Guianas, the national languages are English, Dutch and French, respectively, which adds to the cultural separation from Brazil and Hispanic South America. This is reinforced by the geographic barrier of near-inaccessible rain forests that cover much of the vast, sparsely populated Guianese hinterlands. The Guianas differ from the islands because of their size (the largest island on Guyana's mighty Essequibo River is larger than Barbados) and, culturally, because of the presence of a substantial Amerindian population. The colonial and modern history of Belize (formerly British Honduras) is

11

also closely linked to that of the islands although it is more isolated because of its location in Central America and its Maya heritage.

Geography is fundamentally important to Caribbean culture and art. Maps are of particular interest as definitions of the historical and cultural space of the region. They are commonly used as symbols of identity and feature prominently in the national iconography of Caribbean states, and can also be regarded as diagrams of the power structures that have dominated the region, from the half-imaginary maps of the 'discoveries' to the modern map projections that represent the Caribbean as an appendage of North America. In Puerto Rico and Cuba, two nations where national and personal identity are particularly closely linked to geography, the map is a recurrent theme in contemporary art along with other national symbols such as the flag. The Puerto Rican artist Rafael Ferrer (b. 1933) was among the first to explore the possibilities of the map image. In the series of five lithographs *Istoria de la isla (Island's Tale)* (1974), maps of Puerto Rico were combined with motifs that evoke that country's complex political and cultural history, from its Prehispanic past to its controversial modern status as a commonwealth of the USA. Although the map images seem to shift and fall apart, their outlines remain reassuringly familiar.

The Caribbean region is quite large, but its land mass is small and at once fragmented and united by the Caribbean Sea. The region forms what the Cuban writer Antonio Benítez-Rojo has described as an alternative (and inherently more diffuse) 'island bridge' between North and South America or, culturally, between Anglo-America and Hispano-America. While this definition fails to consider the special cases of the French- and Dutch-speaking territories, it suggests that Caribbean culture is American culture, in its hemispheric sense. The Cuban president Fidel Castro described Cuba as an 'Afro-Latin' country, which calls attention to the African elements in Cuban culture as a distinguishing characteristic, but also to the close association with Latin American culture. Castro's definition can be extended to the other Hispanic islands, although it is untenable to define predominantly Protestant, non-Hispanic countries, such as Jamaica and Barbados, as 'Latin'.

The African presence does not in itself separate the Caribbean from the continent, however, since a significant part of the continental Latin and North American population is also of African descent. The Caribbean region can be placed in the larger context of what has been termed 'Plantation America'. Geographically, Plantation America ranges from the southern United States to north-eastern Brazil. This vast area has a common history as European plantation colonies were sustained by

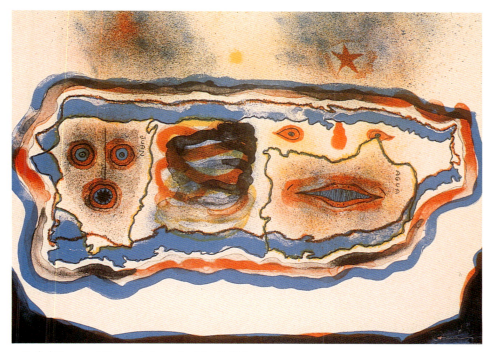

3 Rafael Ferrer, a lithograph from the *Island's Tale* series 1974

African slave labour, an experience that has generated a significant part of 'New World' culture. It is also useful to remember that the Caribbean is an Atlantic culture, which has its primary cultural relations within the Atlantic sphere, between Africa, Europe and America.

There is thus no simple cultural definition for the Caribbean and its specificity derives from combined factors such as the island geography, the long and complicated colonial history, the linguistic and religious variety, the near extinction of the Amerindian population, and the dominant African presence. The Caribbean islands were the first part of the Americas to be colonized by Europe when Columbus and his crew arrived in 1492. And although decolonization started early, with the Haitian revolution (1791–1804), the region's colonial history is one of the longest in the world, continuing into the second half of the twentieth century. This contrasts with continental Latin America where most states became independent in the eighteen twenties and thirties.

The Caribbean was initially controlled by Spain, although France, England and the Netherlands claimed their share in the seventeenth century. The Amerindian population was annihilated during the first decades of European settlement and replaced by West and Central Africans who were brought to the region in large numbers as slaves. They were the ancestors of the majority of the modern Caribbean population. During the nineteenth century, several other ethnic groups started migrating to the region, primarily from India, China and the Lebanon and while these groups remained minorities in most countries, 'East Indians' now make up about half the population of Trinidad and Guyana, and just over one third of Surinam. (In the Eastern Caribbean, the term 'East Indian' is commonly used to differentiate persons of Indian descent from the Amerindians.) The old colonial affiliations have resulted in some surprising migration patterns – about fifteen per cent of the Surinamese population is of Javanese descent and there are Hmong farming settlements in French Guiana.

The Caribbean can thus be described as a repopulated space and its inhabitants as displaced people who, as the Jamaican-born cultural philosopher Stuart Hall has put it, do not 'belong' here but have developed a rootedness in the region (or in those metropolitan areas to which many have in turn migrated). Language has been a significant part of this 'rooting' process – while Latin America is in essence united by language, the Caribbean is divided into four language groups. The Hispanic group is the largest and makes up nearly two thirds of the Caribbean population, the Francophone and English-speaking groups are roughly equal in size and Dutch is spoken by a minority. Dividing the Caribbean according to these official languages is not always tenable, however, since the Creole languages of the masses present a different picture. The Papiamentu of Curaçao and Aruba, which were important mercantile centres in the colonial era, is a mixture of Spanish, Portuguese, Dutch and West African languages and does not even resemble standard Dutch. Similarly, the Creole language of St Lucia is French-based while the official language is English, a result of the country's complicated colonial history. Haitian Creole, while recognizably based on French, also differs substantially from the French that is spoken by the elite.

The four language groups represent broad cultural entities, but there are considerable variations within these groups. This is certainly the case for the republic of Haiti and the French Overseas Departments of French Guiana and the French Antilles, which share French as their official language. The former has, in spite of its considerable social and political difficulties, been independent for nearly two centuries and has a distinctive cultural identity with strong African influences. French Guiana and the French Antilles, on the other hand, have enjoyed relative stability

14

and prosperity and have a closer, albeit ambivalent, cultural relationship with metropolitan France. Migration to North America has further complicated the linguistic balance of the region and has resulted in an ambivalent attitude towards the English language, especially in Puerto Rico where it is associated with US imperialism.

Language plays an important role in Caribbean art. The Cuban artist Consuelo Castañeda (b. 1958), who migrated to Miami a few years ago, has commented on the connection between language and identity in her recent conceptual work. Her installation *To be Bilingual – Lesson # 5: Art* (1995), which is part of a larger series, consists of poster-size enlargements of typical museum labels. Under her name, the country of origin has either been left blank or blocked out, referring to her displaced status. The text is in English, which is also the lingua franca of the international art world, although Castañeda is not yet fluent in this language.

As we have seen, the term Creole has been used to describe the dialects and syncretic languages that have developed in the Caribbean. It initially meant 'locally born' and usually referred to the white colonial elite, although it was also used to distinguish locally born slaves from those who came from Africa. The terms 'Creole' and its derivatives 'creolity' and 'creolization' are now used in a more general sense to describe the syncretic, or, as Benítez-Rojo has termed it, 'supersyncretic' character of Caribbean culture. The notion of 'creolization' is very important in Caribbean cultural theory and provides a useful vantage point from which to understand Caribbean culture and art.

It is now well understood that creolization is an ongoing process and that hybridity, plurality and open-endedness are fundamental characteristics of Caribbean culture. The Cuban anthropologist Fernando Ortiz played a pioneering role in articulating these issues. In 1939, he introduced his famous *ajiaco* metaphor – the *ajiaco* is a traditional Cuban pepper stew of Amerindian origin which is cooked over a long period by continuously adding new ingredients to the simmering mixture. Like the 'ingredients' of Creole culture, additions maintain their identity to varying degrees – some dissolve fully into the mixture or may even evaporate, while others remain more distinct. Ortiz also introduced the term 'transculturation' to describe the complex appropriation and transformation mechanisms that make up the creolization process, as an alternative to the conventional anthropological term 'acculturation' which merely denotes the adaptation of cultural traits from a dominant culture.

Much of this creolization process is involuntary, but the deliberate appropriation of ideas and images is also a central characteristic of Caribbean culture and art. The nineteenth-century Jamaican artist Isaac

5 Isaac M. Belisario *Koo-Koo or Actor Boy* from the *Sketches of Character* series 1837

M. Belisario (*c.* 1795–*c.* 1849) recorded an interesting example of this tendency in his lithography series *Sketches of Character* (1837). The series is best known for its depiction of the Jamaican Jonkonnu masquerade, a tradition that dates from the plantation period when the slaves were allowed free time around Christmas. The 'Actor Boy' character of Jonkonnu wore a white face mask and an elaborate 'aristocratic' European

17

outfit and entertained his audience by reciting random passages from Shakespeare plays. Another Jonkonnu character wore a headdress in the shape of a plantation house, also combined with a white face mask. These so-called fancy-dress Jonkonnu characters were not just imitating, but also parodying the Jamaican plantocracy and its 'European' culture or, to paraphrase the St Lucian author Derek Walcott, what started in imitation ended in invention.

The subversive inversion of images and symbols frequently appears in the modern era as well. Although he does not define himself as Caribbean, it is an important aspect of the work of Eddie Chambers (b. 1960), a British artist and curator of Jamaican parentage. In 1994, he participated in a project for which artists were invited to design flags to be flown at Liverpool Town Hall. This was an interesting challenge for a black artist in Britain where the national flag has sometimes become uncomfortably associated with the extreme right. Chambers replaced the colours of the Union Jack with the Rastafarian red, gold and green, an intervention reminiscent of the African-American artist David Hammons' *African American Flag* (1990) and Chambers' own anti-fascist collages of the early eighties. While the Actor Boy Jonkonnu mockingly adopted a 'white' identity, Chambers imposed a 'black' identity on a quintessentially 'white' symbol. Predictably, the flag was removed after one day, although, unwittingly adding to Chambers' intervention, this was done ceremoniously – he received his flag folded according to the protocol usually reserved for 'real' national flags.

Race is a central issue in Caribbean culture – modern Caribbean society was born out of racial repression and, as we will see throughout this book, racial activism has ever since played a major role in the region's socio-political and cultural development. In spite of the culturally repressive nature of the plantation system, the African heritage is of fundamental importance to Caribbean culture and it is one of the achievements of the post-colonial period that this is now well recognized. Caribbean culture should not however be defined solely as Afro-Caribbean or black culture, as is often done, since this ignores the substantial contribution of other racial and cultural groups such as the Amerindians, East Indians, Chinese, Lebanese and Europeans. Because of colonial history, it is particularly difficult to assess the European elements in Caribbean culture dispassionately, but Europe is certainly a fundamental and authentic ingredient of the Caribbean mix, even though whites are now a racial minority in most Caribbean countries.

As Ortiz' *ajiaco* metaphor reminds us, Caribbean culture is always in a state of flux. Caribbean societies have changed in recent times from

6 Jean-Michel Basquiat *Six Crimee* 1982

predominantly rural to urban and it can be argued that 'the city' has succeeded 'the plantation' as the main generator of Caribbean culture. Havana, Santo Domingo and San Juan now have more than two million inhabitants and Port-au-Prince and Kingston around one million. Mass migration to Europe and North America has reinforced the urbanization of Caribbean culture.

Caribbean policy makers frequently express concerns about North American 'cultural penetration' and with good reason given the remarkable reach of the American mass media, but the fact that Caribbean migrants are helping to shape modern urban culture in North America and Western Europe is often overlooked. Miami, for instance, is *de facto* a Caribbean city with a politically and economically powerful Cuban exile community known for its strong anti-Castro sentiments, and although there are many Jamaicans and Haitians, Spanish is the primary language of southern Florida, largely because of this Cuban presence. Likewise, a substantial part of the population of New York City and environs is of immediate Caribbean descent, mostly from Puerto Rico but also from Haiti, the Dominican Republic, Jamaica and the smaller islands.

The impact of Caribbean migration can be seen in Caribbean and metropolitan art. The painter Jean-Michel Basquiat (1960–88), whose meteoric and self-destructive ascent in the New York art world was emblematic of the eighties, had a Haitian father and a Puerto Rican mother. The Caribbean presence in New York contributed significantly to the graffiti street culture Basquiat used as his point of departure.

7 Hervé Télémaque *Currents No. 2* 1985

Basquiat, who lived in Puerto Rico for two years in his early teens, has in turn become a romantic anti-hero for many young Caribbean artists who see him as a martyr of the 'system'.

Many artists born in the Caribbean, or of immediate Caribbean descent, now work in North America or Western Europe and it is therefore no longer possible to define Caribbean art in strict geographical terms. Although most of these artists have faced marginalization, a few have become part of the artistic mainstream, which has sometimes come at the expense of their perceived 'Caribbeanness'. The Haitian-born painter Hervé Télémaque (b. 1937) moved to France in 1961 and became a noted representative of New Realism. His rebus-like works often contain references to his Haitian background, but he is now commonly described as a French artist. He had the following to say about his relationship with the Western mainstream: 'I want to position myself at the other side of this painting from the Third and Fourth World that is always subjected to interpretations, to slip to the side of those who do the interpretation; but it nevertheless remains that all I do is Haitian.' Télémaque's statement also points to the fact that Caribbean artists have historically had little control over the power structures that determine their access to

20

the metropolitan Western art world, which is after all what 'international' success usually amounts to.

The questions of cultural identity and its relationship to the international status of Caribbean art preoccupies contemporary Caribbean artists. In 1994, the Cuban artist Flavio Garciandía (b. 1954) started a group of paintings entitled *A Visit to the Tropical Art Museum*. They are painted in an eclectic, abstracted 'tropical' style, reminiscent of Lam and his contemporaries. Without being literal or specific, Garciandía's 'museum' explores the paradoxical issue of vernacular artistic language in an eclectic, continuously changing post-colonial culture. His ironic appropriations remind us of the imposed and self-imposed preconceptions about Cuban and Caribbean art and the dilemmas caused by the region's peripheral economic and political status.

Garciandía devised his *Tropical Art Museum* during the severe economic crisis that hit Cuba after the collapse of the Soviet Union, a period that

8 Flavio Garciandía, a work from *A Visit to the Tropical Art Museum* series 1994

coincided with unprecedented international interest in Cuban art. Like many of his contemporaries, Garciandía left Cuba during this time. He now lives in Mexico, but maintains close contact with his home country. Some of his paintings include bean-shaped forms which can be read as a formalist pattern but also as a reference to the beans that are a typical ingredient of the Cuban diet and remind us of the recent food shortages in Cuba and the connection, on a national and personal level, between art and economic survival. The *Tropical Art Museum* thus also comments on the fundamental contradiction of marketing cultural identity.

Economically, the Caribbean is part of the developing world and more often than not the asking party in its relationship with the North. Although mining and agriculture are important, the Caribbean is now the most tourism-dependent region in the world, which in a post-colonial situation has significant implications for cultural development. Although Caribbean tourism depends primarily on the physical beauty of the region, it also involves the marketing of vernacular culture, redesigned, if necessary, to meet market requirements. This places much of the Caribbean in ideological conflict where the plantation era is idealized as a romantic past. The Cuban painter Pedro Alvarez (b. 1967) explores this dilemma by combining appropriations of the work of the nineteenth-century Spanish-Cuban artist Víctor Patricio de Landaluze (1828–89) with tokens of capitalism that are now reappearing in Cuba. Landaluze used to be denounced for his colonialist outlook but now holds an important place in Cuba's cultural marketing efforts.

The relationship between Caribbean tourism and art has always been uneasy. Haiti, in particular, has had art tourism since the late forties when its 'primitive' school came to international attention. This has resulted in a system where most Haitian artists work specifically for certain galleries or dealers who often direct their output according to market demands. Some dealers are in essence wholesalers of Haitian art and cheap, mass-produced Haitian paintings can now be bought as souvenirs throughout the Caribbean. It is ironic, given external preconceptions about authenticity in Caribbean art, that much of the mass-produced 'primitive' art of the Caribbean is specifically created to meet Western expectations. While this extreme commercialization is culturally deplorable, the demand for such Haitian art has provided employment for thousands of people, something that cannot easily be dismissed since Haiti is the poorest country in the Western Hemisphere.

Discussions about Caribbean culture are heavily steeped in perceptions of race and ideology which makes it necessary to pay some attention to terminology. Terms like 'primitive' and 'naive', for instance, are highly

9 Pedro Alvarez *The End of History* from the *Variations on the End of History* series 1994

problematic and, certainly in the Caribbean, heavily burdened with racial and social preconceptions. The Jamaican art historian David Boxer has introduced the term 'intuitive' which emphasizes the untutored, often visionary nature of these artists' work. The term has gained some international currency but is still primarily used to describe the Jamaican 'primitives'. Yet the use of another term does not resolve the questions that surround the categorization of these artists – there are certain thematic concerns and stylistic characteristics that frequently appear in 'primitive' or 'intuitive' art, but it is difficult to separate them convincingly from the artistic mainstream. The real dividing factor is often the social and general educational background of the artist, which reflects the lingering social caste systems of Caribbean societies. Their classification is nonetheless a historical reality, especially in Haiti and Jamaica. I have therefore used the terms 'primitive' and 'intuitive' only for these two countries and if the need for such categorization arises for other countries, I have used 'popular art' as a generic term.

The spelling of Haitian Vaudou is also difficult – until recently, most English-language publications used 'Voodoo', which some feel is burdened with racial and cultural stereotypes. Resistance against this spelling has come mainly from African-American scholars, who prefer 'Vodun', 'Voudun' or 'Vodoun' which emphasizes the African, Dahomean origins of the religion. It is nonetheless important to make a distinction between

Dahomean Vodun and its syncretic Caribbean counterpart and I therefore decided to use 'Vaudou' in this book since this spelling is commonly used in Haiti.

Literature on continental Latin American art has become more widely available, but publications on Caribbean art are still scarce. The few existing general publications are compilations of more specialized essays by different authors and do not present a systematic survey. There are some art histories of the larger islands and a few monographs, particularly on Cuban and Haitian art, but other aspects of Caribbean art have not been documented at all. The study of Caribbean art is an emerging field and critical standards are still evolving so the quality of publications therefore varies considerably. Basic information on Caribbean art is not always readily available and the accuracy of source material is not always verifiable. The perpetuation of errors is therefore a serious and at this point almost unavoidable problem. Because of the polemical context of Caribbean art, it is also important to identify the ideological perspective of publications since this may significantly affect the presented narrative.

Most overseas publications are merely general introductions, published for travelling exhibitions or as chapters in publications on Latin American or black art. Local publications are usually more detailed but are typically produced in small editions and rarely distributed outside their country of origin. Language is of course also a problem and few local publications have been translated, which seriously limits their reach. Illustrations in local publications are usually rudimentary and some contain no illustrations at all, a major drawback for readers who do not have access to the original works (which is in itself often a problem in the Caribbean).

This book seeks to fill this void by presenting a part historical, part thematic introduction to the major trends and developments in Caribbean art, an exciting subject that is still insufficiently known. It offers a critical perspective on the issues that surround Caribbean art and the historical, socio-cultural and theoretical context in which it has developed. As the first of its kind, this book will undoubtedly become a reference for future studies. It is therefore important to note that it is not intended as an encyclopaedia of Caribbean art – artists were selected because their work exemplifies significant developments and issues and this should not suggest that those who are not discussed are less important. Attempting to include all notable artists the Caribbean has produced would come at the expense of clarity and the general understanding this study seeks to provide. Given the polemical nature of Caribbean art, however, this book will no doubt generate its own debates. This, of course, can only benefit the study of Caribbean art.

CHAPTER ONE

Prehispanic and Colonial Art

Although this book is primarily about the twentieth century, the ideas and circumstances that sustain modern Caribbean art have a long ancestry and are easier to understand if placed in a historical context. Prehispanic and colonial Caribbean art provides an important visual record of the social and cultural history of the region.

By the time of the European conquest at the end of the fifteenth century, the Caribbean islands were dominated by two related ethnic groups whose ancestors probably originated from the Orinoco River basin: the Taíno (Island Arawaks) in the Greater Antilles and the Bahamas, and the Island Carib in the east. On his arrival in the Caribbean in 1492, Columbus was met by the Lucayans, the Bahamian branch of the Taíno. The Taíno was the larger and more stable group, with a total population estimated at more than one million, and although they had not yet developed into a coherent nation-state, their territory was divided into loosely associated kingdoms, provinces and villages. They practised trade and farmed – their main crop was cassava (manioc). Taíno religion was based on the worship of a pantheon of *zemis*, nature divinities and ancestral spirits, headed by the sky god, Youcahuna. Their creation myths placed the origin of humanity in Hispaniola – they were obviously firmly established in the region.

The Taíno and their island neighbours did not produce any large-scale stone architecture or monuments, and much of their art was lost or destroyed during the early years of colonization so Prehispanic Caribbean art may seem insignificant when compared with Mesoamerican art. Yet Taíno art, in particular, is now highly regarded for its inventiveness and expressive power. Ironically, this recognition owes much to the controversial quincentenary of Columbus' landing in 1992 that brought the native peoples of the Americas into focus.

There are now significant collections of Prehispanic art in the Caribbean, primarily in the Dominican Republic and Puerto Rico, but most important Amerindian finds made during the colonial period were sent to European museums. Five significant and very rare Jamaican *zemi* woodcarvings – including the so-called 'Bird Man', found in 1792 in a   10

25

10 'Bird Man', found at
Carpenter's Mountain,
Vere, Jamaica, in 1792

cave in south-western Jamaica along with two other important carvings –
for instance, are in the British Museum, London, a matter of some controversy in Jamaica today. The 'Bird Man' represents a highly stylized, hybrid
creature – part man, part bird – and probably personifies the totemic bond
between its makers and the animal world. With its smoothly bulging surfaces and balanced asymmetry, it is a fine example of Taíno woodcarving
which was once described by William Fagg as the 'finest works of wood
sculpture produced in the Americas before or since Columbus'. Although
at least five hundred years old, the 'Bird Man' is in good condition and still
has part of its original shell inlays – incrustations made from gold, *guanin*
(a gold-copper alloy), shell or bone were commonly used in Taíno
carving. Three major Jamaican Taíno woodcarvings were discovered in
1994 and are now in Jamaica's national collection, which compensates
somewhat for the absence of the earlier discoveries.

Perhaps the most remarkable example of Taíno art is a rare, nearly intact
cotton reliquary *zemi* from the Dominican Republic which is now in
the collection of the University of Turin. The figure is ingeniously constructed from woven and wrapped cotton thread on a natural-fibre frame.

11 Cotton reliquary
zemi, Taíno Dominican
Republic

The head was built around the frontal part of a human skull, probably of a
cacique (chieftain), and shell inlays were used for the eyes. The cotton
figure closely resembles surviving wooden and ceramic *zemis*, with its
general stylization and the representation of details like the cotton wraps
the Taíno wore around their limbs. The wide-open mouth, staring eyes
and animated pose make the figure extraordinarily expressive. It is easy to
see why the early Spanish missionaries, with their late medieval sensibilities, described such *zemi* figures as malevolent spirits.

The Taíno became extinct within decades of Spanish colonization due
to disease, ill-treatment and collective suicide. The Island Carib were
more resilient and retreated to the less accessible islands of the Eastern
Caribbean from where they waged resistance against the European colo-
nizers until the eighteenth century. Although there are Amerindian traces
in much of the Caribbean population, the only remaining Amerindians
on the islands are a few hundred racially mixed Carib in the Eastern
Caribbean, mainly in Dominica. The Carifuna of Belize descend from
a group of Afro-Amerindian 'Black Carib' from St Vincent who were
deported there after a confrontation with the British in 1796. Larger

27

groups of ethnically related Amerindians of course still live in the Guianas, where they make up three to four per cent of the population, and where there has also been considerable intermixing with the African and, more recently, the East Indian population.

While the Taíno and Island Carib have left few visible traces on the Island Caribbean, they live on in popular memory and imagination. Their culture still exists in various aspects of Caribbean life – in place names, art, the cuisine, national emblems and the oral traditions – which was helped by the Maroons, freed and runaway African slaves who established communities in remote areas of the Caribbean and absorbed part of the dwindling Amerindian population. There are probably also Amerindian influences in syncretic, primarily Afro-Caribbean religions like Haitian Vaudou and the festival arts of the region, although this is yet to be conclusively studied.

For the Spanish conquistadores, the Caribbean was merely a stepping stone for the colonization of the American continent. It is only in the Greater Antilles, mainly Hispaniola and Cuba, that any substantial settlement took place and so the first colonial art forms appeared in early urban centres on these islands. Historical documents show that several painters and sculptors were involved in the construction and decoration of major churches and public buildings in Havana and Santo Domingo during the sixteenth century, but little is known about these artists and their work is primarily of historical value.

The African slave trade to the Caribbean started in the first decade of the sixteenth century. Tragically, the importation of African slaves was initially justified by advocates like Bartolomé de las Casas as an attempt to save the Amerindian population. In a matter of decades, the black population exceeded the white settlers in most Caribbean territories, except for the Spanish colonies where the rate remained lower. Estimates vary considerably but it is believed that between six and ten million Africans arrived in the Caribbean during the seventeenth and the eighteenth centuries – combined with the numbers sent to the American continent, this makes the Atlantic slave trade the largest forced migration in history. Although the main trading posts were along the west coast of Africa, many slaves were brought from the interior, so it is difficult to establish their exact ethnic origin. As the dominant African cultural retentions in the Caribbean suggest, however, the majority came from West and Central Africa, mainly from the Yoruba, Dahomey, Cross River and Kongo areas.

Despite the violent, repressive nature of the slavery system, the 'African Diaspora' quickly became a major constituent of Caribbean

28

and American culture. Syncretic Afro-Caribbean cultural expressions emerged in response to the new environment and often served as a form of mental resistance. Most of these early Afro-Caribbean art forms related to religion and ritual – seventeenth- and eighteenth-century Jamaican sources mention the production of funerary carvings by the slaves although only utilitarian objects have survived from that period. Even these utilitarian art forms are telling – the Jamaican pottery tradition that originated on the plantations, for instance, combines Taíno, West African, Spanish and English influences and represents a graphic record of the island's complex cultural history.

During the seventeenth century, the other Western European powers challenged the Spanish monopoly. The Caribbean was soon divided – politically, economically and culturally – between France, England, Spain and Holland, with small areas controlled by Denmark, Sweden, and later even Prussia. By the eighteenth century, a certain political stability had been achieved although there were ongoing land disputes between the European powers and frequent slave uprisings. A successful agronomic economy developed, based on slavery and the large-scale cultivation of sugar cane and other export crops like tobacco, spices and indigo. Creole society emerged and the first significant nationalist sentiments were articulated in defiance of central colonial government by the increasingly powerful Creole aristocracy.

This Creole elite aspired to a 'metropolitan' lifestyle and was wealthy enough to patronize the arts. The conditions were therefore right for colonial schools to develop in the larger, economically more successful territories, although differences in settlement patterns also played a role. In the British West Indies, for instance, absentee landownership was common which explains why the West Indian plantocracy was more inclined to patronize itinerant European artists who travelled with them to the region and to commission work in Europe. There are several monuments in Jamaica and Barbados by major English neo-classicists such as John Bacon (1709–87), John Flaxman (1755–1826) and Sir Francis Chantrey (1781–1841).

In the Hispanic Caribbean, the Creole elite was well settled and there was also a substantial professional and mercantile urban middle class. It was in these countries that the first significant Caribbean-born artists appeared – several were active during the second half of the eighteenth century. They satisfied the demand for religious art and portraits of the Creole elite, and, surprisingly, they rarely painted landscapes, but merely used them as backgrounds to their figure compositions. Not many of these artists ever visited Europe and they were exposed to European

12 José Nicholás de Escalera *The Holy Trinity* second half of the eighteenth century

art by what trickled down to the colonies. Apart from a few original European works, this included engravings, painted copies and the occasional treatise on art. Visiting European artists also made their mark.

The work of these early Creole artists was modelled on European art – as their patrons no doubt demanded – and from that perspective we can regard them as minor provincial artists. This applies to the Cuban painter José Nicholás de Escalera (1734–1804) who is often dismissed as an imitator of Murillo. Despite Escalera's obvious limitations, there is some merit to his sober, near monochromatic colour schemes and his insistent use of geometric compositional devices. Others, such as the Cubans Juan del Río (b. *c.* 1748) and Vicente Escobar (1762–1834), and the Puerto Rican José Campeche (1751–1809), were more inventive in their interpretation of European prototypes and so contributed to the development of a vernacular visual language. The 'naive' elements in their work may relate to emerging popular painting traditions.

Campeche was probably the most accomplished Creole artist of the period. His style evolved from decorative rococo to a daringly sober neoclassicism towards the end of his life. He painted religious works and sensitive portraits of the Puerto Rican elite – his paintings were hardly revolutionary but deviated from the Caribbean colonial norm with their

13 José Campeche *Portrait of Governor Ustariz c.* 1792

lively compositions, ornamental colours and penchant for the bizarre. Campeche's official portraits are somewhat stiff but often include historically significant background details, rendered with great precision. His *Portrait of Governor Ustariz* (c. 1792), for instance, includes a unique view of 13 the paving of the streets of San Juan, an accomplishment of Ustariz' administration. As the Puerto Rican art historian Haydee Venegas has pointed out, this urban view is based on a lived experience of the intense light of the tropics rather than on academic convention.

The racial background of these early Creole artists is significant and reflects the colour caste system that was developing in the Caribbean. Campeche was the coloured son of a black slave who had bought his freedom and Escobar was described as a *mestizo*. Escalera's racial background has been disputed although it is traditionally believed he was coloured. While barred from interaction with the white elite on an equal basis, the free coloureds could take up professions, including painting and sculpture. Some acquired wealth and social standing – Campeche's father, for instance, had established himself as a successful guilder and decorative painter.

Several minor European artists travelled to the Caribbean during the eighteenth and nineteenth centuries, often in the company of a wealthy patron such as a high colonial official or planter, and some eventually settled in the region. Their drawings and paintings served as records of the landscapes, scenes of local life and other curiosities seen during these travels, often on the estates of their patrons. Frequently, these works were later published in print or book form to meet the growing European interest in documentary images of the Caribbean.

The Italian itinerant painter Agostino Brunias (1730–96) is a particularly fascinating case. He was in Dominica, a British colony, from 1771 to 1773 as the personal painter of the governor, Sir William Young, and subsequently settled there. He also visited St Vincent, where Young owned land, and probably Barbados and Grenada as well. Brunias' paintings and sketches were later engraved to illustrate the Jamaican planter and historian Bryan Edwards' book, *The History, Civil and Commercial, of the British Colonies in the West Indies*, published in London in 1793. Unfortunately, the engravings fail to reproduce the sensual painterliness of Brunias' originals. Unlike most of his contemporaries, Brunias did not focus on the landscape or portraits of the colonial and Creole elite, instead, he painted the black slaves, the free coloureds and the St Vincent Carib, in picturesque scenes closer to the rococo *fêtes galantes* than the real colonial life. His sensualist preoccupation with the exotic 'other', especially the coloured woman, prefigures orientalism and Gauguin's primitivism.

14 Agostino Brunias *Chatoyer, the Chief of the Black Charaibes, in St Vincent with his Five Wives c.* 1770–80

George Robertson (1748–88), another itinerant artist, came to Jamaica in 1773 with the portraitist Phillip Wickstead, under the patronage of the Jamaican planter-historian William Beckford. Robertson was captivated by the spectacular beauty of the island and painted several landscapes in a lyrical, early romantic style. On returning to England, he successfully exhibited his Jamaican work and had six landscapes published as aquatints. Robertson is an early example of what became a trend of itinerant

15

landscapists in the nineteenth century. Others were primarily scientists, explorers and topographical artists, although their work is often of artistic interest as well. This applies to the famous German naturalist Alexander von Humboldt (1769–1859) who visited Cuba in 1800, during his travels in Central and South America, to study the plantation system there.

The socio-political order of the Caribbean changed dramatically in the nineteenth century. In 1791 a slave rebellion in Saint-Domingue, the wealthy French part of Hispaniola, escalated into a full-scale revolution led by the former slave Toussaint L'Ouverture. His successor, Jean-Jacques Dessalines, proclaimed Saint-Domingue's independence in 1804, changed the country's name to Haiti (its ancient Taíno name) and permanently abolished slavery. While prompted by the French revolutionary ideology of *Liberté, Egalité et Fraternité*, the Haitian Revolution was in effect the only successful slave revolt in Caribbean and American history. Haiti was the second nation in the Americas, after the USA, to become independent and the effect of the Haitian Revolution was felt throughout the hemisphere – Simon Bolívar's campaign to liberate Venezuela from Spanish rule, for instance, set out from Haiti in 1816, with substantial assistance from southern Haiti's president Alexandre Pétion. The Spanish-speaking, predominantly coloured eastern part of Hispaniola seceded from Spain in 1821 but was in turn occupied by Haiti. The area became independent as the Dominican Republic in 1844.

The Cuban sugar and coffee industries, among others, benefitted tremendously from Saint-Domingue's demise, because of the arrival in eastern Cuba of refugee planters and their slaves. Cuba, which remained Spanish, became the wealthiest and most desirable territory in the Caribbean – the USA declared its interest in the region with the Monroe and Manifest Destiny doctrines of the eighteen twenties and made several diplomatic overtures to gain control over the island. Meanwhile, the Cuban independence movement began, leading to the Independence Wars of the second half of the century, a cause that united small peasants and freed slaves with the middle and upper classes. The main ideologist of the Cuban independence struggle was the poet, journalist and art critic José Martí whose ideas about social and racial solidarity, cultural self-affirmation and Latin American unity greatly influenced modern anti-colonial nationalism.

The aftermath of the Haitian Revolution, along with the declining profitability of the plantation system and the Abolitionist campaigns, contributed to the abolition of slavery throughout the Caribbean. The Dutch were the first to do so in 1820, Britain followed in 1834, France in 1848 and Cuba was the last country in the Western Hemisphere to start the

15 George Robertson *Rio Cobre c.* 1773

process in 1880. To provide new labour for the plantations, indentured workers were brought in, mainly from India and China, but also from West Africa, Madeira and, in the case of Surinam, Java. Towards the end of the century, Lebanese merchants settled in the Caribbean. These new waves of migration added to the ethnic and cultural diversity of the region.

In spite of this instability, significant artistic developments took place in the Caribbean during the nineteenth century. Although not much is left, the artistic production of post-revolutionary Haiti is of special interest. Haiti's new black and coloured rulers were active art patrons who commissioned portraits, history paintings and religious works from a surprisingly large number of Creole, European and even American artists, including the Englishman Richard Evans, who is best known for his portrait of Henri Christophe (*c.* 1817), the king of northern Haiti. Evans ran an art school, one of several small, short-lived academies established in Haiti during the post-revolutionary period, at the king's legendary San Souci Palace. Although these artists and their patrons emulated French and English academism, significant shifts took place – for the first time in

35

Caribbean art, black and coloured people were routinely represented with the dignity and decorum until then reserved for the white colonial elite, instead of as subordinates, curiosities or victims. An eyewitness report describes religious paintings in the chapel of San Souci in which Christ and Mary were represented as blacks – it therefore seems justified to speak about a Haitian revolutionary aesthetic that prefigures the artistic ideas of early twentieth-century black nationalists such as Marcus Garvey.

The Haitian Revolution shaped modern Haitian art and popular iconography – historical scenes involving revolutionary heroes are common, especially in the Cap Haïtien School. The revolutionary iconography also influenced Vaudou, which is not surprising since the religion played an important role in the uprising that led to the Haitian Revolution. Certain *loas* (Vaudou divinities) are customarily represented in military and naval uniforms similar to those worn around the time of the revolution. Toussaint and Dessalines even became part of the Vaudou pantheon.

Perhaps the most intriguing painting to have come to us from early nineteenth-century Haiti is an undated view of the palace of San Souci produced by Numa Desroches (*c.* 1802–*c.* 80), a little-known painter who lived at the court of Henri Christophe as a boy. The work, which exists in three versions, is very different from everything else we know from that period. Its intuitive spatial organization, tightly patterned composition and visionary quality recalls the work of the twentieth-century Haitian 'primitives' – especially the fantastic cities of Préfète Duffaut (b. 1923). While Desroches' paintings may have been juvenile work, they also indicate that Haitian 'primitive' painting did not appear miraculously in the middle of the twentieth century but is part of a longer tradition. This is confirmed by rare documents such as a turn-of-the-century photograph made by or for the British explorer Sir Harry Johnston, which is yet to be dated conclusively. The photograph shows what Johnston described as a 'voodoo shrine', adorned with paintings that closely resemble the work of modern 'primitives' like Hector Hyppolite (1894–1948) or Philomé Obin (1892–1986).

Little is known about pre-twentieth-century popular art in the Caribbean. Most of it was linked to religion and ritual, but there were also some secular art forms. The Cuban art historian Jorge Rigol has described a tradition of popular street painting in Cuban cities and towns dating from the latter part of the eighteenth century. In Havana, many streets were named after the central motifs in these paintings that may have served a heraldic function.

Modern Afro-Caribbean religions such as Haitian Vaudou and Cuban Santería use a remarkable array of sacred arts, but the oldest surviving

16 Numa Desroches *The Palace of Sans Souci* n.d.

17 Photograph of a 'voodoo shrine' by Sir Harry Johnston, Haiti *c.* 1900

objects date from the mid-nineteenth century so their earlier history has to be reconstructed from descriptions in historical documents. Some of these sacred arts are ephemeral, such as the intricate *vèvè* ground drawings of Vaudou, or are kept in secrecy, which is inherent to their ritual purpose but also came about in response to cultural repression and, in the colonies of Roman Catholic countries, the forced evangelization of the slave population. It is mainly for this reason that many Afro-Caribbean religions appropriated mainstream Roman Catholic iconography. In Vaudou and Santería, for instance, popular images of saints acquired a double meaning and came to represent divinities of African origin – the Cuban patron saint El Virgen de la Caridad del Cobre also represents Ochún, the Yoruba-derived goddess of love.

Among these popular sacred arts, the Puerto Rican *santos* carving tradition is particularly interesting because it is unusually well documented. The *santos* are small woodcarvings of saints invoked for assistance in domestic rituals. The tradition can be traced back to the late eighteenth century and has survived into modern times. Many were made by artist families whose skills were handed down from generation to generation, like the Rivera family which was active from the mid-nineteenth to the mid-twentieth century. Most *santos* follow conventional Roman Catholic iconography, although there are some interesting transformations – the Three Magi, for instance, were particularly popular with black Puerto Ricans, obviously because of the presence of a black figure. In Puerto Rico, Melchior is the black king instead of Balthazar. Another remarkable type is La Mano Poderosa, which translates as 'the powerful hand'. It is an allegorical representation of the genealogy of Christ consisting of a hand, with each finger surmounted by a tiny representation of a member of the Holy Family. The Puerto Rican scholar Doreen Colón Camacho has suggested that the image is of Franciscan origin. It may also be possible to trace the image to the Islamic influences in Iberian culture since in the Islamic world the hand symbol is associated with the immediate family of the Prophet Mohammed. Although the iconography of La Mano Poderosa is unique, hand symbolism appears frequently in the popular religions and occult practices of the Americas.

Caribbean popular painting and sculpture traditions are closely related to the festival arts, especially the carnival and masquerade traditions. Most of the information we have about the earlier history of these traditions was recorded by mainstream artists interested in the picturesque – for instance, the principal early source on Jamaica's Christmas-time Jonkonnu masquerade is a series of lithographs by Isaac M. Belisario, the first known Jamaican-born artist. The series documents the customs of the black

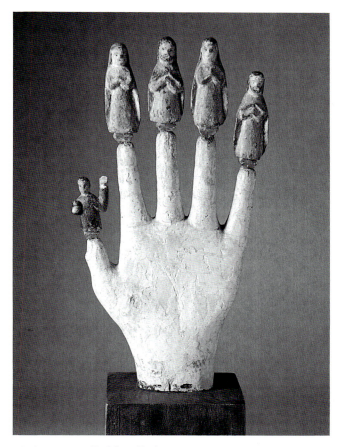

18 Anonymous La Mano Poderosa *c.* 1900

Jamaican population and was made during the four-year 'apprentice' period that followed the abolition of slavery. Belisario published twelve of these drawings as *Sketches of Character* in 1837 with an explanatory text.

Evidence of similar interests can be seen in the work of the Spanish-born painter and caricaturist Víctor Patricio de Landaluze who came to Cuba in 1852. Landaluze is the best-known Cuban exponent of *costumbrismo*, the documentation of picturesque customs and physical types – a significant trend in Latin American painting and literature during the nineteenth century. While also heavily indebted to Goya's early work, Landaluze's images relate closely to the picturesque depictions of popular

Cuban life found on cigar-box labels and in the work of contemporaries such as the French-born printmaker Frédéric Mialhe (1810–81), who was active in Havana from 1838 to 1854.

Like Belisario, Landaluze is important for his documentation of Afro-Cuban traditions in paintings such as *Epiphany Day in Havana*. While accurate in detail, the caricatural nature of his work reflects the racial prejudices of nineteenth-century Cuba, reinforced by his own opposition to the Independence Movement. The coloured woman, the mulata, for instance, is depicted as a willing object of male desire while the black man is represented as a fun-loving buffoon. In spite of this, Landaluze's work chronicles the development of iconographic prototypes that became very important in nationalist twentieth-century Caribbean art – apart from his

19 Víctor Patricio de Landaluze *Epiphany Day in Havana* second half of nineteenth century

20 Víctor Patricio de Landaluze *The Cane Harvest* 1874

masquerade scenes and mulata romances, this also applies to plantation scenes such as *The Cane Harvest* (1874). Like his eighteenth-century predecessors, Landaluze presents an idealized view of plantation life and suggests an almost cordial relationship between the field slaves and the whip-carrying overseer (although he captured, perhaps inadvertently, a glint of defiance in the expression of the cane-cutters).

Although *costumbrismo* can be seen as an early form of primitivism, Landaluze's style suggests that nineteenth-century Caribbean artists were not familiar with avant-garde trends in European art. On the contrary, they were well aware of these developments, aided by the growing mobility and communication between Europe and the region. During the latter part of the nineteenth century, for instance, several major European artists travelled to the Caribbean. Foremost among them was Paul Gauguin (1848–1903) who visited Martinique and Panama in 1887, his first venture into the tropics and although he was ill during most of the trip, his stay in Martinique was the decisive moment in the development of his mature style and consolidated his interest in the exotic. He had no measurable contemporary influence in the region, but his work and ideas heavily influenced the nationalist Caribbean schools of the early twentieth century.

American artists were also attracted to the region. Winslow Homer (1836–1910) visited the Bahamas and Cuba repeatedly during the latter part of his life. The works he produced in response to these visits represent a striking departure from the idyllic, descriptive approach prevailing in pre-twentieth-century Caribbean landscape and genre art. His most famous Caribbean painting, *The Gulf Stream* (1899), dramatically represents humanity's powerlessness against the unpredictable, violent side of nature. Homer's watercolours of Caribbean fishermen and sailors also prefigure the heroic representations of the black working-class male in nationalist twentieth-century Caribbean, especially Jamaican, art.

Several nineteenth-century European artists of note were born in the Caribbean – the French painters Theodore Chassériau (1819–56), who was born in what is now the Dominican Republic, and Camille Pissarro

21 Paul Gauguin *Fruit Gatherers* 1887

22 Winslow Homer *The Gulf Stream* 1899

(1831–1903), whose family were French merchants on the Danish island of St Thomas. While Chassériau's birthplace is of limited relevance to his work, some of Pissarro's early work relates directly to his Caribbean background, specifically the drawings done during, and shortly after, his travels to St Thomas and Venezuela between 1852 and 1855.

A contemporary of Chassériau, the painter Michel-Jean Cazabon (1813–88) belonged to the influential 'French Creole' class of Trinidad, descendants of white and coloured Martiniquans who had settled in Trinidad at the invitation of the Spanish government shortly before the island became British in 1797. Cazabon, who was coloured, studied art in Paris and exhibited there at the salons. He returned to Trinidad in 1852, but lived in Martinique from 1862 to 1870 in a futile effort to find an environment more receptive to his metropolitan artistic interests. Cazabon left behind an eclectic œuvre. His genre scenes reflect his familiarity with the work of Brunias and other itinerant artists, but he is more important as a landscapist. He was influenced by French romantic and realist landscape painting, especially the School of Barbizon, and was at his best in his luminous watercolour landscapes, some of which are surprisingly modern with their tautly structured compositions and stylized details.

23

23 Michel-Jean Cazabon *View of Immortelle Tree on Belmont Hill c.* 1850
24 Henri Cleenewerck *The Yumuri Valley at Dawn* 1865

Although Cazabon worked in relative isolation, he was not the only landscapist in the Caribbean to move from the topographical to the romantic and post-romantic landscape. In Cuba, painters such as Esteban Chartrand (1840–83) and the Belgian Henri Cleenewerck (c. 1825–c. 1903) sought to represent the dramatic essence of the Cuban landscape rather than its anecdotic details. These landscapists are associated with an identifiable Cuban school of painting that appeared during the nineteenth century. The cohesiveness of this school can be attributed to the influence of the San Alejandro Academy in Havana, which was founded in 1817. Its first director was the French painter Jean-Baptiste Vermay (1786–1833), a student of Jacques-Louis David. The academy still functions today and is the oldest art school in the Caribbean.

The urbane, intimate portraits and figure scenes by painters such as Guillermo Collazo (1850–96) and José Arburu Morell (1864–89) are typical products of the Cuban School in the latter part of the century. They were heavily influenced by French and Spanish academism, but these Cuban artists also absorbed some of the European innovations of the time and were responsive to the Cuban ambience. Collazo's *The Siesta*

25 Guillermo Collazo *The Siesta* 1886

(1886) is an evocative depiction of the lifestyle of the wealthy Havana bourgeoisie who were the main patrons of the Cuban School. The image has subtle orientalist overtones and the moody, sensitive treatment of light and atmosphere suggests an awareness of impressionism. With few exceptions, the apolitical, socially conservative nature of nineteenth-century Cuban art is striking, despite Cuba's lengthy independence struggle and Martí's interest in a nationalist art. Collazo, for instance, belonged to a pro-independence family from eastern Cuba and so spent much of his adult life in the United States and France, yet this background is not apparent in his Cuban work.

By the turn of the century, artists began to respond overtly to the social and political changes. Two academic painters, Armando Menocal (1863–1942) and Eduardo Morales (1868–1938), fought on the side of the Independistas and produced several paintings on the heroic events of the Ejército Libertador, the final stage of the Independence Wars in which Martí lost his life. Others, such as José Joaquín Tejada (1867–1943) and Juana Borrero (1877–96), turned towards the urban working class for their subjects. Only three works survive from Borrero's short career, but her best-known painting, *The Little Rascals* (1896), is often cited as a significant step in the development of Cuban art because it depicts Afro-Cubans sympathetically, in keeping with Martí's doctrine of racial solidarity.

It is appropriate to close this chapter with the Puerto Rican painter Francisco Oller (1833–1917) since his work points more decisively towards the future of Caribbean art. Oller studied in Spain and France and spent most of his life travelling restlessly between Puerto Rico and Europe. A friend of Pissarro and Cézanne, he is sometimes credited with bringing impressionism to Spain. Although his landscapes retained impressionist overtones, the work Oller produced in Puerto Rico was in essence realist and heavily influenced by Courbet. Oller made several short-lived attempts at establishing an art academy in San Juan and articulated ideas about a national art. In a speech to the students of the Normal School in San Juan in 1906, he stated: 'The artist must participate in the epoch in which he lives; if he wants to be authentic, he must be of his country, of his people.' His most ambitious painting, *The Wake* (1893), exemplifies these views. It depicts a custom of the Puerto Rican peasantry – a festive vigil held to usher a dead child into afterlife – not for its picturesque interest, but as a reflection of the artist's social and cultural commitments. Surprisingly, Oller's statement that accompanied the work to the 1895 Paris Salon condemned the practice as 'an orgy of brutish appetites under the guise of a gross superstition'. This critical stance may be explained by the social and cultural segregation between the peasantry

26 Francisco Oller *The Wake* 1893

and the educated upper class to which Oller belonged and, perhaps, his insecurities about the European public's response to the subject. Before it was exhibited in Paris, the work was also shown in Havana, where it was well received by the Cuban intelligentsia. While Oller's ideas originated in European romanticism and realism, their application to the Caribbean represents a turning point and prefigures the nationalist schools of the first half of the twentieth century.

27 Víctor Manuel *Gitana Tropical* 1929

CHAPTER TWO

Modernism and Cultural Nationalism

The twenties and thirties were decisive years in the development of modern Caribbean art. It was the golden age of nationalism globally, as new and old nations sought to find their place within a rapidly changing political, economic and social order. In the colonized world, there was a surge of anti-colonial and anti-imperialist sentiments. It is within this context that the first Caribbean national art movements appeared, of which the best known is the Cuban vanguardia.

Although anti-colonial nationalism was also brewing among the peasantry and urban working class, it was essentially articulated and spearheaded by the emerging Caribbean intelligentsia. Many of these intellectuals studied in London, Paris, Madrid or New York, or lived for extended periods in these cities that, paradoxically, became centres of international anti-colonial activism. Paris, in particular, attracted many artists, writers and intellectuals from the Caribbean, Latin America and Africa, which helped to steer Caribbean art towards modernism. The Martiniquan writer and politician Aimé Césaire, for instance, met the future Senegalese president Léopold Senghor there in the late thirties, an encounter that led to the development of the negritude movement, one of the most influential expressions of black cultural nationalism. Shortly before returning to Martinique, Césaire wrote the first version of his epic poem *Cahier d'un retour au pays natal (Notebook of a Return to the Native Land)* (1939), a masterwork of political surrealist poetry. Similarly, most Cuban vanguardia artists lived in Paris for some time. Early Cuban masterpieces such as Víctor Manuel's *Gitana Tropical* (1929) and Eduardo Abela's *The Triumph of the Rumba* (c. 1928) were painted there. 28

Caribbean cultural nationalism is closely related to the Latin America movements that produced, among others, Mexican muralism and Brazilian modernism. Hispanic Caribbean artists, in particular, were visibly influenced by the continental schools and several studied, lived or even taught in Mexico City. Caribbean modernism had its own character, however, and evolved in response to local conditions rather than in imitation of the continent. Although there were some mural projects, muralism did not take hold in the Caribbean, mainly because the necessary public or corporate patronage was not readily available.

The relationship between Caribbean cultural nationalism and developments in African-American culture is also significant. The migration of West Indians to North American cities contributed to this alliance and provided a new channel for intellectual and cultural exchanges. Claude McKay, a key literary exponent of the Harlem Renaissance, was Jamaican, as was Marcus Garvey, the founder of the internationally active United Negro Improvement Association (UNIA). The UNIA was particularly influential in Harlem, where Garvey lived from 1916 until he was deported to Jamaica in 1927. Several important Harlem Renaissance figures travelled to the Caribbean, including the writer and anthropologist Zora Neale Hurston who studied Afro-Caribbean ritual practices in Jamaica and Haiti as a Guggenheim fellow in the late thirties.

The Caribbean nationalist intelligentsia paid considerable attention to the formulation of cultural theories such as negritude that still influence the post-colonial discourse globally. Cultural self-affirmation was deemed a critical part of decolonization and art was recognized as a powerful nation-building tool. The schools that emerged in this context were primarily concerned with the exploration of indigenous aesthetic values and national cultural identity. Many artists and intellectuals turned towards the culture of the masses as the paradigmatic national culture. Consequently, popular Caribbean culture was studied and documented, much of it for the first time. Previously neglected or even actively repressed Afro-Caribbean traditions received special attention – this separates Caribbean cultural nationalism from its continental Latin American counterparts. The Cuban anthropologist and political activist Fernando Ortiz, for instance, advanced the recognition of Afro-Cuban traditions as an integral part of Cuban national culture and published several influential studies on the subject, one as early as 1906. The impact on Cuban art and literature was significant, the trend was known as Afrocubanismo.

Despite the indigenist preoccupation with the traditional, Caribbean cultural nationalism was a progressive, even utopian movement, dedicated to modernity and modernism with typical 'New World' zeal. Artists sampled freely from post-impressionism, symbolism, expressionism, cubism, art deco and, later, surrealism but generally ignored the radical formalist and conceptual explorations of early modernism. It took until the fifties for Caribbean artists to show any significant interest in abstraction – modernism was thus not an end in itself, but served as a vehicle for indigenous content. Gauguin's romantic vision of the tropics was a particularly powerful influence on the nationalist schools. It may seem paradoxical that these schools espoused primitivism, with its close links to the Western colonial world view, but early Caribbean modernists placed the primitivist preoccupation with the 'native' in a nationalist context and used subjects and idioms that were part of their own cultural background.

The educated Caribbean middle classes, to which most artists and cultural theorists of the time belonged, were nonetheless socially and culturally isolated from the masses. The Martiniquan author Frantz Fanon commented on this issue in *The Wretched of the Earth* (1961) where he wrote: 'The culture that the intellectual leans towards is often no more than a stock of particularisms. He wishes to attach himself to the people; but instead he only catches hold of their outer garments. And these outer garments are merely the reflection of a hidden life, teeming and perpetually in motion.' The indigenist use of popular culture indeed sometimes amounted to latter-day *costumbrismo*. Wifredo Lam was conscious of this dilemma and told Max-Pol Fouchet, the author of a monograph on his work (1976), about Cuba in the forties: 'Havana was a land of pleasure, of sugary music, rumbas, mambos and so forth. The Negroes were considered picturesque... I refused to paint chá-chá-chá. I wanted with all my heart to paint the drama of my country, but by thoroughly expressing the Negro spirit, the beauty of the plastic art of the blacks. In this way I could act as a Trojan horse that would spew forth hallucinating figures with the power to surprise, to disturb the dreams of the exploiters.'

The Cuban vanguardia emerged during the repressive regime of Gerardo Machado (1924–33), a period of intense political and cultural activism among young Cuban intellectuals who rediscovered the ideas of José Martí. Their concerns were aptly summarized in the 1927 manifesto of the Grupo Minorista, an influential dissident group. Part of it reads: 'Collectively or individually, our nucleus has fought and is still fighting: for the revision of false and outmoded values; for popular art and, in general, new art in all its diverse forms; for the introduction and dissemination in Cuba of the latest artistic and scientific doctrines, theory and praxis... for Cuban economic independence. Against Yankee imperialism. Against political dictatorships throughout the world, in the Americas, in Cuba.' The signatories included the critics Juan Marinello and Jorge Mañach, the writer and musicologist Alejo Carpentier, the painters Eduardo Abela (1889–1965) and Antonio Gattorno (1904–80), and the sculptor Juan José Sicre (1898–1972). The anti-American tone of the manifesto should not surprise since Cuba was a major target of US interventionism in the Greater Antilles. The USA had gained control over Cuba and Puerto Rico in 1898 after the Spanish-American War and in 1902 Cuba became an independent republic, although the USA

28 Eduardo Abela *The Triumph of the Rumba c.* 1928

retained intervention rights until 1934 under the unilaterally imposed Platt Amendment. The Machado regime, in particular, was supported by the USA.

The *Exhibition of New Art* which opened in Havana in May 1927, a few days after the publication of the Minorista manifesto, is usually cited as the vanguardia's defining moment. This was the first group exhibition devoted to Cuban modernism and included the work of Abela, Gattorno, Carlos Enríquez (1900–57) and his American wife Alice Neel (1900–84), Víctor Manuel García (1897–1969) and Marcelo Pogolotti (1902–88), among others. The exhibition was promoted by the *Revista de Avance*

(1927–30), a periodical associated with the Minoristas and dedicated, as its title implies, to the promotion of the avant-garde. Abela produced the logo for the exhibition, a crude art-deco design that symbolized the event's liberating function – Abela was also a political cartoonist, best known for his anti-Machado cartoon *El Bobo (The Fool)* (1930–34). The San Alejandro Academy had become a conservative force in Cuban art and the espousal of modernism therefore also amounted to a rebellion against academism.

The major vanguardia artists had distinct artistic personalities, but their thematic pursuits were closely related and document a search for archetypal images of 'the Cuban'. In the first phase of the Cuban avant-garde, romanticized depictions of peasant life were most popular – the majority of Caribbean nationalist schools shared this interest which can be explained as a nostalgic reaction against urbanization. Other recurrent themes were the Afro-Cuban traditions, the urban proletariat, the Independence Wars and its heroes, and the physical environment. Portraits were also common and provided a source of income for many vanguardia artists and their Caribbean contemporaries.

Víctor Manuel's *Gitana Tropical* (1929) is representative of the first phase 27 of the vanguardia. While technically a portrait, it represents a Creole archetype of femininity. The *gitana* does not belong to a specific racial or social group, but embodies Cuba's multi-racial, multi-cultural identity. The impact of the School of Paris is evident in the figure's simplified, rounded forms and the contrasting geometric grid structure of the background landscape. The influence of Gauguin is also obvious, although the image is surprisingly sober and restrained, despite its exotic title. *Gitana Tropical* is the classic example of Víctor Manuel's extended series of related images of women, most of them in a more self-consciously primitivist style. He also painted various idyllic views of the parks and streets of Havana and Matanzas.

Víctor Manuel's romantic gitanas and suburban landscapes seem oblivious to the harsh realities of the period. A similar idealization can be seen in the work of Antonio Gattorno although there are hints of social criticism in his emaciated *guajiros* (Cuban peasants) of the thirties. His best-known paintings represent a somewhat sentimental vision of vanishing Cuban country life in a style heavily influenced by post-impressionism and art deco. Gattorno's *Women by the River* (1927), an early 29 painting, lacks the anecdotic detail of his later vanguardia work but clearly documents the search for iconic images. The bathers or the bare, generic background landscape may hardly qualify as typical, but the 'Cubanness' of the scene is inferred by such attributes as the bananas in the still life

29 Antonio Gattorno *Women by the River* 1927

and the banana tree. The presence of the subservient, fully clothed black woman in the background fulfills the same function and reminds of the work of *costumbrista* artists such as Brunias and Landaluze, who frequently juxtaposed seductive mulatas with black attendants. The banana tree is a recurrent, emblematic motif in nationalist Caribbean art along with the palm tree and the sugar cane. With its crisp, elegantly curved lines, the banana tree also lends itself well to art-deco stylization.

The monumental clarity and stillness of Gattorno's style contrasts greatly with the frenzied expressionist language used by Carlos Enríquez. Although Enríquez also painted works that comment on the plight of the working class, he is best known for what he called his 'guajiro ballads', romantic and often frankly erotic fantasies of a Cuban countryside inhabited by voluptuous mulatas and macho mambises, the peasant outlaws of the Independence Wars. In his famous *The Abduction of the Mulatas* (1938) everything conspires to create an image of sensual rapture: the liquid, merging forms of the women, men and horses; the sweltering background landscape; and the luminous, multi-layered paint application. The image was obviously modelled after Rubens' *The Abduction of the*

54

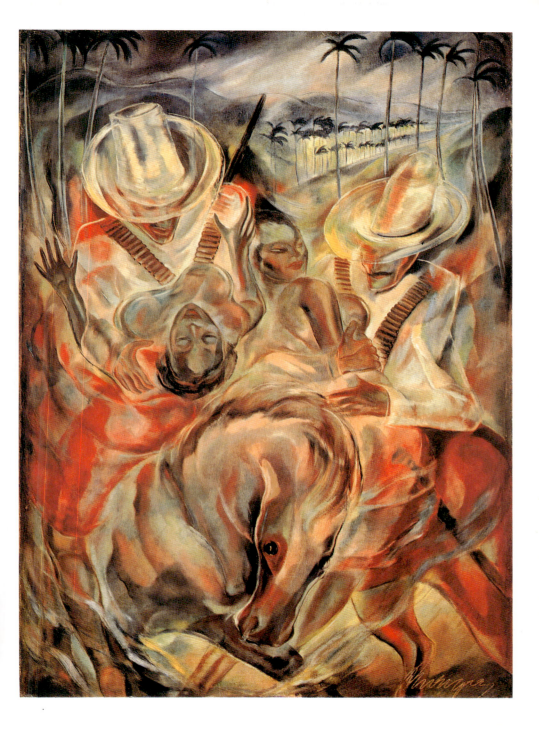

Daughters of Leucippus (1617), although its ecstatic sexuality makes the Rubens seem almost puritanical. *The Abduction of the Mulatas* and related works by Enríquez perpetuate the myth of the sexual availability of the coloured woman. As *Women by the River* also illustrated, sexual, racial and social clichés abound in vanguardia art, showing that there is only a thin line between national icon and stereotype, a fundamental contradiction of Caribbean cultural nationalism.

29

Marcelo Pogolotti's paintings of the mid-thirties offer a very different perspective. Influenced by his involvement with the Turin futurists and the Association des Ecrivains et Artistes Révolutionnaires in Paris, he sought to paint 'the Cuban', but was not interested in the picturesque or the nostalgic. His Cuba was emphatically modern and his 'types' were the worker, the cane-cutter, the guardsman, the clergyman, the bourgeois woman and the capitalist whom he represented as anonymous actors in Cuba's social drama. Large American corporations had established a virtual monopoly over the Cuban sugar industry and invested heavily in other vital areas of the economy, such as banking and light and power, as they did in other parts of the region. Pogolotti's famous *Cuban Landscape*

31 Marcelo Pogolotti *Cuban Landscape* 1933

56

32 Fidelio Ponce de León *Tuberculosis* 1934

(1933) refers to this development and denounces the capitalist exploitation of the Cuban sugar industry and its workers. The work is visibly influenced by the machine aesthetics of Fernand Léger and the purists, with whom Pogolotti was in close contact at the time.

The work of Fidelio Ponce de León (Alfredo Fuentes Pons, 1895–1949) is equally devoid of the picturesque, but, unlike Pogolotti, Ponce was not interested in socio-political statements. Instead, he portrayed a private world haunted by existential anguish, religious mysticism, poverty, alcoholism and disease. As the only major vanguardia artist not to study abroad, Ponce was less visibly inspired by European modernism although he listed Modigliani among his influences, along with El Greco, Murillo and Rembrandt. His work also recalls the angst-ridden expressionism of Edvard Munch. His outlook is perhaps best expressed in *Tuberculosis* (1934), a haunting *memento mori* painted in bleak hospital colours. The painting represents a group of gaunt, elongated figures, almost lovingly gathered around a grimacing skull. Tragically, Ponce later contracted tuberculosis, then a common disease among the Cuban poor. Ponce may not have been interested in indigenist subjects, but *Tuberculosis* reflects a Cuban reality.

57

33 Amelia Peláez *Still Life* 1942

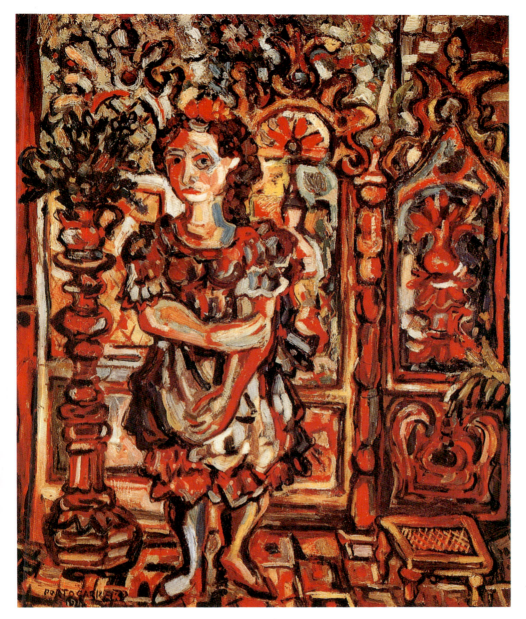

34 René Portocarrero, a work from the *Interiors from El Cerro* series 1943

Machado was overthrown in 1933 and was soon succeeded by the populist military strongman Fulgencio Batista who controlled Cuba until 1944 and again from 1952 until the 1959 revolution. The turmoil of the early thirties was followed by a period of national reconciliation – the vanguardia, which had started as a dissident movement, now received some official support. The first acknowledgment was the establishment in 1935 of a national salon, sponsored by the newly installed Directory of Culture. These salons included modernist and academic art, exhibited in separate rooms. Several vanguardia masterpieces in the Cuban national collection were acquired from these exhibitions – *The Abduction of the Mulatas, Gitana Tropical* and Abela's *Los Guajiros (The Cuban Peasants)* from the 1938 salon. The authorities also sponsored a few mural projects such as the now destroyed murals at the General José Miguel Gómez municipal school that included paintings by Enríquez, Víctor Manuel and Ponce. Another important initiative was the foundation of the Free Studio of Painting and Sculpture in 1937, whose main organizer and director was Abela. The school received a subsidy from the Directory of Culture and, as in the Mexican free schools, tuition was available free of charge to anyone interested. Teaching methods were innovative and encouraged the exploration of indigenous subjects. Although the Free Studio lasted less than a year, it was the first significant alternative to the elitist San Alejandro Academy.

During this period, Cuban modernism entered what Cuban art historians have called its 'classical phase'. The emerging second generation was generally less interested in socio-political issues even though the Mexican School had replaced European modernism as the most distinct outside influence. While the Cuban avant-garde was from its onset closely allied with literary developments, this association intensified in the forties. Two literary figures were particularly influential: Alejo Carpentier, who was in Cuba during the early forties, and the poet and critic José Lezama Lima. The latter edited the internationally acclaimed arts journal *Orígenes* (1944–56) that published the work of most important Cuban artists of the time. Of particular interest in the writing of Lezama Lima and Carpentier is the notion of *barroquismo*, the eclectic, baroque orna-mentalism they identified as a fundamental characteristic of the Cuban and Latin American aesthetic.

While other indigenist themes remained popular, artists such as Amelia Peláez (1896–1968) and René Portocarrero (1912–85) found a new nationalist paradigm in the ornate, eclectic colonial architecture of the Cuban capital. This new direction in Cuban art is often referred to as the School of Havana. Chronologically, Peláez belongs to the vanguardia generation, although her best-known work dates from the forties and fifties and is closer in form and spirit to that of the younger painters. She brought a personal, feminine perspective to the search for 'the Cuban'. Her *Still Life* (1942) is typical of her mature style and reflects her main thematic pursuits: the still life, the interior and architectural ornamentation. The frontality of the image, its brilliant colours and heavy, interlocking black outlines remind of the fan-shaped, stained-glass windows found over doorways in the colonial mansions of Havana. The work also reflects her interest in pictorial structure. This formalism separated her from her Cuban contemporaries and was influenced by her studies with the Russian constructivist Alexandra Exter in Paris. 33

Portocarrero's sumptuous *Interiors from El Cerro* (1943) depict the same interiorized urban life that inspired Peláez, although his compositions have a more nervous, expressionist quality. His themes also ranged wider and included the rural and urban landscape, popular culture and religion. These thematic interests are summarized in *Homage to Trinidad* (1951), a fanciful view of the historical city of Trinidad, painted the year before he started his famous visionary panoramas of Old Havana. The crowned female figures in the religious procession in the foreground herald the popular saints of his *Colour of Cuba* series on Cuban folklore of the early sixties. 34

The Second World War brought together Caribbean intellectuals and exiled members of the European avant-garde, and provided a new impulse in the development of Caribbean art. It was during this period, for instance, that Wifredo Lam returned to Cuba. After fifteen years in Spain, during which he fought on the Republican side in the Civil War, in 1938 Lam had been accepted into the Paris avant-garde as a protégé of Picasso. At the start of the Second World War, Lam fled to Marseilles where he joined the circle around André Breton and rapidly assimilated the language and methods of surrealism. He made the long, nerve-racking passage to Martinique in 1941, in the company of Breton and his entourage.

While in Martinique, Lam and Breton met Aimé Césaire who had returned to his 'native land' just before the start of the war. Césaire's negritude aesthetics deeply influenced Lam's mature work. After a brief stop in the Dominican Republic, Lam finally arrived in Cuba in the summer of 1941 and lived there, with some interruptions, until he moved back to Paris in 1952. In Havana, he befriended Carpentier and the folklorist Lydia Cabrera who encouraged him to explore Afro-Cuban traditions. This reacquaintance with his heritage was a turning-point in Lam's development – it resulted in dramatic, powerful works such as *The Jungle* (1943) and *The Eternal Presence* (1945) that contrast greatly with his earlier, somewhat anaemic cubist paintings.

The Jungle is usually cited as Lam's masterwork and surely ranks with Picasso's *Guernica* (1937) as one of the most haunting images created this century. The mask-like faces of the four figures are visibly indebted to Picasso, although Lam brought an explicit anti-colonial agenda to Picasso's primitivism. Like most of Lam's mature work, *The Jungle* incorporates allusions to traditional Afro-Cuban iconography such as the scissors, a motif associated with herbalism. The imagery was clearly inspired by the overwhelming, sexually suggestive tropical flora of the Caribbean and embodies the central pantheist notion of most Afro-Caribbean religions that nature is humanity's point of contact with the transcendental. The backdrop of sugar cane and tobacco leaves, which Lam also used in other works of the period, reminds of Fernando Ortiz' allegorical study of Cuban culture, *Cuban Counterpoint of Tobacco and Sugar* (1940). The choice of vegetation is significant to the political meaning of the work – sugar cane and tobacco, Cuba's traditional crops of the Plantation period, form the 'backdrop' of the island's colonial history and are heavily charged with connotations of slavery and exploitation, but also of resistance and revival. Because of this association, *The Jungle* is perhaps best understood as an allegory of Plantation America.

While the socio-political prevails in *The Jungle*, other Lam works of the period, such as *The Chair* (1943), are more directly associated with Afro-Cuban traditions and rituals. *The Chair* may seem like a casual garden still life, but the image reminds of the altars to the *orishas* (divinities) Santería practitioners keep in their homes or gardens. This interpretation is confirmed by the more anecdotic Santería altars Lam painted the following year and the association of chairs or stools with the divine and the ancestral in several traditional West African religions. Significantly, the vase on the chair contains an 'offering' of tobacco leaves, the crop Ortiz associated with the ritualistic, primarily Afro-Amerindian element in Cuban culture.

Although Lam's Cuban work reflects ideas that were current in the Caribbean, he remained an outsider to the Cuban School and was critical of the bourgeois outlook of contemporaries like Peláez. Lam's presence nonetheless affected the course of Cuban art and resulted in a renewed interest in Afro-Cuban subjects among the younger generation. Roberto Diago (1920–57), himself of Afro-Cuban descent, was most visibly indebted to Lam, although he brought his own imagination and a strong sense of plasticity to the subject. Other artists took a more illustrative approach, as can be seen in the contemporary work of Portocarrero,

35 Wifredo Lam *The Chair* 1943

36 Mario Carreño
Afro-Cuban Dance 1944

Mario Carreño (b. 1913) and Luis Martínez Pedro (1910–89). Carreño
had, like Lam, frequented the surrealist circles in Paris in the late thirties
and also studied in Mexico, where he was exposed to muralism. Works
like his *Afro-Cuban Dance* (1944) reflect these combined influences.

The Cuban vanguardia was the first Caribbean School to receive attention in Europe and North America. In 1944, a major exhibition of
modern Cuban painting was staged at the Museum of Modern Art in
New York. Lam declined to participate and instead had a solo exhibition
at Pierre Matisse's gallery. The Museum of Modern Art actually acquired
Cuban works, most notably Lam's *The Jungle* in 1945. These initiatives
were part of a larger programme of Latin American exhibitions and
acquisitions, in keeping with President Roosevelt's Good Neighbour
policy. After the war, Cuban art also found its way to Europe. In 1951, for
instance, there was a major exhibition of Cuban art at the Musée National
d'Art Moderne in Paris.

Haitian art began to receive international attention in the forties,
especially after it was represented in two major UNESCO exhibitions of
modern art in Paris, in 1946 and 1947. The spectacular upsurge of Haitian
art in the mid-forties is usually attributed to the establishment of the

Centre d'Art in May 1944, a joint Haitian-American venture that served as a school and gallery. It was initiated and directed by the American watercolourist DeWitt Peters (1902–66) who had come to Haiti in 1943 to teach English. While the Centre d'Art had a pivotal role in the development of Haitian art and its international promotion, the origin of modern Haitian art more correctly dates from the thirties. As in Cuba, anti-American sentiments played a significant role in the increase of Haitian cultural nationalism, especially during the US occupation of Haiti from 1915 to 1934. The Haitian scholar Jean Price Mars called for a revaluation of Afro-Haitian popular culture in his influential collection of essays *Ainsi parla l'oncle (Thus Spoke the Uncle)* (1928). It became the foundation text of Haitian indigenism, mainly a literary movement, but it also influenced the visual arts.

Haiti's first modern artist, Pétion Savain (1906–73), started painting local landscapes and scenes in the early thirties in a modest, realist style. He was encouraged to explore indigenous subjects by the African-American artist William E. Scott (1884–1964) who visited Haiti in 1930. Savain in turn influenced younger artists with similar interests, such as Georges 'Geo' Remponneau (b. 1916). In 1939, Savain published an illustrated novel, *La Case de Damballah (Damballah's Shack)*. The novel reflects the ideas of Price Mars, who had declared Vaudou to be Haiti's national religion at a time when it was still illegal. Savain's illustrations, while formally crude, mark the first deliberate use of Vaudou as a paradigm of 'the Haitian' in the visual arts. Savain later became famous for his much-copied geometrically stylized market scenes.

Indigenist Haitian art was nonetheless conventional and even feeble compared to the Cuban vanguardia. The artistic climate became more energetic in the mid-forties, galvanized by the activities of the Centre d'Art and increased intra-regional contacts. Césaire came to Haiti in 1944, which established a tangible link between negritude and indigenism. The Centre d'Art's programmes included exchanges with the Cuban avant-garde like the showing of the MOMA exhibition of Cuban art in 1945 and other exhibitions. Several Cuban artists also visited which reinforced their interest in Afro-Caribbean culture – Lam came along with Breton in 1945 and stayed for four months as guests of Pierre Mabille who was then French cultural attaché in Port-au-Prince, Enríquez visited in 1945 and Portocarrero in 1946.

The contacts with the Caribbean and European avant-garde were decisive in the development of Haitian artists such as Lucien Price (1915–63) and Luce Turnier (1924–94). Price, whose small œuvre on paper is scarcely known, was the first Caribbean artist to venture into full abstraction in the mid-forties, although he simultaneously produced drawings on indigenous and African themes. While Haiti's intelligentsia was absorbing modernism, the 'primitive' movement emerged with the 'discoveries' of Philomé Obin, Hector Hyppolite, Castera Bazile (1923–66), Rigaud Benoit (1911–86) and Wilson Bigaud (b. 1931), among others. The Centre d'Art soon became the main promoter of the 'primitives', especially after the American writer Selden Rodman became co-director in 1947. In spite of the controversy that followed, the Centre d'Art provided opportunities for talented artists, who might otherwise not have attracted the attention of Haiti's elitist cultural establishment, and opened the floodgates of popular creativity.

That the nationalist ideas of the Caribbean intelligentsia were, with some variations, paralleled by those of the working class is well illustrated by the work of the early Haitian 'primitives'. Many of them openly produced Vaudou-related work, for instance, reflecting the changing attitudes towards the religion. Of the early 'primitives', the 'popular realist' Obin qualifies most readily as a nationalist artist. Apart from his depictions of life in his hometown Cap Haïtien and his autobiographic works, Obin applied his narrative and allegorical talents to patriotic subjects such as the Haitian Revolution and modern political events, including several emotionally charged paintings on the death of Charlemagne Péralte, the leader of the *cacos* (peasant rebels) in northern Haiti during the US occupation.

Obin's work illustrates that popular art is in constant dialogue with the artistic mainstream – his historical works, for instance, were painted in a formal style that can be traced to Haiti's creolized academic tradition. He also produced paintings that verged on geometric abstraction. Obin had been painting for some thirty years before he joined the Centre d'Art, which again shows that 'primitive' Haitian art did not appear suddenly. He managed a branch of the Centre d'Art in Cap Haïtien and became the patriarch of what is now known as the Cap Haïtien School. The main exponents of this school are his brother Sénèque Obin (1893–1977) and various younger members of the Obin family.

Most patronage of the 'primitives' came from Europe and North America where they were enthusiastically received as the 'authentic', 'unspoiled' Haitian artists, while the work of their modernist counterparts was criticized for being too derivative. Rodman's ground-breaking book on Haitian art, *Renaissance in Haiti* (1948), also championed the 'primitives', as did his later publications on the subject. Predictably, this did not go down well with the Haitian intelligentsia and a divisive polemic developed that still lingers today. In 1950, a group of disgruntled artists left the Centre d'Art and founded the Foyer des Arts Plastiques (Home of the

37 Philomé Obin
*Toussaint L'Ouverture
in his Camp c. 1945*

Visual Arts). The dissident group consisted mainly of modernists, including Price, but also a few 'ex-primitives' such as Dieudonné Cédor (b. 1925). While the Centre d'Art was trying to safeguard the 'purity' of the 'primitives', the artists at the Foyer sought to integrate them into the mainstream and aimed to translate modernism into something more relevant to the Haitian public. The defensive situation in which they found themselves seems to have come at the expense of critical standards, however, and the results were problematic. The more inventive modernists Max Pinchinat (1925–85) and Roland Dorcely (b. 1930) left for Paris, and Price became ill and stopped working. Most other artists at the Foyer espoused a gloomy naturalism that provided a lacklustre alternative to the thriving 'primitive' school at the Centre d'Art.

The early Cuban and Haitian Schools are the best known and documented, but historical and artistic developments elsewhere in the Caribbean were very similar. The Dominican Republic was also occupied by the US marines, from 1916 to 1924, and as in Haiti and Cuba, this resulted in a surge of nationalist sentiments that influenced cultural

38 Yoryi Morel *At the Fiesta* 1948

development. Celeste Woss y Gil (1890–1985), for instance, shocked the conservative, racially prejudiced Santo Domingo bourgeoisie with her candid nude paintings of coloured women, in a modernized academic style influenced by Gauguin. The Dominican nationalist school also includes Yoryi Morel (1901–78), a regional artist who painted the people and views of his native city Santiago and its environs. His *Peasant from Cibao* (1943) qualifies as a national icon and compares thematically with the *guajiro* paintings of the Cuban vanguardia, be it in a more traditional, academic form.

Early Dominican modernism was shaped by two major influences: Mexican muralism and Spanish modernism. This is illustrated by the early work of the painter and critic Darío Suro (b. 1917), who studied in Mexico, but most of all by Jaime Colson (1901–75), who is arguably the most underrated early Caribbean modernist. A restless traveller throughout his life, Colson studied in Spain and moved to Paris in the mid–twenties where he was accepted into the cubist milieu. By the early thirties, he had developed a distinct style influenced by purism, Picasso's classicism and surrealism. Colson moved to Mexico in 1934 and taught at the Workers' Art School where Mario Carreño was among his students. His exposure to Mexican cultural nationalism led him to explore indigenous subject matter around his return to the Dominican Republic in 1938 in works such as *Merengue* (1937) in which he infused an indigenous theme with the coolly dramatic, sexually ambiguous atmosphere of his surrealist work.

The US occupation of the Dominican Republic was followed by the dictatorship of Rafael Trujillo who was in power from 1930 to 1961 with an increasingly corrupt and repressive regime. In 1937, Trujillo orchestrated a horrifying ethnic cleansing incident, known as the 'Dominican Vespers', in which thousands of Haitian border workers were killed. Eager to restore its public image, the Trujillo regime provided some artistic patronage during the early forties, establishing the National School of Fine Arts and the National Biennial in 1942. The Spanish influence in Dominican art was reinforced when Trujillo offered asylum to Spanish Civil War refugees. Some feel this was an attempt to 'whiten' Dominican society in keeping with Trujillo's anti-Haitian policies. Between 1939 and 1940, some five thousand Spaniards came, including several noted artists, which gave the isolated Dominican art world a

39 Jaime Colson *Merengue* 1937

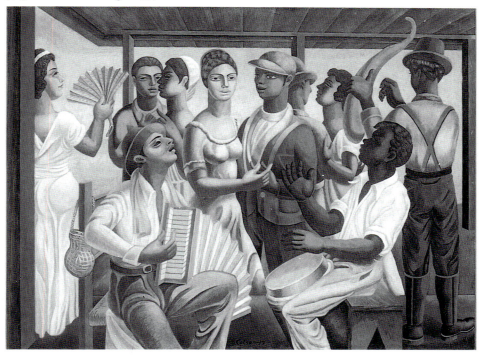

more cosmopolitan outlook. The most influential ones were the painters Eugenio Fernández Granell (b. 1912) and Josep Gausachs (1889–1959), the painter and sculptor Angel Botello (1913–86) and the muralist José Vela Zanetti (b. 1913), who helped to reconcile Dominican subject matter with modernist ideas. Granell came to the Dominican Republic as a writer and musician and started painting there, influenced by the visits of Lam and Breton in 1941 and his subsequent contact with the surrealists. This again shows how crucial the international exchanges of the early forties were for the development of Caribbean art and the later phase of surrealism generally. Granell was co-founder of the literary journal and group *La Poesía Sorprendida* (1943–47), which infused avant-garde ideas into Dominican literature. His presence reinforced the surrealist current in Dominican art and, although he left in the fifties, the influence of his whimsical, graphic style can still be detected today.

Despite Francisco Oller's ground-breaking work, it took until after the Second World War for Puerto Rican artists to discover modernism and, more importantly, for any truly significant artists to appear. This lack of cultural vigour is usually attributed to the cultural dislocation caused by the American annexation of the island in 1898. Nationalist resistance was brewing, however, led by the radical independence activist Pedro Albizu-Campos who came to prominence in the late twenties – the artistic product-ion of the time reflects this nationalist ferment. As in Cuba, traditional rural life was idealized and the white Puerto Rican peasant, the *jíbaro*, was elevated to a national emblem. The theme was so prevalent that a noted Puerto Rican scholar described it in 1936 as an 'empire of jíbarismo'.

The painter Ramón Frade (1875–1954) is an early representative of this development, although in fact his work is closer to late nineteenth-century academism than to Caribbean modernism. Frade said that 'since all that is Puerto Rican is being swept away by the wind…I seek to per-
41 petuate it in paint'. His best-known painting *Our Daily Bread* (c. 1905) is one of the earliest examples of nationalist art in the Caribbean. It presents a sober, monumental image of an elderly *jíbaro* holding a bunch of plantains, Puerto Rico's national food. Frade is often mentioned along with Miguel Pou (1880–1968), the first Puerto Rican artist to study in the United States. Pou lived in Ponce, Puerto Rico's prosperous second city, and, like Frade, he painted a nostalgic vision of Puerto Rico, although his work has a more informal, impressionist quality. Apart from his luminous landscapes and portraits of the Puerto Rican elite, Pou painted Puerto
42 Rican 'regional types'. His most famous work, *A Race of Dreamers: Portrait of Ciquí* (1938), a portrait of a popular baseball player, is, despite the title's benevolent racial stereotyping, a rare and sensitive portrait of a black

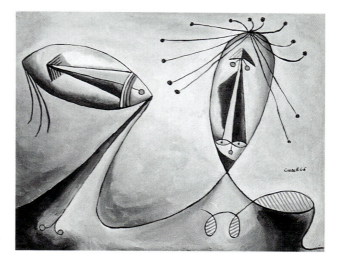

40 Eugenio Fernández Granell *Nostalgia of an Indian in Love* 1946

person in a country that has never quite come to terms with the African elements in its heritage.

Jamaica was the sole remaining European colony in the Greater Antilles and was relatively isolated from the artistic developments in the neighbouring islands until the fifties. Despite this isolation, artistic developments were remarkably similar to those already discussed. The early Jamaican School was dominated by the sculptor Edna Manley (1900–87), who was born in England to a Jamaican mother and an English father. Her first Jamaican sculpture, *Beadseller* (1922), was probably the most radically modernist work created in the Caribbean at the time and reflects her interest in vorticism. While the work has autobiographical implications, it was inspired by a market scene, a classic indigenist theme. *Beadseller* could have marked the start of a nationalist school, yet the small, typically colonial Jamaican artistic community was not yet receptive to such ideas. In the twenties, Manley exhibited in Britain, where she was acclaimed as a promising young modernist sculptor, and in 1930 she was accepted into the London Group along with Henry Moore and Barbara Hepworth.

West Indian independence was negotiated gradually and mainly on a political level. The cultural climate changed dramatically in the thirties and a spirited nationalist, anti-colonial movement emerged throughout the British West Indies, fuelled by labour unionism and racial activism. Manley's husband Norman was a leader of the Jamaican nationalist movement and later became premier. The West Indian labour movement emerged from a series of riots and strikes that racked the West Indies from 1935 to 1938 and gave the working class a political voice. Racial activism

71

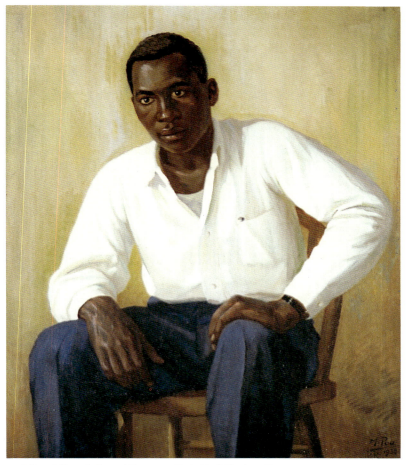

42 Miguel Pou *A Race of Dreamers: Portrait of Ciquí* 1938

was particularly pronounced in Jamaica, which can be attributed to the influence of Garveyism and other emerging forms of black nationalism such as Rastafarianism. Marcus Garvey used Jamaica as his base from 1927 to 1935, when he left for Britain.

It was in this ideologically charged context that Manley created her *Negro Aroused* (1935), the undisputed icon of Jamaican cultural nationalism. It was the first of a series of explicitly political carvings that celebrated the black working class. While some are more anecdotic, such as *Market Women* (1936) or *Diggers* (1936), the carvings stand out among

43

73

41 Ramón Frade *Our Daily Bread c.* 1905

contemporary Caribbean art because of their emphatic 'blackness' and the heroic treatment of the figure. Although the graphic work of William Blake was Manley's most consistent iconographic influence, her work of the thirties parallels that of the Harlem Renaissance. The silhouette quality and symbolism of *Negro Aroused*, in particular, remind of the work of Aaron Douglas which Manley may have known at the time.

Similarly, there is a striking resemblance between Manley's *Horse of the Morning* (1943) and the horse in the foreground of Enríquez' *The Abduction of the Mulatas*, although it is far less likely that she was familiar with her Cuban counterparts. In both works, the quintessentially romantic image of the horse is associated with energy and male sexuality. While Manley and Enríquez of course drew from the same sources, the similarity of their visual language reflects the conscious and unconscious crosscurrents within the Caribbean. *Horse of the Morning* belongs to Manley's *Dying God* series of the forties, in which she developed a romantic-surreal iconography with autobiographical overtones, based on the motifs of the sun, the moon and the horse. Although no longer explicitly political, the series was inspired by the spectacular Jamaican Blue Mountain landscape.

30

43 Edna Manley *Negro Aroused* 1935

 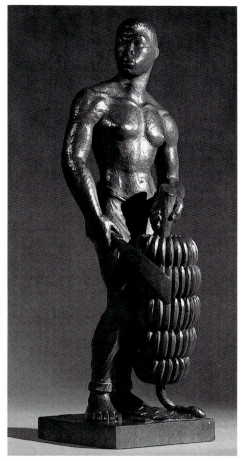

44 Edna Manley *Horse of the Morning* 1943   45 Alvin Marriott *Banana Man* 1955

The dominance of sculpture and, specifically, woodcarving in early modern Jamaican art is exceptional, even in the Caribbean context, and may be attributed to the revival of the African traditions in Jamaican culture that accompanied cultural nationalism. The sculptor Alvin Marriott (1902–92), like Manley, started his career in the twenties, although at first independently from her. In 1929, he was cited by Marcus Garvey as the most outstanding West Indian sculptor, not surprisingly since his work embodied Garvey's academic preferences. Marriott was at

45   his best in his exquisitely crafted woodcarvings, such as *Banana Man*
      (1955), that combine his academic approach to the figure with a slight art-
      deco stylization. These works reflect the influence of Manley and the
      avant-garde Jamaican furniture designer Burnett Webster for whom
      Marriott did decorative carving. Like Manley's work of the late thirties,
      Banana Man is an iconic image that glorifies labour and the black race.

      The changing cultural climate led to a number of initiatives that
      encouraged the development of Jamaican art. The Institute of Jamaica,
      which was founded in 1879 for the promotion of art, science and litera-
      ture, adjusted its typically colonial policies under pressure of the national-
      ist intelligentsia. In 1937, Manley's *Negro Aroused* was acquired by public
      subscription and became the first modern Jamaican work of art to enter
      the Institute's collection. Manley became an influential cultural organizer
      and in 1940 started free art classes at the Institute of Jamaica which stimu-
      lated the development of a coherent artistic community and led to the
      establishment of the Jamaica School of Art in 1950.

      The work of Albert Huie (b. 1920) exemplifies the interests of this
      'Institute Group'. Although he is now best known as a landscapist, many
47   of his earlier images relate to labour – his *Crop Time* (1955), for instance,
      provides an anecdotic depiction of the cane harvest, with allusions to the
      dignity of labour and the positive role of sugar in the Jamaican economy.
      It is a relatively small painting, but the epic quality of the composition
      reflects the influence of Mexican muralism, which reached Jamaica some-
      what later than the Hispanic Caribbean. The moderate post-impressionist
      and art-deco influences are also typical for the Institute Group. Another
      member of the group, David Pottinger (b. 1911), found his inspiration in
      the old working-class neighbourhoods of Kingston, where he has always
48   lived. His *Nine Night* (1949) depicts a traditional Afro-Jamaican wake in a
      sombre, awkward expressionist style reminiscent of the early work of
      Pétion Savain.

      The painter and sculptor John Dunkley (1891–1947) belongs to the
      same generation, but he is usually classified as an 'intuitive' and discussed
      in isolation from the nationalist Jamaican School. His dark, brooding
      landscapes are indeed private visions that may seem far removed from the
      nation-building images of the Institute Group, yet his work compares sur-
      prisingly well with that of his mainstream Caribbean contemporaries.
      The consciously or unconsciously sexualized character of Dunkley's
      imagery, for instance, brings to mind Wifredo Lam's contemporary work
      and his pantheist notion of the spiritual 'murmur' of nature. On a more
      descriptive level, paintings such as *Banana Plantation* (c. 1945) compare
      with the iconic Caribbean landscapes of the nationalist schools. Dunkley's

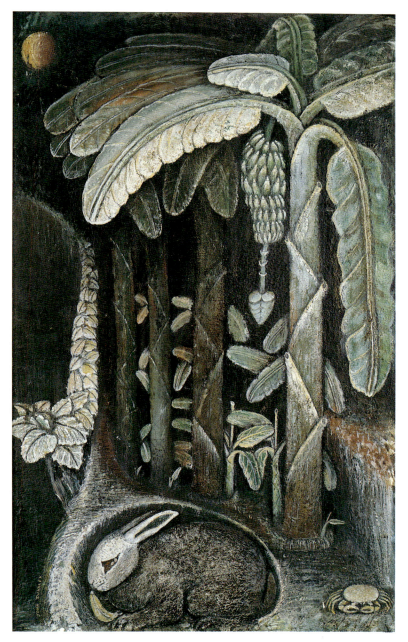

46 John Dunkley *Banana Plantation c.* 1945

47 Albert Huie *Crop Time* 1955

48 David Pottinger *Nine Night* 1949

49 Ronald Moody *Johanaan (Peace)* 1936

50 Boscoe Holder *Portrait of Louise de Frense Holder* 1938

compositions were visibly influenced by art deco, which testifies to the popularity of the style in the Caribbean.

The sculptor Ronald Moody (1900–84) was an outsider of the early Jamaican art movement and made his career in Britain and France. The hieratic monumentality, frontal emphasis and silent inwardness of early carvings like *Johanaan (Peace)* (1936) reflect his interest in Ancient Egyptian and Buddhist sculpture. Although his brother Harold Moody was politically active in Britain as the leader of the League of Coloured Peoples, Moody's work was not guided by the nationalist agenda of his Jamaican-based contemporaries. Instead, his sculptures express a complex personal philosophy, influenced by his study of Indian and Chinese metaphysics and, later, the experience of the Second World War. With their simplified, monumental forms, his early work is nonetheless stylistically akin to the contemporary carvings of Manley and Marriott, with whom he shared his mastery of woodcarving.

Even though the Eastern Caribbean produced internationally acclaimed literary and political figures such as Aimé Césaire and the Trinidadian C. L. R. James, developments in the visual arts were slower and comparatively modest, which may be explained by the lack of art patronage in these smaller societies. Trinidad is larger and less isolated than the other Eastern

79

51　Sybil Atteck, a work, *c.* 1950s

Caribbean islands, but the artistic developments were typical for that part of the Caribbean region. The first inkling of a national art movement was the foundation of the Society of Independents (1929–38), a small group of young upper-class artists. The bohemian lifestyle of its main exponents Amy Leon Pang (1908–89) and Hugh Stollmeyer (1913–81) scandalized the Port of Spain bourgeoisie. Artistically they were not of great consequence although the references to *obeah* (Afro-Caribbean sorcery) in Stollmeyer's work parallel developments elsewhere in the Caribbean, but they did influence others. The painter, dancer and musician Boscoe Holder (b. *c.* 1920), for instance, was encouraged by Leon Pang as a young artist. While much of his later work suffers from facile exoticism, his 1938 portrait of his mother shows him as a sensitive portraitist of the black race.

The Trinidad Art Society, which was founded in 1943, was more specifically committed to the development of a national art movement. Among the early members of the society, Sybil Atteck (1911–75) was most adventurous in reconciling abstraction and stylization with emblematic Trinidadian subjects such as the landscape and the popular festivals. She greatly influenced the following generation of Trinidadian artists.

50

CHAPTER THREE

Popular Religion, the Festival Arts and the Visionary

As we have seen in the previous chapter, popular traditions featured prominently in the iconography of the nationalist schools of the Caribbean. Throughout the development of modern Caribbean art, popular culture has been a fertile source of conceptual, thematic and formal possibilities. Two aspects of popular culture, the religions and the festival arts, are particularly important to the visual arts, as subjects and as sources of artistic production in their own right. In this chapter, the role of popular culture in Caribbean art is examined further, with emphasis on those artists who bridge the two realms.

Caribbean popular religions such as Vaudou, Santería and Rastafarianism typically have a strong visual emphasis and use an eclectic array of ritual and emblematic objects and images. Several well-known Caribbean artists started as makers of such sacred items and crossed over into the domain of 'museum art', often after being encouraged by talent-scouting art patrons. This phenomenon has been most pronounced in Haiti. Major 'primitive' painters such as Hector Hyppolite, Robert Saint-Brice (1898–1973), André Pierre (b. 1916) and Lafortune Félix (b. 1933) were *houngans* (Vaudou priests) before becoming artists and many others have been closely associated with the religion.

Even though Vaudou plays an important role in Haitian life as the traditional religion of the Creole-speaking masses, it was repressed by the ruling class, culminating in the anti-superstition campaign of 1942–43. Its practice was finally legalized in 1946, which helps to explain why Vaudou-related art came to prominence in the late forties. It was not his involvement in Vaudou, however, that brought Hyppolite to the attention of the Centre d'Art but his work as a house painter, his main source of income before he became famous. He was approached by DeWitt Peters and the Haitian novelist Philippe Thoby-Marcelin because of the striking floral panels and name sign he had painted for a small bar in the village of Mont-Rouis. Hyppolite moved to Port-au-Prince in 1945 and rose to international attention within months, aided by the enthusiastic endorsements of André Breton, Wifredo Lam and Pierre Mabille. His short but intense career ended abruptly when he died of a heart attack in 1948.

52 Robert Saint-Brice
The Queen Erzulie 1957

53 Hector Hyppolite
The Great Master 1946–48

Hyppolite painted fanciful romantic scenes, still-life compositions and even an occasional portrait, but his work was fundamentally linked to Vaudou. He claimed to work in a state of possession, on the instruction of John the Baptist (although it should be remembered that he consciously produced for the Centre d'Art, like most contemporary Haitian 'primitives'). His most memorable works depict major *loas* of the Vaudou pantheon with considerable iconographical freedom. The majestic, emblematic figure with a double nose and three eyes in *The Great Master* (1946–48), for instance, is an image without known precedent in Haitian art and probably represents the chief god of the Vaudou pantheon. With its symmetrical frontality and lack of ornamental detail, the composition is unusually stark for Hyppolite, although the bold, fiery colours add to the visionary power of the image.

The candour of Hyppolite's paintings makes a striking contrast to the enigmatic, spectral images of Robert Saint-Brice whose informal, almost tachist painting style prefigures later developments in Haitian art such as the Saint-Soleil School. The singularity of Saint-Brice's style does not mean his work is unrelated to popular iconography – his early painting *The Queen Erzulie* (1957) represents the temperamental Vaudou goddess of love in her double identity as the black Virgin Mary.

82

Vaudou was also essential to the work of Georges Liautaud (1899–1992), the master of the Haitian *feroniers* (iron sculptors). He was a black-smith by profession and started his career by making iron graveyard crosses in his hometown of Croix-des-Bouquets, today the centre of Haitian ironwork. The designs of his crosses resemble the *vèvè* ground drawings of Vaudou. Graveyard crosses are also associated with Baron-la-Croix, the guardian of the graveyard in the Vaudou pantheon. Most of Liautaud's sculptures were made from recuperated metal – *Sirène Diamant (Diamond Mermaid)*, one of his most exquisite works, was ingeniously forged from a long iron railway nail, a material he used for several major works in the early fifties. It is an early representation of Liautaud's favourite *loa*, the mermaid goddess La Sirène. The poetic title refers to the light effects created by the fish-tail pattern perforations of the figure. In the mid-fifties, Liautaud started cutting silhouette forms from sheet metal recycled from oil drums, the method also used by younger feroniers such as Murat Brierre (b. 1938) and Serge Jolimeau (b. 1952). Similarly, 'primi-tive' painters often started working with recycled and improvised mate-rials (Hyppolite painted with a chicken feather) although most turned to more conventional materials when they entered the gallery system.

The painter Préfète Duffaut, another early member of the Centre d'Art, is best known for his fantastic cities, painted in a colourful, meticu-lous graphic style. Although they are formally inspired by the spectacular, mountainous landscape around his hometown Jacmel in southern Haiti, Duffaut's cities evoke the supernatural rather than the natural. His *Heaven and Earth* (1959), for instance, juxtaposes a heavenly and an infernal realm, a recurrent theme in his work. The image embodies the dualist world view of Vaudou and other Afro-Caribbean religions, where good and evil are seen as complementary, interconnected forces. Other works are more directly associated with Vaudou iconography, particularly his awe-inspiring representations of Erzulie as the Virgin on the Mountain.

It would nonetheless be reductive to define Haitian 'primitive' art as 'Vaudou art', as authors like Sheldon Williams have done. Neither are all 'primitives' Vaudou practitioners. Philomé Obin, for instance, was a devout Protestant and primarily a secular artist, but even his occasional religious paintings were unrelated to Vaudou. Obin's best-known relig-ious works are his contributions to the mural cycle at the episcopal Cathedral of the Holy Trinity (1950–51) in Port-au-Prince.

The Holy Trinity mural project was executed by the major 'primitives' attached to the Centre d'Art at the time. It was initiated and directed by Selden Rodman and enthusiastically supported by Bishop Alfred Voegeli, an early patron of the Haitian art movement. The first section to be

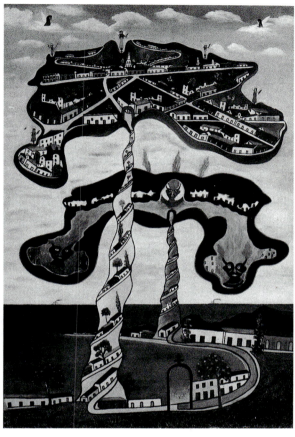

55 Préfète Duffaut *Heaven and Earth* 1959

54 Georges Liautaud *Sirène Diamant* n.d.

56 Rigaud Benoit, Philomé Obin and Castera Bazile, *The Nativity*, *The Crucifixion* and *The Ascension*, Cathedral of the Holy Trinity, Port-au-Prince, 1950–51 (detail)

completed was the apse, with three major murals, *The Nativity*, *The Crucifixion* and *The Ascension* by Rigaud Benoit, Philomé Obin and Castera Bazile, respectively. Despite the distinct painting styles of each contributor, the apse murals form a surprisingly coherent whole, although the sugary angels and tumbling rosebuds by Gabriel Lévêque (b. 1923) in the upper section detract from the more formal compositions below. Obin also painted the stately *Last Supper* in the west transept chapel and Wilson Bigaud the spectacular *Wedding at Cana* in the east transept. The mural cycle includes smaller paintings by Bazile and several other artists. In 1954, Bishop Voegeli added a terracotta choir screen by Jasmin Joseph (b. 1923).

The biblical events represented in the Holy Trinity murals were placed in a modern, recognizably Haitian context, a revolutionary departure at the time. The actual biblical figures were represented according to conventional Christian iconography, although most were 'Haitianized' by combining Caucasian features with a darker skin. Some murals include Vaudou-related motifs, such as the drums and sacrificial animals in Bigaud's *Wedding at Cana*. While several participating artists were Vaudou practitioners, this does not mean the murals are disguised Vaudou art since the references to Vaudou were included to depict typical Haitian life. Not

86

57, 58 Philomé Obin *Last Supper*, Cathedral of the Holy Trinity, Port-au-Prince, 1950–51 (details)

all of this happened spontaneously, however, and contemporary accounts reveal that Rodman encouraged the artists to include anecdotic Haitian details, to the point where some felt he was interfering. While the results were generally successful, the mural project illustrates that the 'primitives' were already then willing and able to adapt to the demands of patronage.

Predictably, the project was at first highly controversial in Haiti. Some members of the establishment felt the murals were sacrilegious and inappropriate for a mainstream Christian church. The Holy Trinity murals were executed during the conflict about the promotion of the 'primitives' by the Centre d'Art and in fact contributed to the crisis. The importance of the murals to Haitian art is now well recognized, although they are in urgent need of restoration.

Vaudou is not the sole explanation for Haitian art, but it has been an important source for mainstream Haitian artists, starting with the indigenist painter Pétion Savain. The interest in Vaudou took a new turn with the foundation of the Poto-Mitan school in 1968 by the artists Tiga (Jean Claude Garoute, b. 1935), Patrick Vilaire (b. 1942) and Frido (Wilfrid Austin, b. 1945). The term 'poto-mitan' refers to the central pole in the main room of the *hounfort* (Vaudou temple), which symbolizes the link between the spiritual and the earthly realm. The artists associated with Poto-Mitan turned to Vaudou cosmology and Prehispanic culture as the basis of their aesthetic investigations.

Tiga, the main organizer of Poto-Mitan, has been active as a ceramist, painter, musician, educator and cultural organizer and has devised several elaborate artistic theories, all based on his belief in the mystical interconnectedness of things. Tiga's views are exemplified by an untitled work on paper (1995) that, according to him, inadvertently augured the presidential secession from Bertrand Aristide to René Préval (the image indeed bears some resemblance to both men). The work is part of an ongoing series created with a chance technique he calls *soleil brulé* (burnt sun). The monochrome brown colours and textured surfaces of these works remind of his background in ceramics.

Apart from his own work, Tiga is best known as the initiator of the Saint-Soleil experiment in the early seventies. The project started as an application of his theories about spirituality, spontaneity and interdisciplinary art. Art materials were given to a group of peasants who had never painted before and a 'cultural community' was formed in Soissons-la-Montagne, a village in the mountains above Port-au-Prince. The results were astounding and several major artists emerged from the experience, including Prospère Pierre-Louis (1947–96), Dieuseul Paul (b. 1953), Levoy Exil (b. 1944), Denis Smith (b. 1954) and one of very few female

60

'primitives', Louisianne Saint-Fleurant (b. 1924). Like Saint-Brice, they portray the spirit world of Vaudou in amorphous, intuitive forms and only occasionally represent identifiable *loas*. There are no attempts at realism in their paintings, which separates them from most other Haitian 'primitives'. Even though each Saint-Soleil member maintained a distinct style, the group developed a recognizable idiom, characterized by intricately patterned psychedelic colours and two-dimensional, frontal compositions defined by heavy black outlines.

The Saint-Soleil group came to international attention after the visit of André Malraux in 1975, another example of the role of Western endorsements in the development of Haitian 'primitive' art. Malraux was particularly impressed by the tomb paintings members of the group had made at the local cemetery. He discussed their work at length in his study of religious iconography *L'Intemporel* (1976) and described Saint-Soleil enthusiastically as 'the most arresting and the only controllable experience of magic painting in our century', thereby perpetuating the myth that Haitians are a people of natural painters. Saint-Soleil was originally also conceived as an alternative to the commercialization of Haitian art, but the work of the group soon found its way into overseas galleries and collections. The community fell apart in the late seventies, but most participants are still painting, although their work has become routine, like that of so many other Haitian artists. Saint-Soleil has nonetheless revitalized Haitian art and inspired several younger artists such as Stevenson Magloire (1963–94), Louisianne Saint-Fleurant's son, who combined motifs that relate to Haiti's modern realities, such as armed militiamen, with elements of the Saint-Soleil idiom.

Since the Haitian Revolution, Vaudou has been linked to politics, often to the discomfort of the Francophone ruling class. The dictator François Duvalier ('Papa Doc'), who was president from 1957 to 1971, ruthlessly exploited Vaudou beliefs to reinforce his corrupt and violent regime. His personal appearance was carefully modelled after Baron Samedi, the fearsome *loa* of death. Unavoidably, there was a backlash against Vaudou when his son and successor Jean-Claude Duvalier ('Baby Doc') was deposed in 1986 – a *hounfort* with murals by André Pierre in Croix-des-Bouquets, among others, was destroyed. Despite this reaction, which is still lingering, younger mainstream Haitian artists have become more comfortable using Vaudou iconography and, more generally, the idiom of the 'primitives'. The leading representative of this development is the painter and installation artist Edouard Duval-Carrié (b. 1954) whose work evokes the magic and mystery of the Vaudou universe and comments on Haiti's history and socio-political realities with sharp, surreal wit.

59 Mallica 'Kapo' Reynolds *Revival Goddess Dina* 1968

In Jamaica, also, popular religion has deeply influenced the visual arts. Jamaican Revivalism, used here as a generic term to describe the traditional Afro-Jamaican cults, generally resembles Vaudou and combines Christian elements with African-derived ancestor worship and healing practices. The biblical elements are more prominent, however, and stem from inspirational Protestantism rather than Roman Catholicism. The reason for this is that the evangelization of the Jamaican masses was primarily the work of Baptist, Methodist and Moravian missionaries, who also played an important role in the Abolitionist movement.

The Jamaican intuitive sculptor and painter Mallica 'Kapo' Reynolds (1911–89) was a Revivalist bishop and, like most other Caribbean artist-priests, he claimed to have received divine instruction to start carving and painting. His subjects vary widely, from biblical figures, angels and Revivalist rituals to the landscape or market scenes, yet even his secular works portray the social and physical context of Revivalism. Many paintings and sculptures are autobiographical and include self-images of Kapo

60 Prospère Pierre-Louis *Spirit* n.d.

in his capacity as church leader. Some of his most outstanding works are about women and reflect the prominence of women in the cult.

The spirit pantheon of Jamaican Revivalism is rudimentary compared with Vaudou and Santería. The title of Kapo's sculpture *Revival Goddess Dina* (1968) should therefore not be taken literally. Instead of representing an identifiable divinity, it is a homage to the spiritual power of a matriarchal, possibly ancestral figure and to women in general. The figure's horn-shaped hair signifies her spiritual involvement and her pose captures the typical swirling motion of Revival ritual dancing. The figure was carved along the natural shape of the wood (the branches became the arms), a technique that later became a stereotype in Jamaican 'airport art'.

Kapo produced some ritual items for the church he established in West Kingston, although his paintings and sculptures were from early on consciously created as 'art' and sold via Kingston dealers such as the Hills Galleries in the fifties and sixties or directly to visiting patrons. The sale of his work provided a source of income for his extended family and church community. Although Kapo's works were also bought by overseas collectors, much of his patronage came from local collectors and academics. His most prominent Jamaican patron was Edward Seaga, a sociologist and politician who became prime minister of Jamaica in the eighties. The local availability of patronage and the support of national institutions like the National Gallery of Jamaica have so far protected the Jamaican intuitives from the excessive commercialization that has plagued their Haitian counterparts, although there has always been some mass production for the tourist sector.

Jamaican Revivalism is a declining tradition, in part because of the competition from Pentecostalism, the new North American evangelical churches and Rastafarianism. The latter emerged in the thirties as a counterculture in the economically depressed urban and rural areas. The pioneers of the cult identified Haile Selassie, the young emperor of Ethiopia, as the black Messiah and Ethiopia as the legitimate home of the 'African Diaspora'. They were heavily influenced by Marcus Garvey and his frequent metaphorical references to Ethiopia as the African Zion. This African Zionism is not unique to Garveyism and Rastafarianism but is rooted in the popular resistance to New World slavery and colonization. Vaudou practitioners, for instance, believe they will return to 'Guinée' after death, which they define as the ancestral place 'across the waters' where the *loas* reside.

Of all Afro-Caribbean religions, Rastafarianism most explicitly unites the religious and the political, and developed as a conscious African nationalist alternative to Christianity and Creole nationalism. Early

Rastafarians were defiant of government authority and the social establishment. This anti-establishment stance was reinforced by the long, matted 'dreadlocks' hairstyle of orthodox believers and the ritual use of *ganja* (marihuana). Most Afro-Caribbean religions use emblems and symbolic colours but this is surely most pronounced in Rastafarianism, a consequence of the nationalist character of the cult. Rastafarian symbols derive from an eclectic array of sources such as the red, gold and green Ethiopian flag and the star of David.

Predictably, Rastafarianism was initially repressed by the Jamaican and colonial authorities, but by the mid-fifties, the movement began to attract academic attention and by the sixties, there was a certain amount of public acceptance. It is during this period that the intuitive painter and sculptor Everald Brown (b. 1917) came to national and international attention with the wall paintings, ritual objects and decorated musical instruments he had made for his small church, a self-appointed mission of the Ethiopian Orthodox church. Many early Rastafarians embraced the Ethiopian Orthodox church as an authentically African form of Christianity, although their beliefs were only partly compatible, especially where the divinity of Haile Selassie is concerned.

The images Brown represents in his paintings and sculptures come to him in dreams and meditations – he combines elements of Rastafarian, Ethiopian Orthodox, Revivalist, Judaic, Masonic and East Indian iconography with his own unique visions, a good illustration of the eclecticism and individualism of Rastafarianism. Brown frequently uses polymorphic images, which he reinforces with verbal punning – the title of the painting *Ethiopian Apple* (1970) is a pun on the Otaheite apple, a common fruit 61 in Jamaica. The central figure in the composition is at once an Otaheite apple tree and a hieratic figure, and symbolizes humanity's sacred oneness with nature, a central notion of Rastafarianism and other Afro-Caribbean religions. The colours of the tree and its backdrop also form the Rastafarian tricolour. As was noted in the introduction of this book, verbal and visual punning are common in Caribbean culture, particularly in Rastafarian circles where it is usually based on mystical association. In Brown's work, it became a powerful visionary tool that took his imagery far beyond the conventional Rastafarian iconography.

While Brown is a professed apolitical artist, the militant side of Rastafarianism is represented by the work of Albert Artwell (b. 1942) who uses the apocalyptic 'fire and brimstone' rhetoric of the cult to express an African supremacist world view. This is well illustrated by his *Judgment Day* (1979) where the only white persons are among the 62 damned in hell. The frontal, hieratic quality of the composition and the

93

61 Everald Brown *Ethiopian Apple* 1970

vertical stacking of the figures reflect the popularization of Ethiopian religious painting in Rastafarian circles. The Rastafarian colours are again used in the rainbow motif over the head of the Christ figure. It is interesting to compare Artwell's *Judgment Day* with a work on a similar theme, *The Judge of Nations* (1989) by Gladwyn Bush ('Miss Lassie', b. 1914), who is from the nearby Cayman Islands, where the Christ figure is white and the congregation is multi-racial. Although Bush is also of African descent, her representation of race and religion reflects the more Eurocentric outlook of the Cayman Islands, where racial activism has been limited.

Revivalism appears as a subject in mainstream Jamaican art, but Rastafarianism has been a far more visible influence, especially since the late sixties when black nationalism entered Jamaican mainstream ideology. This is illustrated by the work of the painter and sculptor Osmond Watson (b. 1934). While not a Rastafarian himself, Watson has used the cult (and occasionally Revivalism) as a paradigm of black nationalism. His

94

62 Albert Artwell *Judgment Day* 1979

63 Gladwyn Bush *The Judge of Nations* 1989

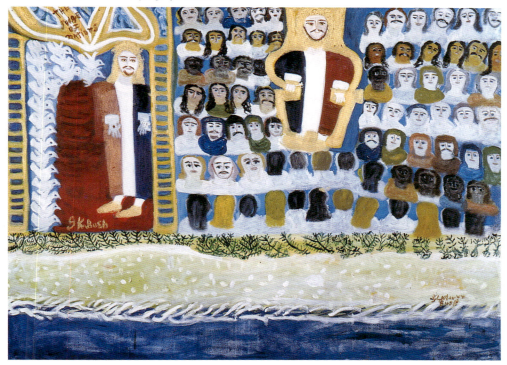

64 Osmond Watson *Peace and Love* 1969

65 Leonard Daley *The Pickpocket* 1984

painting *Peace and Love* (1969), for instance, is at once a self-portrait and a 'Rastafarianized' Christ image. The work also reflects the influence of Ethiopian Orthodox icon painting.

Rastafarianism has in recent years lost much of its impact in Jamaica, although the movement has spread throughout the 'African Diaspora' and even to sub-Sahara Africa. Two of Barbados' leading contemporary artists, Ras Akyem Ramsay (b. 1953) and Ras Ishi Butcher (b. 1960) are Rastafarians and use recognizable Rastafarian imagery in their work. The international familiarity with Rastafarian imagery also stems from its association with reggae music and the work of graphic designers such as Neville Garrick (b. 1950), a Jamaican Rastafarian who was Bob Marley's art director and designed most of his record covers. Aspects of Rastafarian imagery have been popularized by the Jamaican and Caribbean tourist industry to the point where the colours and other symbols are used on anything from beach towels and souvenir T-shirts to beer and rum bottles, with little consideration for their religious and political meaning.

161

As with Vaudou, there is a tendency to overuse the label 'Rastafarian art'. The Jamaican intuitive painter Leonard Daley (b. 1930) is often described as a Rastafarian artist, although his work is only indirectly related to the cult. Daley had been painting on all sorts of surfaces in his living environment for many years and came to the attention of the Jamaican art establishment in the early eighties. While his personal philosophy is loosely associated with Rastafarianism, he rarely uses identifiable Rastafarian imagery. His cryptic, hallucinatory paintings are in essence autobiographic and can best be defined as cathartic parables of good and evil, which he sees as equally important parts of human nature. This dualism, as we have seen before, is a common notion in Caribbean popular philosophy.

Daley's visionary images are too individual to accommodate any religious or ideological label. The same can be said of the work of the Guyanese painter and sculptor Philip Moore (b. 1921). Moore is associated with the Jordanites, an inspirational Guyanese church, but his work

97

expresses a very personal, utopian vision of Guyana, an ideal of community in a country that has a history of racial and political divisiveness. Like Everald Brown in Jamaica, Moore frequently uses polymorphic imagery, but his brilliantly coloured, symbol-laden pattern structures are even more intricate. Moore's *The Cultural Centre* (1996) is a personification of the National Cultural Centre in Georgetown and an allegory of multi-cultural Guyana. The figure-building is crowned with symbols of Guyana's five national religions and supported by Greenheart – Guyana's national tree – caryatid pylons, an example of Moore's unique interpretations of national symbols.

The Cuban painter and woodcut maker Gilberto de la Nuez (1913–93) pursued similar formal and thematic interests in his intricate, visionary compositions. He often referred to Afro-Cuban traditions such as the bembé dance ritual of Santería, but in fact his work stemmed from a broader interest in documenting the history and customs of Cuba. Surprisingly, de la Nuez was a marginal figure in Cuban art and it is only

66 Philip Moore *The Cultural Centre* 1996

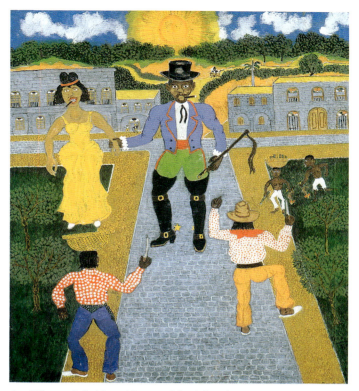

67 Gilberto de la Nuez *Memory of the Colonial Past* 1989

now that Cuba is beginning to recognize its untrained painters and sculptors. In spite of this, the Cuban explorations of popular culture have been extensive and sophisticated, particularly with Afro-Cuban culture. As we have seen before, Afrocubanismo was an important influence on vanguardia art, but mainly as a source of picturesque indigenous subject matter. Wifredo Lam revolutionized this by approaching Afro-Cuban culture as an 'insider' and emphasizing its ideological significance. Since then, Afrocubanismo has remained an important current in Cuban art.

Even though the black population of Cuba is comparatively small, African traditions have been unusually well preserved, largely because local colonial policies allowed the various African ethnic groups to maintain their cultural identity. The Santería religion (*regla de ocha*), for instance, is primarily of Yoruba origin, and its main counterpart, Palo Monte (*regla de Congo*), is derived from Kongolese traditions. Policies of revolutionary Cuba towards Afro-Cuban religions may have been ambivalent, but they are more popular than ever and have spread far beyond the black population.

Manuel Mendive (b. 1944), a major exponent of contemporary Afro-cubanismo in the visual arts, was born in a Santería-practising family. He received a conventional artistic schooling at the San Alejandro Academy, but turned to popular culture as his formal and conceptual source. Mendive is an initiate in Santería and Palo Monte, but his work has no ceremonial function, instead, he practises what the Cuban critic Gerardo Mosquera has termed 'living mythological thought' and uses Afro-Cuban imagery to examine the questions of contemporary life. This is well illustrated by *Oya* (1967), a work from his so-called 'dark period', which was inspired by the orisha Oya, who is associated with storms, the gates to the graveyard and the dead. This became a point of departure for what Mendive has described as a meditation on death, as an aspect of life. Mendive is one of several Caribbean artists to have appropriated popular idioms in his work. The academically trained Dominican sculptor Gaspar Mario Cruz (b. 1929), for instance, has adopted the visual language of the traditional *santos* carvings of the Hispanic Caribbean to create moving religious works.

Mendive's 'dark period' was followed by his more narrative, sometimes political paintings of the seventies. His travels to Africa in the early eighties gave new energy and depth to his work and he adopted a more informal idiom that expresses an animist, sexually suggestive vision of nature acted out by hybrid, amorphous figures similar to those of Saint-Brice and the Saint-Soleil School in Haiti. The most significant innovation in Mendive's work, however, has been his involvement in performance art. His performances are loosely choreographed, interdisciplinary pieces acted out by a troupe of performers and involve body painting, dance, music, sculpted and ready-made objects, and even the artist himself in the act of painting. The performances allude to Afro-Cuban rituals, but again without being literal or descriptive.

It is indeed an easy step from the ritual performances and assemblages of Afro-Caribbean religions to the performances and installations of contemporary art. Interestingly, one of the first artists to tap this source was

120, 121 Ana Mendieta (1948–85), who had been sent to the United States as an adolescent in 1961. For Mendieta, Afro-Cuban rituals provided an insight into her identity as a Cuban exile and a woman. Her first major work on this subject was *The Burial of the Nañigo* (1976), one of her silhouette installations, which refers to burial rites of the all-male Abakuá secret society of Western Cuba. (The Abakuá society is of West African Ejagham

68 Manuel Mendive *Slave Ship* 1976

69 Manuel Mendive, live performance at the Havana Biennial, 1997

70 Gaspar Mario Cruz, a mahogany carving, *c.* 1950s

origin and *Nañigo* is the general term for an Abakuá member.) The identification with an exclusively male ritual also addressed the issue of male domination and its relationship to cultural and personal identity. Mendieta has been very influential on younger Cuban and Caribbean artists, especially since her visits to Cuba in 1980 and 1981.

The Cuban generation of the eighties turned overwhelmingly towards Afro-Cuban rituals to explore issues of identity, although most have no traditional involvement in these religions. In these works, the spiritual and the political often meet. The installation *For América* (1986) by Juan Francisco Elso (1956–88), for instance, is a ritualized representation of José Martí, the 'sacred warrior' of Cuban independence. The carved image of Martí was treated as a power object and covered with mud mixed with blood and items personally significant to him and his wife, the Mexican

71 Juan Francisco Elso
For América 1986

72 José Bedia *Island Playing at War* 1992

artist Magali Lara. The dart-like objects that are sprouting from the body can be read as arrows, blood or flowers and are reminiscent of the St Sebastian iconography and Mesoamerican regeneration rituals. Like Mendieta, Elso became a near mythical figure in the Latin American art world after his early death.

Another major Cuban artist of that generation, José Bedia (b. 1959) went further and became an initiate of Palo Monte in 1984. His interest in non-Western, aboriginal cultures also led to a residency with the Dakota Sioux in 1985. His paintings, drawings and installations remind of Kongo cosmograms, Afro-Cuban altars, Abakuá ideographic writing and Sioux pictographs. As a true heir of Wifredo Lam, Bedia uses Afro-Cuban and Native American culture in a poetic, yet critical, dialogue between the Third World and the West. His images are graphic and simple and are often elucidated with text, which reinforces their didactic overtones.

Until recently, the Afro-Caribbean components in Caribbean popular culture have received most academic attention. From an art-historical point of view, this is not surprising since Afro-Caribbean traditions have most obviously influenced the visual arts. The contributions of other ethnic groups are nonetheless also significant and are now beginning to attract attention. The East Indians of Trinidad and the Guianas have started claiming their space in national culture and this is reflected in contemporary visual art. The Trinidadian artist Wendy Nanan (b. 1955), for instance, used popular religion as an ironic token of hope in the at times very troubled 'marriage' of multi-racial, multi-cultural Trinidad in her relief construction *Idyllic Marriage* (1989). It represents 'La Divina Pastora' in a wedding scene with Lord Krishna. La Divina, as she is popularly known, is a wooden statue of a black Virgin Mary in the town of Siparia in southern Trinidad that is venerated by Hindus and Roman Catholics alike for its purported miraculous powers. As a sacred sculpture of uncertain, probably Hispanic or Amerindian origin, La Divina embodies the syncretism of Creole Caribbean culture. Although the 'bride' seems reluctant, her 'marriage' to Lord Krishna challenges the perception that the East Indian population of the Caribbean has retained its own culture and does not participate in the creolization process.

The Caribbean has a wide range of festival traditions, mainly pre-Lenten carnivals and Christmas season masquerades that originated during the plantation period. While these festivals are primarily Afro-European, other ethnic groups have brought their own traditions such as the East Indian Hosay festival and the Chinese New Year celebrations. The Caribbean festival traditions are as such beyond the scope of this book, although the costumes and body decorations are often of considerable artistic merit. Some are traditional, while others are designed for the occasion, usually a highly competitive enterprise. Where there are dominant festival traditions, as in Trinidad and the Bahamas, the festival arts have also contributed to the development of a vernacular aesthetic that influences the entire cultural spectrum, including the visual arts.

The traditional carnivals are found in countries with a Roman Catholic heritage such as Cuba, Puerto Rico, Haiti, the Dominican Republic and Trinidad. In these carnivals, the sacred and the secular meet. The Haitian *rara* Lenten carnival, for instance, is closely associated with Vaudou and Cuban carnival incorporates Afro-Cuban ritual practices such as the masqueraders of the Abakuá secret society. These *ireme* masqueraders were already documented by the nineteenth-century *costumbrista* artist Víctor Patricio de Landaluze and reappear throughout modern Cuban art. In revolutionary Cuba, the *ireme* figure has become a national symbol and

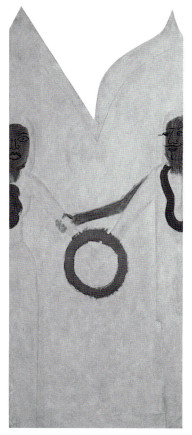

73　Wendy Nanan, a work from the
Idyllic Marriage series 1989

carnival was moved to the last two weeks of July to coincide with the
anniversary of the revolution. The status of the *ireme* figure in Cuban
national culture is illustrated by works such as René Portocarrero's *Little*
Devil No. 3 (1962), part of his *Colour of Cuba* series, a celebration of Cuban
popular culture.

　　The origins of Trinidad carnival or 'mas', as Trinidadians prefer, are primarily French Creole and West African. Mas has grown into the premier
pre-Lenten carnival of the Caribbean and is regarded as the focal-point of
modern Trinidadian culture. It is impossible to draw a clear line between
the mas designers and visual artists of Trinidad – the most spectacular case

74

74 René Portocarrero *Little Devil No. 3* from the *Colour of Cuba* series 1962

of overlap has been the work of Peter Minshall (b. 1941), a theatre designer who revolutionized mas in the early eighties and became one of Trinidad's most influential artists. He challenged the stereotypes of sequins, lamé and feathers and brought a new social consciousness to the festival. Minshall's bands are unusually large, sometimes involving more than two thousand people, and act out morality plays on the fundamental existential issues of modern life in a spectacular, filmic form. Not surprisingly, Minshall cites Cecil B. DeMille as an influence, although more recent film epics such as the *Star Wars* trilogy also come to mind.

Minshall's spectacular 'king' and 'queen' costumes, in particular, are elaborate kinetic constructions, animated by the wearer and sometimes also by mechanical devices such as the electric compressor in the king costume *ManCrab* (1983) that pumped 'blood' over a canopy of white silk. *ManCrab* was the king of the 1983 band *The River*, an allegory of the destructive nature of modern life. The band acted out a battle between good and evil, between *ManCrab*, a Lucifer-like creature that represented the evils of modern technology, and the queen *Washerwoman*, the embodiment of purity and harmony. *Washerwoman* was 'killed' at the end of the 1983 carnival, a surprising and unconventional victory of evil. *The River* was the first of a trilogy that also included *Callaloo* (1984) and *The Golden*

106

75 Peter Minshall *ManCrab* from the Trinidad Carnival *The River* 1983

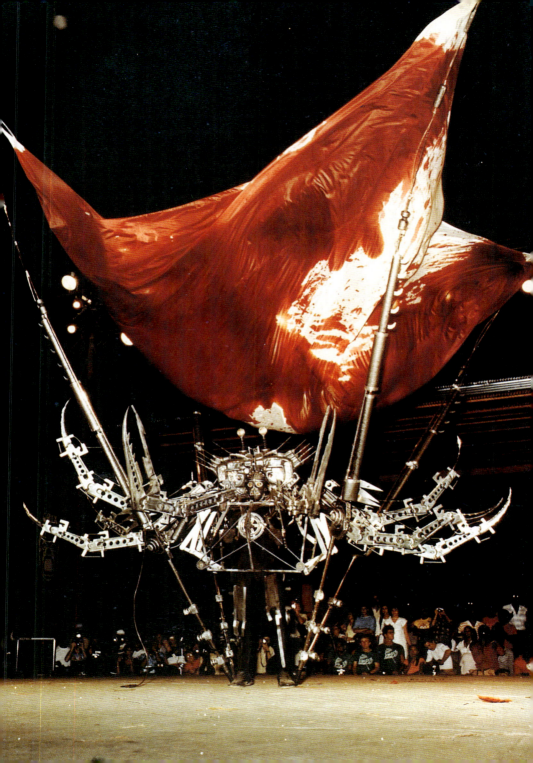

76 Gaston Tabois *John Canoe in Guanaboa Vale* 1962

Calabash (1985), in which these themes were explored further. While the East Indian and Chinese contributions to Trinidad mas have not always been acknowledged, Minshall's bands are emphatically multi-cultural. In *The River*, for instance, he appropriated East Indian elements such as the small, portable *tassa* drums and the East Indian *phegua* (*holi*) spring festival in which coloured dyes are thrown on participants.

In predominantly Protestant countries like Jamaica, other traditional festivals exist such as the Christmas season Jonkonnu masquerade. Like the *ireme* masqueraders in Cuban art, Jonkonnu has fascinated artists since the mid-nineteenth century when Isaac M. Belisario first documented the tradition. In the twentieth century, Jonkonnu appears in the work of artists who are concerned with 'the Jamaican' such as Osmond Watson and the intuitive painter Gaston Tabois (b. 1931). The latter is a keen observer of Jamaican life and the surreal overtones of his precisely crafted Jonkonnu paintings remind us that reality and the fantastic intersect in masquerade. Although there have been several attempts to revive Jonkonnu, among others through Jamaica's midsummer Independence Festival, it is a waning tradition.

Unlike its Jamaican near-namesake, which never really entered mainstream culture, the Bahamas Junkanoo has evolved into a spectacular Boxing Day street parade in which various organized bands compete with floats and masqueraders. The modern Junkanoo attire consists of a body costume and headdress, both elaborately decorated with brightly coloured crêpe-paper strips. As in Trinidad, several noted Bahamian artists are involved in Junkanoo design – Stan Burnside (b. 1947), John Beadle (b. 1964) and Jackson Burnside (b. 1949) are associated with the 'One Family' Junkanoo Organization. Junkanoo frequently appears as a subject in modern Bahamian art and has led to a recognizable Bahamian aesthetic of flat, brilliant colours and simple yet dynamic forms. One such example is *Junkanoo Ribbons* (1984) by Brent Malone (b. 1941) which is part of a larger series of part photo-realist, part surrealist portrayals of the festival. Junkanoo is also an important theme in the work of the popular painter Amos Ferguson (b. 1920) and even his paintings that are not directly related to the masquerade reveal its influence.

The Caribbean festival traditions have travelled with Caribbean migration to North America and Europe. The larger Caribbean carnivals

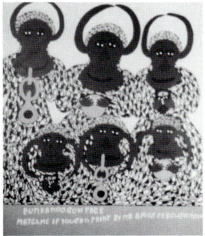

78 Amos Ferguson *Junkanoo Cow Face: Match Me If You Can* 1990

77 Brent Malone *Junkanoo Ribbons* 1984

79 Tam Joseph *Spirit of the Carnival* 1983

in cities such as Brooklyn, Toronto and London were modelled after Trinidad mas, although they attained broader significance as celebrations of Caribbean heritage, black solidarity and multi-cultural goodwill. Unavoidably, however, these festivals have also been channels for racial and political dissent. The Notting Hill Carnival in London, for instance, erupted into large-scale race riots in 1976, one of the first major episodes of unrest among the black population in Britain.

Tam Joseph (b. 1947), a London-based artist who was born in Dominica, started his career during this turbulent period and has devoted much of his work to exploring the cultural and racial stereotypes that prevail in multi-cultural Britain. He commented on the politicized nature of carnival in his *Spirit of the Carnival* (1983). The work reminds of the stereotype media images of black rioters in confrontation with the police and incisively satirizes the typical overreaction of the British security services to matters involving the black population.

CHAPTER FOUR

Revolution, Anti-Imperialism and Race Consciousness

Caribbean art entered a new phase in the fifties and sixties, which was characterized by a radicalization and polarization of artistic views. Some artists rebelled against the indigenist canons of the nationalist schools and sought a more universal artistic expression in formalist modernism. Almost simultaneously, social and political subjects became more prominent and several schools of political art emerged. This chapter examines the ideologically motivated art forms of this era and their relationship with abstract and experimental art.

This was one of the most turbulent periods in the socio-political history of the Caribbean – the Cuban Revolution of 1959 was a watershed event in Caribbean history and gave the entire region unprecedented international attention. It placed Cuba in opposition to the United States in the midst of the Cold War and influenced the course of politics throughout the Americas. The assassination of the dictator Trujillo in the Dominican Republic in 1961 marked the start of several years of social and political unrest that culminated in civil war in 1965. Anxious to avoid 'another Cuba', the United States sent a massive intervention force of twenty thousand marines and restored the status quo. The following year, the former Trujillo aide Joaquín Balaguer was elected president. It was during this period, also, that François Duvalier came to power in Haiti and established one of the most repressive regimes in modern Caribbean history.

There were fundamental changes in the political status of most Caribbean countries. In 1958 the British territories were united into the West Indies Federation, but it fell apart when Jamaica and Trinidad seceded to become independent from Britain in 1962. Barbados and Guyana followed in 1966 and most smaller islands have since then also become independent. While the failure of this federation experiment shows that the region was not ready for a pan-Caribbean state, it generated greater regional consciousness and stimulated cultural exchange. Puerto Rico, in contrast, became a Commonwealth or 'Associated Free State' of the USA in 1952, a controversial compromise between integration and independence. The French Antilles and French Guiana opted for full assimilation with France as Overseas Departments in 1946 and similarly, the Dutch territories became part of the Netherlands in 1955, with internal self-government, although Surinam opted for independence in 1975.

Whereas local conditions varied, there was a general increase in political activity throughout the region. Anti-imperialist sentiments ran high and several Caribbean nations asserted themselves as a part of the Third World, in the political sense of the Non-Aligned Nations movement. In many instances, the nationalist leaders and intellectuals of the previous decades became the governing politicians, which allowed them to turn anti-imperialist nationalism into official policy. There was a pervasive, undeniably utopian belief that a more equitable socio-political order had finally become possible. This view was perhaps best summarized by the Trinidadian historian and politician Eric Williams who said in 1961: 'Massa day done', the slave-master's time is over.

This new breed of politicians was acutely aware of the social and political importance of culture in post-colonial society and this led to an unprecedented level of government involvement in the arts and, occasionally, incidents of interference. New art schools, museums and other supporting facilities were established in the larger Caribbean countries, most of them with government funding, which helped to broaden the scope of Caribbean art. The Cuban government, in particular, has devoted considerable resources to artistic and cultural promotion, more so than most Third World nations. There is a comprehensive art education system that is offered free of cost – the flagship of this system is the Higher Institute of Art (ISA) in Havana, the influential national post-graduate art school, which opened in 1976.

Despite the initial optimism, internal tensions emerged in several Caribbean countries and the new political establishment was soon challenged by dissident, usually more radical factions. Marxism was important, but race was a central issue in this radicalization process, especially in Jamaica, Trinidad and Guyana, where black nationalism gained widespread support and became an important political force. Other ethnic groups asserted themselves, especially the fast-growing East Indian populations of Trinidad and Guyana, who frequently found themselves at odds with radical black nationalism. Caribbean migrants and their descendants also participated in racial activism in North America and Europe, as they had done earlier in the century. Malcolm X, for instance, was of part West Indian descent (his mother was from Grenada).

It may seem contradictory that Caribbean artists became interested in abstract art during this era of ideological radicalization. The two were not mutually exclusive, however, since the Caribbean ventures into abstraction often amounted to rebellion against being typecast, whether by the Western or the Caribbean cultural establishment. The Guyanese-born painter and critic Frank Bowling (b. 1936) has vocally defended his right of access as a black artist into the modernist mainstream of London and New York, where he has lived for some forty years. These developments were reinforced by the shift from Paris to New York as the focal-point of the metropolitan avant-garde and the increased exposure to these trends through overseas study, travel, migration and international art journals.

Predictably, however, abstract art has been highly controversial in the Caribbean and has been rejected by many as a concession to North American cultural imperialism. It is too simplistic to attribute these developments to the influence of the New York School, however, since abstraction and formalism are firmly rooted in twentieth-century Latin American art. Starting with the Uruguayan Joaquín Torres-García (1874–1949), Latin American artists have been among the pioneers of constructivism and concrete art and its offshoots into kinetic art and op art. The critique of indigenism also started early in Latin America, especially in Argentina where cultural nationalism was already rejected in the twenties by the artists and intellectuals associated with the *Martín Fierro* journal. It is therefore no coincidence that abstraction emerged in Caribbean art at a time of intensifying intellectual and artistic contacts with Latin America and that it flourished mainly in the Hispanic Caribbean.

Cuba and Puerto Rico represent two political extremes in the Caribbean and have produced the most distinctive schools of political and abstract art. It is therefore useful to examine the developments in these two countries in some detail and to compare them with related trends elsewhere in the Caribbean. Cuba had a well-established national school, but in the first half of the twentieth century Puerto Rican art had been practically dormant. A cohesive, assertively nationalist Puerto Rican School finally appeared in the fifties, at a time when indigenism was being challenged throughout the Caribbean and Latin America, and this initially left limited room for abstract art. The emergence of the Puerto Rican School coincided with the country's change in political status from colony to commonwealth of the USA and the launching of *Operation Bootstrap*, an ambitious social and economic reform programme based on industrialization and US investment. These reforms took place during the administration of the first locally born governor, Luis Muñoz Marín.

The Puerto Rican School was more radically populist in orientation than the earlier nationalist schools in the Caribbean and found its most distinctive expression in the graphic arts, which can be distributed widely and at low cost. Although the Mexican workshop, *Taller de Gráfica Popular*, was clearly an inspiration, Puerto Rican printmaking was directly influenced by the social reform programmes of *Operation Bootstrap*. The main agency involved in this process was the Division of Community Education (DIVEDCO) of the Department of Health, a rural education agency established in 1949. The agency used film, posters and other graphic media in its educational campaigns, which reinforced the notion of art as a social mobilization tool and encouraged the development of printmaking. Most emerging Puerto Rican artists of that era were at some point associated with the DIVEDCO screen-printing workshop.

The decisive event in the evolution of the Puerto Rican School was the establishment of the Centre of Puerto Rican Art (CAP) in 1950 by Lorenzo Homar (b. 1913), Rafael Tufiño (b. 1918), José Torres Martinó (b. 1916) and Julio Rosado del Valle (b. 1922). CAP served as a training centre, print workshop and exhibition venue. Its first collaborative print portfolio, entitled *The Puerto Rican Print* (1951), was accompanied by a statement that outlined the organization's objectives and can be read as a manifesto of nationalist Puerto Rican art. It stated that: 'This portfolio...is the fruit of the collective labour of a group of artists interested in the development of Puerto Rican art. They are of the view that the print permits the artist to reach a broader public; that in Puerto Rico art should spring from a complete identification of the artist with the people; and that only by working together and engaging in collective discussion of their work and problems, with views to self-improvement, will artists be able to bring new life to Puerto Rican art.'

CAP was short lived and closed in 1952, but it had galvanized the energies of young Puerto Rican artists, many of whom had recently returned from studies in Europe, North America and Mexico. The early graphic work of Tufiño and Homar is characteristic of this period – they collaborated on the *Portafolio de Plenas* (1953–55), a portfolio of linocuts inspired by the Puerto Rican *plenas*, popular songs on topical subjects. One of Tufiño's prints in the portfolio, *Temporal (Storm)*, was inspired by a song about the San Felipe hurricane that devastated the island in 1927. Tufiño represented the storm as a malevolent giant who swept away the defenceless people and ramshackle houses of the poor neighbourhoods of San Juan. *Storm* closely resembles a contemporaneous print by Carlos Raquel Rivera (b. 1923), *Hurricane from the North* (1955), in which the storm became a metaphor for the destructive influence of North American materialism on Puerto Rican society, one of the first openly anti-American statements in Puerto Rican art.

81

114

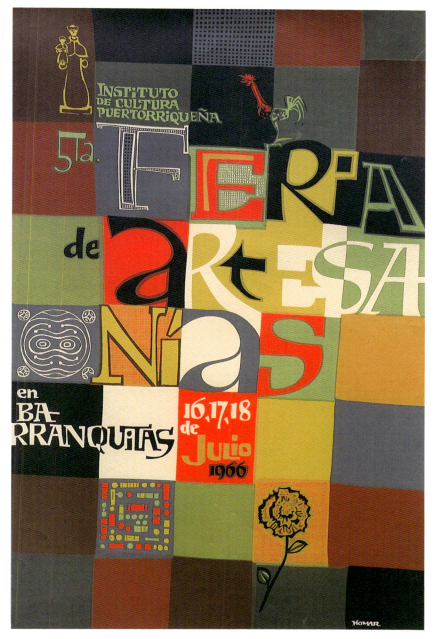

80 Lorenzo Homar, poster for the *5ta Feria de Artesanías de Barranquitas* 1966

81 Rafael Tufiño *Storm* from *Portafolio de Plenas* 1953–55

While the early Puerto Rican prints were thematically and formally inventive, the paintings by the same artists were usually more conservative social realist. There were exceptions, however, such as the surreal visions of Raquel Rivera or the heroic figure scenes of Augusto Marín (b. 1921), who was visibly influenced by the Mexican muralist Orozco. Abstraction also appeared in the mid-fifties, most notably in the paintings of Rosado del Valle. At first, Rosado del Valle used indigenous subjects as his point of departure – his painting *Vejigantes (Carnival Devil)* (1955), for example, captured the shapes, colours and patterns of the horned masqueraders of the Ponce carnival in a composition reminiscent of synthetic cubism. Rosado del Valle's work became more radically abstract in late fifties, although he returned to representation in the seventies.

As the Argentinean-born critic Marta Traba later observed, the resistance against cultural assimilation with the USA has been a fundamental characteristic of modern Puerto Rican art. Not surprisingly, therefore, Rosado del Valle and other early abstractionists were criticized for adopting a North American artistic concept. Migration and overseas studies meant that the influence of the New York School was inevitable, although it must be noted that New York had become a meeting place for

82

Caribbean and Latin American artists, as Paris had been in the twenties and thirties. Rosado del Valle had studied under the Cuban Mario Carreño, a pioneer of Cuban abstraction, at the New School for Social Research in New York in the mid-forties.

Except for the isolated case of Lucien Price in Haiti in the previous decade, Cuban artists took the lead in the Caribbean assimilation of abstraction. Alongside this, political events were leading up to the Cuban Revolution. Fulgencio Batista had seized power in 1952 and resistance against his dictatorship started the following year when Fidel Castro's rebels attacked the Moncada Barracks in Santiago de Cuba. Artistically, 1953 was also an important year that saw the establishment of, among others, *Noticias de Arte*, a journal favouring geometric abstraction, and of *Los Once (The Eleven)* (1953–55), an informal group of artists with abstract expressionist leanings.

The editorial council of *Noticias de Arte* included Carreño, Martínez Pedro and Sandú Darié (1908–91). As we have seen, Carreño and Martínez Pedro had been involved in the second phase of the indigenist avant-garde which contained the rudiments of abstraction, particularly in the surreal stylizations of Lam, the pattern structures of Portocarrero and the decorative formalism of Peláez. Afrocubanismo was an important influence on geometric abstraction in Cuba, as is illustrated by Carreño's work of the late forties to mid-fifties (he moved to Chile in 1957). This is not surprising, since Afro-Cuban ideographic writing, cosmograms and colour symbolism provided ready-made models for the reconciliation of abstract form with indigenous content, the 'creolized' approach to abstraction most Caribbean artists have taken. The Dominican painter Paul Giudicelli (1921–65), for instance, also used symbols derived from Taíno and Afro-Caribbean sources in his highly abstracted, linear compo- 83 sitions. In Cuba, this was also evident in Portocarrero's geometric abstractions of the early fifties, which were still recognizably linked to the Cuban folklore and the architecture of Old Havana.

Darié, on the other hand, represented the experimental side of Cuban abstraction. He was born in Romania but moved to Cuba in 1941 to escape the Second World War and started producing abstract art in 1950. Paintings such as *Spatial Multivision* (1955) reflect his concern with picto- 84 rial structure, space and movement and his lack of interest in indigenous content. Darié befriended Gyula Kósice of the Argentinean avant-garde group Madí, sharing the group's emphasis on construction and invention, which could be seen in works such as his participatory *Transformable Structures* (1956) and kinetic environments such as his *Cosmorama* (1960). Whereas most Cuban abstractionists later returned to representation,

82 Julio Rosado del Valle *Vejigantes (Carnival Devil)* 1955

83 Paul Giudicelli *Untitled* 1963

Darié remained faithful to concretism throughout his career. The radical formalism of his work was unusual for the Caribbean, although there have been a few younger artists with comparable interests, such as the Dominican artist Soucy de Pellerano (Jesusa Castillo de Pellerano, b. 1928), who started making her whimsical kinetic sculptures in the late seventies.

The *Los Once* artists were also committed to modernism and were particularly critical of the regionalism and exoticism of the School of Havana. Raúl Martínez (1927–95), who joined the group shortly after its establishment, deliberately restricted colour in his gestural abstracts of that period. In spite of their formalist interests, the *Los Once* members were politically active. Martínez explained the group's position to the American art historian Shifra Goldman in 1982: 'We believe[d] that art is for art's sake, but what one does with the art is a problem of individual conscience, and that is already political.' The group's main political act was the organization of the so-called *Antibiennial* at the University of Havana in 1954 in protest against the *Hispano-American Biennial*, a joint project of the Batista and Franco regimes.

84 Sandú Darié *Spatial Multivision* 1955

85 Soucy de Pellerano
Machine Lever Structure 1990

86 Luis Martínez Pedro
Territorial Waters No. 14 1964

87 Luis Hernández Cruz *Composition with Ochre Shape* 1976

Castro and his rebels came to power in 1959 and officially embraced communism in 1961. Although the Cuban Revolution caused a shift towards political art, abstraction did not suddenly disappear. Martínez Pedro's *Territorial Waters* paintings of the mid-sixties, for instance, present a highly abstracted, 'hard-edge' evocation of the wave movement and optical effects of the sea, although the title inevitably evoked Cuba's uncertain territorial status during those eventful years.

While abstract art was on the wane in Cuba, it gained greater credibility in Puerto Rico with initiatives like the exhibition *The New Abstraction* (1967) at the University of Puerto Rico. Noemí Ruiz (b. 1931) and Luis Hernández Cruz (b. 1936) were among the Puerto Rican artists who adopted minimalism and geometric abstraction in the sixties, a more fundamental 'universalist' departure from the nationalist norm than their predecessors. The work of Hernández Cruz is a good example of the eclecticism of Caribbean abstraction, however, and usually combines organic forms with elements of constructivism and op art. Many of his paintings and sculptures also include references to the figure or the Puerto Rican landscape.

Hernández Cruz has been important as an advocate of experimentation and greater openness for Puerto Rican art. He was influential as art professor at the University of Puerto Rico (1968–93), and was a founder of the Puerto Rican Frente group in 1977, with Lope Max Díaz (b. 1943), Paul Camacho (b. 1929) and Antonio Navia (b. 1945). Max Díaz stands out among this group with his immaculately crafted mixed-media reliefs, based on the square and rectangle, that reflect a more orthodox constructivist vision. Frente was one of many artists' associations that were formed in the Caribbean during this period – other influential groups were Proyecta (1968) and Nuevo Imagen (1972) in the Dominican Republic and the Contemporary Jamaican Artists' Association (1964–73) in Jamaica. Whereas local conditions varied, the general objectives of these

88 Lope Max Díaz *Ancestral Penetrations* 1982

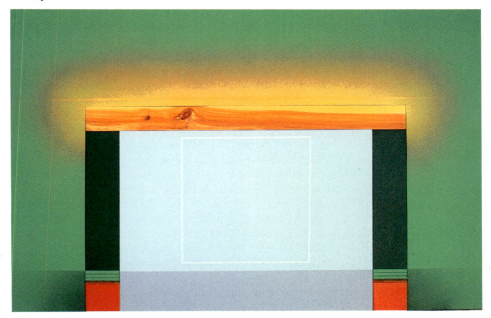

groups were very similar: they challenged the established artistic order and promoted the development of contemporary art in their country.

Abstract art became more prominent in Puerto Rico, but it remained controversial, largely because the Puerto Rican art public resisted anything that deviated significantly from the nationalist norm. Rafael Ferrer, a former student of the Spanish surrealist Eugenio Fernández Granell at the University of Puerto Rico, defied moral and artistic conventions with his sexually suggestive assemblages and installations made from industrial waste. The public response was hostile and included the picketing of his first major exhibition in 1961. Ferrer left for the USA in 1966 and settled in New York the following year.

The debates about Puerto Rican art became increasingly polarized between universalist and nationalist factions, which echoed the political climate. Although *Operation Bootstrap* had generated some prosperity, it did not fulfil expectations and by the late fifties there was a growing disenchantment with the political situation, fuelled by the Cuban Revolution and the struggles of Puerto Rican migrants in the USA. This led to an intensification of nationalism and pro-independence activism, especially among the intelligentsia, but also to growing pro-statehood sentiments.

The artistic impact of this political radicalization is evident in the screen-print portfolio *The Alacrán Cards Deck* (1968) by Antonio Martorell (b. 1939), which satirized the elections of that year. This portfolio took the form of an oversized cards deck, with Lyndon B. Johnson as the joker. It was produced at the Taller Alacrán (1967–71), a print workshop established by Martorell in an economically depressed area of San Juan. The name of the workshop, which means scorpion, refers to a gang-related scarification pattern. It was the first of several independent, community-based workshops with a more radical political orientation. The Taller Alacrán also produced posters, which became a major art form in Puerto Rico and Cuba in the sixties.

Some of the most beautiful Puerto Rican posters were made for the Institute of Puerto Rican Culture, an institution established in 1955 for the study and advancement of Puerto Rican culture. Lorenzo Homar directed the Institute's graphics workshop from its inception in 1957 until 1973. While there, he produced several classic Puerto Rican posters such as the one for the *5ta Feria de Artesanías de Barranquitas* (1966), an annual craft fair. This poster stands out because of its colourful abstract design and the dominant, playful lettering, one of Homar's special interests. It is also an early example of the use of motifs derived from Taíno art and the *santos* carvings in modern Puerto Rican art.

80

89 Antonio Martorell
Joker from *The Alacrán
Cards Deck* 1968

In Cuba, the appearance of poster art was directly linked to the Revolution and the need of the Cuban government and its agencies to communicate political ideas and information to a large audience. Cuba's new alliances in Eastern Europe reinforced this development and Polish poster design was a notable influence. Cuban poster design was spearheaded by artists such as Raúl Martínez, who had worked in advertising before, and Alfredo González Rostgaard (b. 1943). The posters were primarily produced for educational initiatives such as the nationwide literacy campaign of 1961 and for cultural organizations such as the Cuban Cinema Art and Industry Institute (ICAIC), the Cuban Artists and Writers Union (UNEAC) and the Casa de las Américas. As in Puerto Rico, screen-printing was the medium of choice, although in Cuba this was caused in part by the lack of functional lithographic presses after the USA imposed its economic blockade in 1962.

The designs for ICAIC included Martínez' famous poster for *Lucia* (1968), a film by Humberto Solas. With its brilliant colours and compartmentalized composition, the *Lucia* poster reflects the legacy of Amelia Peláez and, therefore, the continuities in Cuban art, despite Martínez' earlier criticisms of the School of Havana. A poster-making workshop was also established at the Casa de las Américas, an organization established to

92

125

foster cultural exchanges with the Caribbean and Latin America – the best-known example of what was produced was Rostgaard's poster for Canción Protesta (1967), a protest song concert. This poster became an international icon of the period when it appeared on the cover of the book *The Art of Revolution, Castro's Cuba: 1959–1970* (1970) by Dugald Stermer and Susan Sontag. The emblematic simplicity of Rostgaard's design – a stylized rose with a bloodied thorn – contrasts with the more complex designs by Martínez, showing that there was no official style for Cuban poster art.

The Canción Protesta poster illustrates that the political and the cultural were not clearly separated in Cuban poster art. This was less apparent in Puerto Rico, although the cultural posters had strong nationalist overtones. While most Puerto Rican designs were elaborate, occasionally involving as many as twenty colours, the Cuban designs were simpler, in part because of the shortage of printing ink that forced artists to use less colours and more open space. Cuban and Puerto Rican poster-makers both used abstraction in their designs – which again shows that abstraction and political content are not mutually exclusive – although the Cuban posters were more distinctly modernist, in keeping with the revolutionary

90 Raúl Martínez *Island 70* 1970

91 Edouard Duval-Carrié
J.C. Duvalier as Mad Bride 1979

ethos of modernity. Because of the considerable artistic value of these hand-made posters, they became collectibles and inevitably lost some of their public function, especially in Puerto Rico. The Institute of Puerto Rican Culture posters, for instance, were printed in small editions and given only limited public exposure. Some smaller private workshops, such as the Taller Alacrán, also resorted to selling their posters to recover costs.

Apart from his work as a graphic designer, Martínez was also the prime exponent of Cuban revolutionary painting. After a series of works on political subjects in a style influenced by Robert Rauschenberg, he produced *Martí and the Star* in 1966. It was the first painting in which he used his trademark graphic stylization and repetition of the image, techniques borrowed from his screen-printing experience. Similar paintings followed, primarily of Cuban revolutionary heroes such as José Martí, Ché Guevara and Fidel Castro, although he portrayed anonymous Cuban types as well. Martínez' work of this period is often compared with Andy Warhol's multiple screen-printed images, but although he was visibly aware of US pop art, his work was rooted in the ideology and visual culture of the Cuban Revolution rather than in Western consumerism and its upbeat, purposefully political character was far removed from Warhol's dispassionate, mechanical approach.

90   Martínez' mural-size triptych *Island 70* (1970) is in essence a summary of his work of the late sixties and reminds of the propaganda billboards that have proliferated in revolutionary Cuba. It was painted during the year of the Cuban Government's ill-fated campaign to produce ten million tons of sugar on its state-run plantations and is a subtly ironic image of a utopian world in which various Cuban types (and a cat and a gorilla) mingle with the heroes of the revolution as one happy, smiling 'Cuban family'. The sugar cane and factory in the background refer to what had become the official doctrine of *la zafra* (the sugar crop) as the engine of the revolution rather than an agent of oppression. The political significance of *Island 70* is reinforced by the prominence of reds and oranges in the colour scheme and the inclusion of the logo of the Committee for the Defense of the Revolution (CDR), a stylized image of a cane harvester.

Apart from Martínez, other artists expressed the early revolutionary ideology – for instance, Servando Cabrera Moreno (1923–81) and Adigio Benítez (b. 1924). Whereas Cabrera Moreno's flamboyant depictions of the Cuban peasantry were rooted in the vanguardia tradition, particularly 95   the work of Carlos Enríquez, the more sedate, stylized images of welders by Benítez were formally indebted to the abstract trends of the previous decade. Wifredo Lam, who had by then settled in Europe, made his public

92 Raúl Martínez, poster for *Lucia* 1968

93 Alfredo González Rostgaard, poster for Canción Protesta 1967

endorsement of the Cuban Revolution with *The Third World* (1966), 94 which he painted for the presidential palace in Havana. This mural-size work is a good example of his later, more graphic style.

Cuban art of the sixties was far more imaginative than the dull socialist realism of the Soviet Union or China, but most of it was propaganda art and cultural policies left little room for deviations from the official norm. Anti-government protest art was not tolerated and artists with 'bourgeois' interests were systematically castigated by orthodox critics. This led to the alienation of the neo-figurative painter Antonia Eiriz (1929–95), one of 124 the most interesting Cuban artists of the era. She stopped painting in 1969 and dedicated the rest of her active life to community craft work for the CDR. By the mid-seventies, Cuban art had lost much of its early revolutionary enthusiasm and photo-realism had become the dominant style. In 1976 the Cuban constitution incorporated the following statement: 'Artistic creation is free as long as its content does not oppose the Revolution. Forms of expression are free.' However, what 'opposing the

129

Revolution' means is a matter of interpretation, which helps to explain the inconsistency of Cuban artistic policies that have wavered between liberalism and dogmatism.

The Cuban revolutionary school was a unique phenomenon in the Caribbean and elsewhere 'propaganda' art was usually limited to official portraits and public monuments. While these works document the development of official iconography in these post-colonial societies, which is historically and culturally significant, most are of limited artistic interest. In comparison, social and political protest art flourished throughout the region, not surprisingly, given the political turbulence of the era. Artists actively participated in the events surrounding the Dominican Civil War of 1965, for instance, and represented their political views in their work – this can be seen most notably in the early work of Ramón Oviedo (b. 1927). Although most artists refrained from direct political comments during the succeeding Balaguer administration, the civil war period left a legacy of social and political involvement in Dominican art that is still evident today.

Overt political protest art can, of course, only exist when there is freedom of expression. The conditions in Haiti under the Duvaliers did not allow for overt political dissent and most artists therefore turned to general existential, social and cultural issues, often from a black nationalist perspective. It is no coincidence that there was a revival of Vaudou-related art, as we saw in the previous chapter. There are notable exceptions, however, such as the work of the 'primitive' artist Jasmin Joseph, who had abandoned sculpture for painting in the late fifties. His fable-like animal scenes often allude to socio-political events and personalities, although most of these references are so subtle that they can only be understood by those who are intimately familiar with Haiti's current affairs. Edouard Duval-Carrié also uses quasi-naive, surreal imagery, but has been more candid with his comments on Haitian politics, perhaps because he has spent most of his adult life outside Haiti. His early painting *J. C. Duvalier en Folle de Marié (J. C. Duvalier as Mad Bride)* (1979), for instance, is a daring satirical reference to rumours about Baby Doc's sexual preferences and unstable character.

As these Haitian examples illustrate, allusions and metaphors are powerful tools in political art, especially when overt political commentary is restricted. The seemingly conventional idyllic landscapes the Guyanese artist Bernadette Persaud (b. 1946) painted from the mid-eighties to early nineties quietly decried the militarization of Guyana by the inclusion of barely visible, but heavily armed, soldiers in camouflage outfits. The series was inspired by the botanical gardens that surround the official residence

96

91

97

94 Wifredo Lam *The Third World* 1966

95 Adigio Benítez *Welders* 1963

96 Jasmin Joseph, title unknown, *c.* 1980 (detail)

of Forbes Burnham, who was president of Guyana from independence in 1966 until he died in 1985. The policies of the Burnham administration, which instituted an idiosyncratic form of socialism, were isolationist and intolerant of opposition. Most Guyanese artists therefore avoided the overtly political, like their Haitian and Dominican counterparts.

In comparison, freedom of expression was well established in the English-speaking islands, for instance in Jamaica, where artists commented freely on the political crisis of the late seventies. Michael Manley, the son of Edna Manley, had become prime minister in 1972 and under his administration Jamaica espoused democratic socialism and became a vocal exponent of the Third World movement. Culturally, it was a particularly fertile era, during which the visual arts flourished and reggae music, another form of protest art, came to international attention. The atmosphere became increasingly tense, however, with rapid economic decline, outbursts of partisan violence in Kingston's inner-city areas and rumours of destabilization plots and CIA interference. The unrest culminated in the violent 1980 elections that brought the Manley era to an end.

One of the many artists who responded to these events was Carl Abrahams (b. 1913), a contemporary of the Institute Group, who presented a moving image of hope and reconciliation with his *Christ in Rema* (1977). (Rema is one of Kingston's most volatile inner-city neighbourhoods.) Others presented a more critical and pessimistic view – such as

98

97 Bernadette Persaud *A Gentleman at the Gate* 1987

98 Carl Abrahams *Christ in Rema* 1977

Eugene Hyde (1931–80) in his *Casualties* series (1978). The abstracted, bandaged figures that dominate these paintings refer to the street people of Kingston, which Hyde used as a metaphor of the deteriorating socio-economic conditions. As is typical for political art, the series relies heavily on colour symbolism – the yellow, green and black in *Good Friday* (1978) are the colours of the Jamaican flag whereas the red refers to communism, which Hyde perceived as an imminent threat to Jamaica. The *Casualties* series also reveals his indebtedness to the American artist Rico Lebrun, particularly his *Casualties* series of 1959. Hyde was a pioneer of abstraction in Jamaican art in the early sixties and a founder of the Contemporary Jamaican Artists' Association.

Trinidad had one of the strongest economies in the Caribbean, due to its oil reserves, but its political life was far from stable. Race riots and fears of an army mutiny resulted in a seven-month long state of emergency in 1970–71. This atmosphere of crisis was graphically represented by Isaiah James Boodhoo (b. 1932), who is better known today for his lyrical, semi-abstract landscapes and evocations of East Indian life, in *Breakdown in Communications* (1970). It is a vitriolic comment on the policies of Eric Williams, the Prime Minister of Trinidad from 1962 until he died in 1981. Williams is represented as a skull-faced demon, with his trademark sunglasses, hearing aid and tie with the logo of his political party. The flag

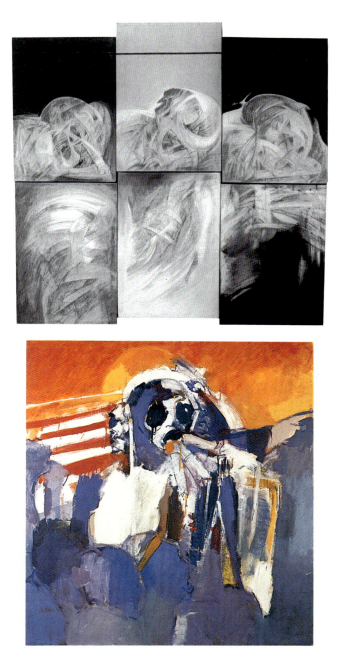

99 Eugene Hyde *Good Friday* from the *Casualties* series 1978

100 Isaiah James Boodhoo *Breakdown in Communications* 1970

101 Stanley Greaves
The Annunciation
from *There is a
Meeting Here
Tonight* series 1993

next to him is the 'stars and stripes', not the Trinidadian flag, an indict-ment of his political and economic concessions to the USA and an expression of the growing anti-American sentiments in the Caribbean.

Boodhoo's portrayal of Williams contrasts sharply with Martínez' cheerfully propagandist images of Castro, although both depict the stock image of the Caribbean political patriarch as public speaker, a tantalizing subject for political satire. *There is a Meeting Here Tonight* (1993) is a suite of three paintings by the Guyanese artist Stanley Greaves (b. 1934), who has lived in Barbados since 1985, which without being specific satirizes the demagogic tendencies in Caribbean politics and reflects the recent disenchantment with Caribbean political culture. In the first panel, *The Annunciation*, the literally double-talking political activist seems unaware that he is standing in a garbage can, ready to be carted away. Political sub-jects are, however, rare in the work of Greaves, although his precise 'meta-physical' paintings usually contain references to his Guyanese background.

Compared with the rest of the Caribbean, there was little political activity in the French Overseas Departments of the French Antilles and French Guiana, although there were some separatist rumblings, especially in Guadeloupe. However, the changed relationship with the 'metropolis' did cause new social, racial and cultural dilemmas and led to a renewed need for cultural definition in art. This is illustrated by the work of the Martiniquans Louis Laouchez (b. 1934) and Serge Hélénon (b. 1934), who joined forces in 1970 as the Ecole Négro-Caraïbe (Negro-Caribbean School) and defined their work as Afro-Caribbean art with universalist aspirations. Their cultural allegiances are reflected in Laouchez' pictographic painting style, which reminds of African and Caribbean Amerindian rock paintings. Hélénon has been more explicitly critical of social conditions in his recent *Expressions-Bidonvilles (Ghetto-Expressions)*, a series of painted wood assemblages inspired by the slums that still exist in the French Antilles, despite the artificial prosperity generated by the Overseas Department status.

As several examples already cited in this chapter illustrate, racial consciousness was an increasingly important influence on art from the English- and French-speaking countries. Black nationalist art predominated, although East Indian nationalism also emerged in, for instance, the work of James Boodhoo. Most black nationalist artists refrained from direct references to the racial tensions of the sixties and seventies and instead emphasized the philosophical and cultural aspects of race. This is evident in the work of the Trinidadian painter and poet LeRoy Clarke (b. 1938), whose visionary paintings explore the existential dimensions of 104 race and post-colonial identity. For more than twenty years, Clarke has

102 Louis Laouchez *Free Brothers and Sisters* 1986   103 Serge Hélénon *Sun Inside* 1990

worked on an extended series called *The Poet* – of which the recent *Pantheon* series is a continuation – in which he has developed a complex iconographical programme on the black experience in the New World, from oppression to transcendence. The central symbols of *The Poet* derive from the geography of Trinidad: the second highest mountain El Tucuche represents the pinnacle of human achievement while the highest mountain Aripo is used as a symbol of the divine. His imagery draws heavily from Afro-Trinidadian religion and folklore, reflecting the growing appreciation of popular Afro-Caribbean culture among black nationalist artists. This is also illustrated by the work of the Jamaican Osmond Watson who, as we have seen before, appropriated the militant, visionary language of Rastafarianism.

Caribbean migration to Europe and North America peaked in the post-war era. Mass migration to the colonial and neo-colonial 'mother countries' caused fundamental cultural changes in the Caribbean and the destination countries alike. The political and cultural sensibilities of these migrants and their descendants were sharpened by the marginalization they faced in these new environments. Predictably, many identified with the struggle of local 'minorities' for social and political justice, especially in the USA during the Civil Rights campaign. This was epitomized by the Young Lords party, the Puerto Rican equivalent to the Black Panthers, who coupled radical Puerto Rican nationalism with Hispanic and Black Power activism.

Artists of Caribbean descent were closely involved in these developments and joined with other 'minority' artists in questioning the exclusion of black, Hispanic and women artists from the metropolitan mainstream. One particularly influential pressure group was the Art Workers' Coalition in the USA, which included among its members Rafael Montañez Ortiz (b. 1934), an artist of Mexican and Puerto Rican parentage. Ralph Ortiz, as he was known then, gained notoriety in the sixties with his *Theatre of Destruction* performances in which he demolished pianos and sacrificed chickens, artistic 'guerrilla' acts that challenged the social and cultural stereotypes of Latinos. Around the same time, Rafael Ferrer attacked the exclusivity of the New York art world with interventions in prime exhibition spaces such as the Museum of Modern Art, which consisted of impromptu installations made from messy, ephemeral materials such as ice, autumn leaves and grease.

This cultural activism led to the establishment of specialized cultural facilities and organizations, usually with a strong community orientation. In New York, El Museo del Barrio (1969) and the Studio Museum (1967) in Harlem were set up to promote Hispanic and African diasporal art,

104 LeRoy Clarke, a work, *c.* 1980

respectively. Both museums have Caribbean art in their collections and have employed art professionals of Caribbean origin – Ralph Ortiz, for example, was the founding director of El Museo del Barrio and LeRoy Clarke was attached to the Studio Museum as programme coordinator and artist-in-residence from 1971 until 1974, when he returned to Trinidad.

The Puerto Rican collaborative workshop model was transplanted to New York with the Taller Alma Boricua, founded in 1969 by a group of 'Nuyorican' artists, including Armando Soto (b. 1945), Marcos Dimas (b. 1943) and Adrían García (b. 1948). The Taller Boricua, as it is more commonly known, became a meeting place for Puerto Rican artists in New York. The collaborative's nationalist orientation was reflected in its name, which is derived from the Taíno word for Puerto Rico, and the frequent use of Taíno symbols by the participating artists. The workshop was initially housed in a building across from the East Harlem head-quarters of the Young Lords and produced several posters for the party. An early workshop member, Martín 'Tito' Pérez (1943–74), was arrested for playing music in the New York subway and died under controversial circumstances while in police custody. His tragic death gives special poignancy to the crucifixion-like self-image of his *Untitled* (1972–74). 106

Cultural and racial awareness was also growing among the West Indian migrants in Britain. Namba Roy (Roy Atkins, 1910–61), who was born in the Jamaican Maroon village of Accompong, but lived in Britain for most of his adult life, produced consciously neo-African ivory carvings. He 105

139

105 Namba Roy *Jesus and his Mammie* 1956

came from a family of traditional story-tellers and used his Maroon heritage as a source for his sculptures, novels and story-telling projects. Although he is now recognized as an important name in Jamaican art history, he worked on the margin of the British art world, as was the fate of most black artists of his generation.

West Indian artists and writers became more visible in Britain with the establishment of the Caribbean Artists' Movement (CAM) (1966–72). CAM helped to articulate the debates on race and multi-culturalism that dominate black British art today and influenced developments in the Caribbean as well, since several members later returned to the region. The group was dominated by writers and philosophers such as Edward Kamau Brathwaite, Stuart Hall and Andrew Salkey but also included notable visual artists such as Ronald Moody and Aubrey Williams (1926–90) from Guyana and Errol Lloyd (b. 1943) from Jamaica. While the first two dealt with broader existential and cultural issues in their work, Lloyd was one of the first West Indian artists to represent the black experience in Britain, although his expressionist paintings lack the militancy of black British art of the eighties.

Most Caribbean migrants were attracted to the USA by the economic opportunities, but many Cubans went there for political reasons after the revolution. In spite of this, the work of Cuban exile artists such as Ana Mendieta and Luis Cruz Azaceta (b. 1942), who both left Cuba in their teens, deals with the general existential issues of exile and identity

120, 121

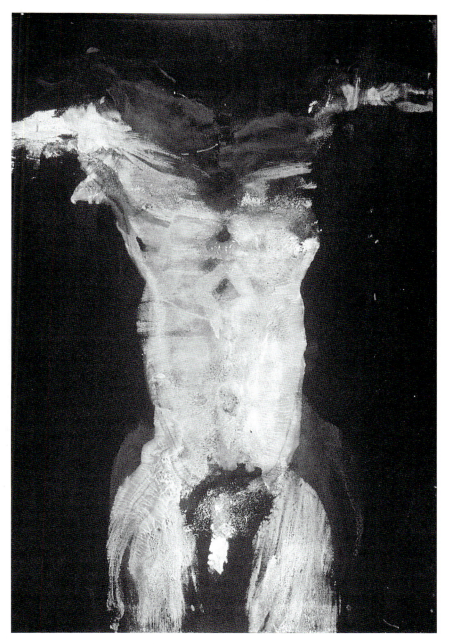

106 Martín 'Tito' Pérez *Untitled* 1972–74

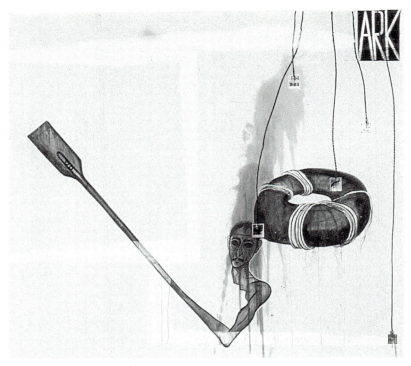

107 Luis Cruz Azaceta *Ark* 1994

instead of the political questions that surround their experience. As we
have seen, Mendieta even established a working relationship with the
Cuban government.

While Mendieta's work implied that redemption is possible, Azaceta's
tormented neo-expressionist paintings present an entirely pessimistic
view of post-modern urban life. During the seventies, he used grotesque
cartoon images to represent the urban violence of New York, where he
then lived. His recent work is more distinctly autobiographical and often
refers to his Cuban background, although he continues to comment on
broader social problems such as the AIDS epidemic – self-images appear
in most of Azaceta's recent paintings, usually as a gaunt, naked figure with
hybrid, insect-like limbs. In *Ark* (1994), which was made during the
Cuban boat people crisis, he presents himself as a Cuban rafter, with an
oar-shaped arm, surrounded by Polaroids of attacking sharks. Like his
New York paintings, it is a gripping image of an archetypal individual in a
hostile, alien environment.

CHAPTER FIVE

Nature in Caribbean Art

The natural beauty of the Caribbean region has been a source of inspiration to artists, native and foreign, since Prehispanic times and a source of
metaphorical and formal possibilities for many modern Caribbean artists.
As the most predictable subject matter of Caribbean art, however, run-
of-the-mill depictions of the natural environment tend often to be
conventional in style and format and usually present an idealized, even
stereotypical view of the Caribbean. Much of this work is mass produced
in response to market demands, especially from tourism – including the
standardized Haitian jungle paintings, replete with tigers and giraffes, that
owe more to Le Douanier Rousseau than to the local environment. There
are nonetheless artists who have dealt in their art with nature and the
landscape in more complex and reflective ways, for instance through
formal experimentation, or by linking it with ideological issues such as
environmental conservation or explorations of identity. In Wifredo Lam's
mature work, nature embodied the spiritual realm, but, in contrast, nature   94
was primarily a formal inspiration for the geometrically abstract *Territorial*   86
Waters paintings of the mid-sixties by Lam's compatriot Luis Martínez
Pedro. While these examples are very dissimilar, the natural environment
in both cases alludes to the region's turbulent socio-political history.

The overwhelming, menacing quality of Lam's nature imagery reminds
us that Caribbean nature is bounteous and fertile, but also unpredictable
and uncontrollable. The region is prone to natural disasters – hurricanes,
floods, volcanic eruptions and earthquakes – and this unpredictability has
been used by artists and writers alike to evoke the volatility of the
Caribbean experience, most poignantly by the poet Aimé Césaire who
employed the volcano as a metaphor of a convulsive, explosive self. The
related theme of humanity's powerlessness against nature often appears in
Caribbean art, for instance, in the American Winslow Homer's *The Gulf*   22
Stream (1899) and Rafael Tufiño's *Temporal (Storm)* (1953–55) and is, sym-   81
bolically, also a central tenet in the visionary work of John Dunkley.   46

Dunkley's work also demonstrates that nature is an important subject
in the work of Caribbean popular artists whose interpretations of the
natural environment range from the fanciful 'realist' landscapes of Gaston   76

143

Tabois to the mystical visions of Préfète Duffaut, Philip Moore and Everald Brown. The 'popular realist' approach to the landscape is evident in the work of Justo Susana, a little-known Dominican artist who has been painting his colourful, part imaginary views of the waterfront areas of Santo Domingo and environs since the sixties. Like many other Caribbean popular artists, Susana often includes his country of origin in his signature. While this is primarily to satisfy foreign patrons who may buy such works as souvenirs, it reminds us that portraying the 'national' landscape is also an assertion of national identity and pride.

Unless an artist's intentions are purely documentary, landscape painting usually stems from a deep personal identification with nature and the land. The English-born painter Alison Chapman-Andrews (b. 1942) has been painting the landscape of Barbados since she moved there in 1971 and while her early works were in essence realist, with a slight degree of stylization, her depiction of the landscape gradually became more
abstracted and internalized. The patchwork-like quality of her compositions derives from a process of abstraction, but also captures the fragmented quality of the Barbadian landscape that consists of windswept, heavily cultivated rolling hills intersected by steep, densely overgrown gullies with tall royal palm trees. The Barbadian gully groves are the remnants of the primeval forest that covered the entire island before the sugar plantations were established, which imparts an environmental subtext to Chapman-Andrews' work. In her recent paintings, these gullies have been transformed into surreal cosmic visions.

In the last few years, the degradation of the environment has become a major concern in the Caribbean which has a unique but very fragile ecology. Not surprisingly, many artists address environmental issues in their work, but since concerns about the environment have also become fashionable it is often difficult for artists to find a balance between attention-seeking opportunism and genuine activism. One artist who has dedicated much of his recent work to the environment is the St Lucian painter and printmaker Llewellyn Xavier (b. 1945). He gained exposure on the London art scene in the early seventies with a series of mail-art exchanges with George Jackson, one of the Soledad Brothers, with contributions by celebrities such as James Baldwin, Jean Genet, the British politician Peter Hain, John Lennon and Yoko Ono. Xavier now lives in St Lucia again and has applied this contributory approach to the environmental movement in a series of collages, *Global Council for the Restoration of the Earth's Environment*, first exhibited in 1992. These collages were made entirely from recycled materials such as brightly coloured handmade paper and nineteenth-century zoological prints. Although there is a

144

108 Justo Susana, a landscape, *c.* 1970s

very active environmental movement in St Lucia, the images Xavier appropriated are not specifically related to the Caribbean but reflect a more global interest in the environment. Each collage is endorsed with stamps and signatures from environmental activists like his compatriot Derek Walcott, the 1992 Nobel Laureate for literature, and environmental organizations such as the World Wildlife Fund. Some of the collages in the series are overly decorative, with rather precious details like ribbons, although the more successful examples have visionary overtones.

Caribbean landscape and nature art often present an aestheticized and even escapist representation of the realities of the region. As we saw in the previous examples, however, such works are not necessarily devoid of socio-political content. In fact, as Bernadette Persaud's 'militarized' landscapes of the eighties illustrate, even the most idyllic scenes sometimes address political issues. This also applies to the work of Colin Garland

97

145

109 Alison Chapman-Andrews *A Last Day in the Country* 1987

(b. 1935), an Australian-born artist who moved to Jamaica in 1962. While the figure usually dominates his fanciful, fairytale-like images, nature and the landscape are also important elements. The content of his paintings and sculptures is often personal, with ambiguous erotic overtones, although his images are laced with ironic allusions to social and political issues. The triptych *In the Beautiful Caribbean* (1974), for instance, presents a dazzling panorama of an imaginary Caribbean landscape filled with tokens of the local flora and fauna (including Caribbean and Floridian kitsch icons such as the pink flamingo and the hibiscus flower) and references to spiritual practices such as Vaudou and Rastafarianism. These are combined with equally 'quaint' and 'typical' reminders of foreign invasions, economic poverty and the police and the military, all highly visible components of the Caribbean socio-political 'landscape'.

Garland's highly marketable surreal-poetic style has been influential in the Caribbean, particularly in Haiti through Bernard Sejourné (1947–94),

110 Llewellyn Xavier *Red Vermillion* from *Global Council for the Restoration of the Earth's Environment* series 1992

111 Colin Garland *In the Beautiful Caribbean* 1974

the founder of the School of Beauty, who was his student in Jamaica in the late sixties. Garland and the artists of the School of Beauty can be placed in the larger context of a rather disparate surrealist and magic realist trend in Caribbean art, which also includes the Haitian painter Gesner Armand (b. 1936). While the artists of the School of Beauty focused on the human figure, particularly the black woman, Armand's genteel, decidedly apolitical images are based on nature and the landscape. With their seductive, high-keyed colours and soft-edged forms, his paintings could be dismissed as merely 'pretty' were it not for the startling, ironic allusions to Haitian popular culture and the transitoriness of life.

This aestheticizing trend is also represented by the work of the Cuban photo-realist Tomás Sánchez (b. 1948), who is best known for his serene, crepuscular vistas of Cuba's coastal wetlands. His emphasis on the formal relationships within these landscapes reminds of the work of René Magritte who has been a significant influence on surrealist and magic realist trends in Caribbean and Latin American art. Sánchez joined the recent exodus of Cuban artists to the USA and now lives in Miami. He has become one of the 'best-selling' Cubans, no doubt because of his remarkable technical mastery and the sleek 'tropical' quality of his images. His recent work has moved in different directions, however, and includes ominous representations of environmental issues such as solid-waste pollution.

112 Gesner Armand *Cemetery* n.d.

113 Tomás Sánchez *Relations* 1986

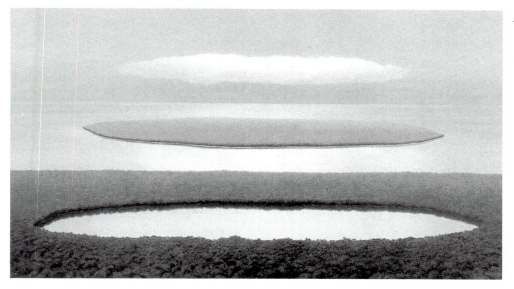

114 Winston Patrick
Mahogany Form 1974

115 Hope Brooks *Nightfall – The City* from *The Nocturne* series No. II 1991

Nature has been the point of departure for many Caribbean abstractionists, again showing how formalism is not necessarily divorced from
the local realities. This is well illustrated by the semi-abstract, biomorphic
carvings by the Jamaican sculptor Winston Patrick (b. 1946), which are
made from local hardwoods. His tactile, erotically suggestive *Mahogany
Form* (1974) is a technical marvel of illusionist woodcarving inspired by
the shape of banana leaves.

Nature is the primary inspiration for the 'minimalist' paintings of Hope
Brooks (b. 1944), another Jamaican artist, who, in spite of her formalist
emphasis on texture, pattern and structure, is a subjective observer of
nature and her paintings are rooted in introspection. Her extended *Garden*
series (1986–89) was inspired by a small interior garden in her house, a
controlled, self-contained environment for interaction with nature.
Although some paintings in the series contain vestigial images, they are in
essence highly abstracted evocations of fleeting moments of light and
atmosphere. The multi-panel format of most works in the *Garden* series

suggests not only a window structure, but also a sequential, almost filmic development. The *Garden* series evolved into the *Nocturne* series (begun 1990) in which she has been exploring the overwhelming sensory experience of the tropical night and the use of black as a colour.

Lyrical abstraction has been prevalent in the Caribbean and is often based on the landscape and the flora, which serve as vehicles for emotional associations. This is exemplified in the work of the Guyanese abstract painter Aubrey Williams. Although he is better known for his use of Mesoamerican and Guyanese Amerindian symbols and his leading role in the 'Amerindian revival' in Guyanese art, the lyrical, atmospheric quality of his abstracted images evokes the opulent vegetation of the Guyanese rain forests. As the Guyanese poet Wilson Harris has pointed out: 'Aubrey Williams is not a painter of landscapes, but his brush dips into landscapes to become a filter of associations into abstract reverie and moods.' This description could also be applied to the work of the Trinidadian painter Kenwyn Crichlow (b. 1951), who presents an emotionally charged vision of the tropical environment with his calligraphic brushstrokes and brilliant, atmospheric colours. Williams lived in England for most of his adult life and his work reflects a nostalgia for the Caribbean environment shared by other expatriate Caribbean artists.

While Williams maintained strong links with Guyana and the English-speaking Caribbean, his compatriot Frank Bowling has exhibited only once in Guyana since he left to settle in Britain in 1950 and has made his career in near isolation from the Caribbean art world. As we have seen before, Bowling has been militant about his self-definition as a formalist modernist although his paintings are haunted by his childhood memories of Guyana, especially the shimmering light of the rivers and the tidal flats of the Atlantic coast. Rivers and water still play an important role in Bowling's everyday life: his London studio is near the Thames and his Brooklyn studio overlooks the East River. After a neo-figurative phase, he produced his well-known series of map paintings, in the late sixties – contour maps of South America and the Western hemisphere are covered with thinly poured, aqueous layers of paint that are perhaps reminiscent of the stained waters of the Guyanese rivers. More recently, he has been using pigment and objects embedded in thick layers of acrylic gel, a medium that brings to mind a sense of solidified water. Although Bowling is not a political painter, his images and titles are often charged with the 'flotsam and jetsam' of history. The map paintings, for instance, inevitably evoke the middle passage, migration and Guyana's socio-political position within the Western hemisphere. Similarly, his epic painting
Chaguaramusbay (1989) takes its title from the treacherous stretch of water

116 Aubrey Williams
*Olmec Maya – Night and
the Olmec* 1983

117 Kenwyn Crichlow
Whispers in the Rainforest
1985

118 Frank Bowling *Chaguaramusbay* 1989

that separates Trinidad from Venezuela, an area associated with the slave trade and colonial and post-colonial territorial disputes.

The marine character of the Caribbean environment is essential to the work of Bendel Hydes (b. 1953), a New York-based painter from the Cayman Islands. His recent paintings are informal, abstract evocations of light, water and atmosphere, superimposed on nautical map images that evoke the sea-faring history of his home country. Before the Cayman Islands became a tourist and offshore banking paradise, its main source of income was fishery and shipping is still an important industry today. Paintings such as *Roncador Cay* (1995) refer more specifically to the cays off the coast of central America where Cayman fishermen used to journey.

Perhaps no Caribbean artist has taken the identification with nature as far as Ana Mendieta who sought to become part of nature and the earth

154

119 Bendel Hydes *Roncador Cay* 1995

itself in her quest for personal identity as a Cuban exile. Her extended *Silhouette* series of the seventies, in particular, consists of ritualistic performances and interventions in the landscape for which she used her body, or a symbolic silhouette outline in a quasi-sacrificial manner. She explained these works as follows: 'I have been carrying on a dialogue between the landscape and the female body (based on my own silhouette). I believe this has been a direct result of my having been torn from my homeland (Cuba) during my adolescence. I am overwhelmed by the feeling of having been cast from the womb (nature). My art is the way I reestablish the bonds that unite me to the universe. It is a return to the maternal source. Through my earth/body sculptures I become one with the earth.'

Interestingly, this statement was written in 1981, the year she made her *Rupestrian Sculptures* in Cuba. She was the first and until recently the only Cuban exile artist to receive permission to work there by the Cuban

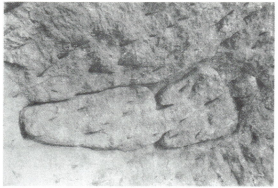

120, 121 Ana Mendieta *Guanaroca (First Woman)* (left) and *Guanbancex (Goddess of the Wind)* (above) from the *Rupestrian Sculptures* series 1981

authorities. The *Rupestrian Sculptures* are a series of carvings made into the rock walls and caverns of the Jaruco forest near Havana, which had also been used by Prehispanic Amerindian artists. The carvings consist of stylized, slightly smaller than life-size female figures that can also be seen as vaginal forms, consistent with Mendieta's metaphor of the earth as womb. To create these images, she used existing bumps and cavities in the rock surfaces, as the prehistoric artists would have done; some forms were also enhanced with paint. These carvings were named after female figures from Taíno mythology such as Guanaroca, the first woman, and Guanbancex, the goddess of the wind, another reference Mendieta makes to Cuba as her 'maternal source'. In their ephemeral character and dependence on nature, Mendieta's earth works allude to the cycle of life and the transience of the human experience.

Such themes also dominate the work of the Puerto Rican ceramist and installation artist Jaime Suárez (b. 1946), who has taken the use of clay well beyond the traditional confines of ceramics. In his work, clay is used as earth, as a token of the land, and his methods have strong ritualistic overtones. Basic ceramic forms are broken and reassembled, deliberately eroded with water or vinegar, rubbed with oxides and combined with other materials such as wood or stones. He also uses clay as a printmaking medium in his so-called 'barrografías' that are made by pressing clay surfaces onto paper.

Suárez' ceramic reliefs, totemic structures, vessels and installations explore the closely related themes of architecture, the land and ritual.

He was trained as an architect and his weathered architectural relief structures are representations of a man-made environment. On a broader metaphorical level, they also allude to civilization and its decline. Nature is represented by his highly abstracted 'earthscapes' or 'topographies', as he calls them, that remind of the parched, fissured soils of the arid mangrove swamps that exist in most Caribbean islands. They also refer to the degradation of the natural environment. The ritualistic character of his work comes to the fore in his sober, unadorned vessel forms and carefully staged installations. Most of these works evoke funerary rituals, death as the ultimate surrender to the earth.

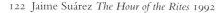
122 Jaime Suárez *The Hour of the Rites* 1992

CHAPTER SIX

The Self and the Other

As this book amply illustrates, identity is the cardinal issue in modern and contemporary Caribbean art. Most examples discussed so far address questions of identity from a social, political or cultural perspective, although the work of artists such as Fidelio Ponce de León, John Dunkley or, more recently, Ana Mendieta demonstrates that identity may ultimately be an individual, existential concern. In the sixties, while the political and abstract schools were at their peak, there was also a growing emphasis on existential subject matter, a development that has greatly influenced the present course of Caribbean art. While this was partly in reaction against dogmatic indigenism, it was also a departure from direct political commentary, on the one hand, and formalist abstraction on the other.

This new subjectivity in Caribbean art was influenced by existentialist philosophy and was related to Latin American neo-figuration of the sixties and was perhaps most evident in the dark, macabre paintings and drawings of the Cuban Antonia Eiriz, which are formally and thematically akin to the work of continental artists such as the Mexican José Luis Cuevas and the Venezuelan Jacobo Borges. Like these artists, Eiriz was evidently indebted to Goya and Ensor. Her preoccupation with the macabre, however, relates to the Cuban caricature tradition, the work of certain vanguardia figures such as Ponce de León and Rafael Blanco (1885–1955) and even the early work of Manuel Mendive, although her interests were far removed from Afrocubanismo.

Eiriz' short artistic career was contemporaneous with the early years of the Cuban Revolution and she occasionally alluded to political rhetoric and events. One such example is the pen and ink drawing *My Comrade* (1962) in which her 'comrade' is death, in the form of a grinning skeleton. While she takes no clear political position in this work, its sarcastic tone contrasts greatly with the propaganda art of the period, which surely contributed to the negative critical response she received. Most of Eiriz' works are, in fact, recognizably linked to contemporary Cuban life, unlike those of her continental counterparts – *La Muerte en Peloto (Death at the Ball Game)* (1966) was inspired by baseball that is, ironically, as popular in

32
68

124

123 Angel Acosta León *Metamorphosis* 1960

Cuba as in the USA. It is hardly a nationalist image, however, and Eiriz used formal analogy to transform the protective headgear of the players into skull-like masks and the audience into an accumulation of grimacing skulls reminiscent of the Mesoamerican skull racks.

Whereas Eiriz is best understood in her cultural and historical context, the work of her compatriot Angel Acosta León (1930–64) is entirely idio-syncratic and depicts the hermetic, private world of a tormented man (he committed suicide at the age of thirty-four). His surreal, hybrid imagery, which combines mechanical, animal and human forms, may at first seem like a delightful fantasy but it also expresses alienation and pain, even if in a highly aestheticized form. One of Acosta León's fantasies was to be a bus driver and wheel motifs appear throughout his work – in some instances they suggest escape, not unlike the ladder motifs of the German artist Wols, while in other works, particularly those that involve his cruelly stretched humanoid figures, the wheel is an instrument of torture and restraint.

123

While Eiriz and Acosta León explored new thematic and formal directions in their work, most of their contemporaries opted for a more conventional approach to existential subject matter. This is reflected in the prominence of figure and portrait painting in Caribbean art of the sixties and seventies and even today, in a variety of modes ranging from realist to surrealist and expressionist. Although the figure and the portrait

124 Antonia Eiriz *Death at the Ball Game* 1966

125 Luce Turnier *Little Girl* 1974

had also been important in the nationalist schools, primarily as expressions of national identity, there was a shift in emphasis towards the individual significance of these subjects.

This is illustrated by the sober, psychologically perceptive portrayals of black Haitians by Luce Turnier, an early member of the Centre d'Art. The Jamaican painter Barrington Watson (b. 1931) also represents the traditionalist, humanist side of Caribbean art. Although his later work is often overly academic, his paintings of the sixties have an appealing, unaffected immediacy. One such example is his iconic, subtly humourous *Mother and Child* (1958), which was inspired by his own family. The racial identity of the persons depicted by Turnier and Watson may seem almost incidental, but it is important to remember that these paintings were made in an era of militant black activism. As we have seen before, however, most Caribbean artists who have specifically dealt with race in their work, such as the Trinidadian LeRoy Clarke or the Jamaican Osmond Watson, have treated it as a matter of ideological, cultural and existential significance, a good reminder that these approaches are not mutually exclusive.

Barrington Watson is also noted for his candid erotic paintings of the seventies, a reflection of the increasingly liberal approach to sexuality in Caribbean art. This trend towards an eroticized representation of the figure is also evident in the work of the Surinamese painter and sculptor Erwin de Vries (b. 1929), who has been a regular exhibitor in Jamaica,

126

161

126 Barrington Watson *Mother and Child* 1958

with among others, Watson. De Vries' principal subjects are the female nude and the couple, in a painterly, expressionist style that contrasts with Watson's more formal treatment of the figure.

The figure dominates the work of the Puerto Rican painter and print-maker Myrna Báez (b. 1931). Her still, contemplative images of female nudes in interior settings, painted in dream-like, transparent colours represent a distinctly feminine perspective and defy convention with their emphasis on older women, who are represented with great serenity but without idealization. An exception is her *Nude in Front of Mirror* (1980) which depicts a younger, more conventionally beautiful woman. Whereas the personal prevails over the ideological in her figure scenes, Báez' nationalist convictions are more obviously expressed in her depictions of the Puerto Rican landscape and flora. The formal characteristics of Báez' paintings, such as the use of transparency and large, simplified colour

127 Myrna Báez *Nude in Front of Mirror* 1980

128 Erwin de Vries
Dancing Woman 1994

areas, clearly relate to her experience in printmaking, a common feature of modern Puerto Rican painting.

During the Dominican Civil War, Ramón Oviedo, who was from the Dominican Republic, began his career as a painter of social and political subjects, turning towards existential issues in the mid-seventies in a period of personal crisis. His work of this era was typically neo-figurative, with surrealist overtones, as can be seen in *Sterile Echo* (1975), one of a series of paintings in which he explored the questions of birth, life, sexuality and death. Much of the emotional tension of his work derives from the contrast between the self-contained plasticity of the tumbling figures, which include an anguished self-image, and the spatially ambiguous, blood-red background. Oviedo's work of the mid-seventies lacks specific references to his Dominican background, but his later, more abstracted works often include motifs derived from Taíno art.

Expressive colour also played an important role in the hallucinatory, often violent images of the Haitian painter Bernard Wah (1939–81). He came out of the social realist tradition of the Foyer des Arts Plastiques and developed a personal, surreal idiom based on quasi-mechanical stylizations of the figure, although the interlocking, rounded forms he used are

132

129 Jean-René Jérôme *Woman with Pigeon* 1973

typical for mainstream Haitian art of that period. He lived outside Haiti for most of his adult life, in Paris in the mid-sixties and in New York from 1966, but his work also reflects the anxieties of the Duvalier era. On the other side of the spectrum of Haitian art was the School of Beauty, whose main representatives were Bernard Sejourné, Emilcar Similien (Simil, b. 1944) and Jean-René Jérôme (1942–91). The elegant, serene 'dream surrealism' of the School of Beauty can be regarded as an escapist reaction to the socio-political conditions in Haiti. The female figure was the main focus of their work, which was presented as a celebration of black female beauty.

The School of Beauty was the first mainstream Haitian school to challenge the commercial supremacy of the 'primitives' with some success. Sejourné, Jérôme and Simil were eagerly patronized by the Haitian 'elite' (as the local upper class is usually called) and their work was in demand on the international market as well. No doubt because of this commercialization, their work deteriorated into beautifully crafted, ornamental luxury objects that lacked conceptual depth or emotional authenticity. There were exceptions, however, such as Jérôme's *Woman with Pigeon* (1973), a more thoughtful image painted after the death of his teenage daughter.

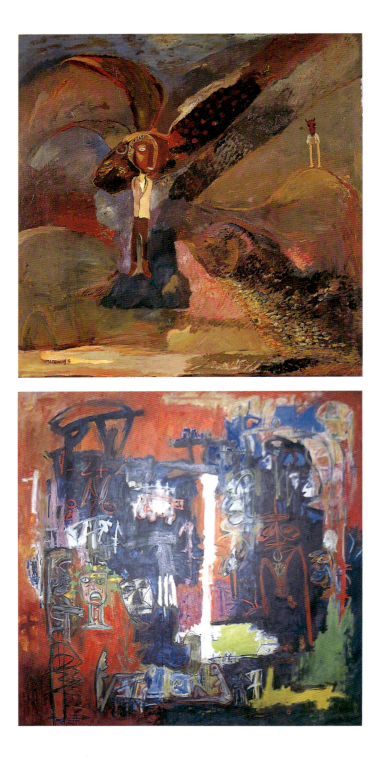

132 Ramón Oviedo *Sterile Echo* 1975

In recent years, autobiographical subjects have become increasingly important in Caribbean art, especially in the new wave of figurative expressionist painting that appeared in the eighties. The Jamaican painter Milton George (b. 1939) is a key representative of this new autobiographic expressionism – his sensually painted, instinctive images are directly linked to his personal life, especially his turbulent relationships with women, although he occasionally refers to social and political issues in Jamaica as well. Milton George has said that all his paintings are self-portraits and many include self-images, usually as a tiny, naked figure, with recognizable features or disguised with a horned mask, a tragi-comical counterpart to the tormented self-images of the Cuban-American artist Luis Cruz Azaceta. While Milton George's work is often humorous and sometimes frankly carnal, it is also deeply anguished and death is always lurking, as in *The Ascension* (1993), which was painted during a period of illness and personal turmoil.

This autobiographical expressionist trend is also represented by the recent work of the Dominican artist José Perdomo (b. 1943), particularly his extended series of highly improvisatory mixed-media paintings entitled *The Magical World of JOP* of the nineties. The acronym 'JOP' stands for the initials of his name – the series is an ongoing visual diary in which he comments on events in his life and in society by means of free associations and appropriated images, which include references to Taíno art. The graffiti-like quality of his imagery reminds of the work of Jean-Michel Basquiat, who has been a notable influence on contemporary Caribbean expressionism. While Perdomo paints the world as he sees it, he is not recognizably present in his paintings.

In contrast, the self-portrait is central to the work of the Jamaican artist and art historian David Boxer (b. 1946) that documents, as he put it, 'the thoughts and memories, the fears and drives, of one twentieth-century man who lives through a life on one small, complex, disturbing Caribbean island'. Boxer introduced the autobiographical in his work with his 'assaulted self-portraits' of the early seventies that were visibly influenced by his doctoral research on the early work of Francis Bacon. His later work is more political, with strong nationalist and anti-imperialist overtones, although the autobiographical element has remained. Boxer's work is unified by his interest in the general themes of oppression and conflict, whether personal or political – the annihilation of the Jamaican Taíno, the cultural conflicts caused by colonization and the threat of a nuclear holocaust are particularly important recurrent themes within this context.

Boxer develops these subjects into complex, open-ended iconographical programmes, often through the appropriation of existing images from

133 David Boxer, installation view of *The Passage*, 1997

a variety of historical and contemporary sources such as traditional African art, Italian Renaissance painting and the modern electronic media. He is a pioneer of assemblage, installation and video art in Jamaican art, media that are particularly suitable for his appropriation techniques. His paintings are more directly autobiographical, however, as can be seen in *Self-Portrait with Four Brain Patterns* (1988), where he probes 134 his multi-racial and multi-cultural identity, and the multiple guises of the self in its relationships with others. The painting also appropriates Marcel Duchamp's famous profile, an example of the art-historical references in Boxer's work.

134 David Boxer *Self-Portrait with Four Brain Patterns* 1988

The self-image also dominates in the mesmerizing, visionary paintings of the Puerto Rican Arnaldo Roche Rabell (b. 1955) – one of his many disguised self-portraits, *You Have to Dream in Blue* (1986) is a provocative statement on racial identity. In addition to being a general indictment of racial prejudice, it more specifically challenges the common denial of the 'blackness' of the Puerto Rican population, although the incongruous blue eyes of the black figure also remind of its hybridity. The work compares in subject and form to Boxer's *Self-Portrait with Four Brain Patterns*, an illustration of the similarity of interests across the Caribbean, despite the limited artistic contact between the different language groups.

You Have to Dream in Blue was produced with Roche's trademark frottage technique of rubbing and carving into thick, wet layers of paint, often with his bare hands. In other works, he places the canvas on top of a model, often his mother or other close associates, and traces their body into the wet paint. He also uses imprints of decorative surfaces such as plant leaves and paper lace-mats into the wet paint, another example of

135 Arnaldo Roche Rabell
You Have to Dream in Blue
1986

136 José García Cordero
Bilingual Dog 1993

the impact of printmaking on Puerto Rican painting. The intense physical involvement in the process of painting gives Roche a strong presence in his work, even when there is no recognizable self-image.

As the last few examples illustrate, there are no certainties in the recent explorations of identity in Caribbean art. Similarly, the Dominican painter José García Cordero (b. 1951), who has described his recent work as images for times of crisis, uses grotesque metaphorical images, such as his alarmingly humanoid dogs, to comment on social and political issues relevant to the Dominican Republic and neighbouring Haiti. The dog metaphor is disturbingly open-ended and even in his famous images of 'boat dogs', it is not certain whether the dogs are the victims or 136 aggressors. The dog image also appears in *Bilingual Dog* (1993), a pun on hybridity, double entendre and duplicity, although the issue of bilinguality can also be taken more literally, since García Cordero lives in both Santo Domingo and Paris.

As a major aspect of the modern Caribbean experience, migration raises new existential questions, primarily of displacement and otherness. These themes appear in the recent installations of Antonio Martorell who, like many Puerto Rican artists, lives in Puerto Rico and in New York. The title of his installation *Pasaporte Portacasa* (1993) is a pun on the Spanish words for home and passport. With its playful allusions to official documents, the home, popular culture, colonization, racial prejudice and economic need, the installation refers to the realities and historical context of Caribbean migration and celebrates the 'portable' but irrepressible cultural identity of the Caribbean diaspora.

The effects of migration can also be seen in the work of the Jamaican-born artist, writer and curator Keith Morrison (b. 1942) who left to study art in Chicago in the early sixties and settled in the USA. The visceral, figurative style of his recent work is rooted in the Chicago School rather than in Caribbean expressionism. In these recent paintings, Morrison explores his multi-cultural identity by means of eclectic, often satirical references to his childhood memories of Caribbean folklore, modern African-American life and mainstream Western culture. He also 140 frequently comments on social issues – his *Crabs in a Pot* (1994), for instance, summarizes the African diasporal experience with references to ancient Africa, slavery and Afro-Caribbean popular culture, but also refers to the self-destructive 'crab barrel' mentality of placing individual over communal progress. As a grotesque memento mori, the scene is surmounted by a urinating skeleton.

The AIDS epidemic has taken its toll in the Caribbean, which has surely contributed to the growing thematic emphasis on mortality and

137 Antonio Martorell *Pasaporte Portacasa* 1993

the transience of life. This is evident in the work of the Puerto Rican artist Carlos Collazo (1955–90) whose earlier, photo-realist work was somewhat slick and decorative, but his art took on new urgency when he was confronted with disease and death, first of a close friend and then of himself. His later paintings examine the questions raised by his terminal illness in a sober but emotionally gripping manner. The most poignant of these works are the monumental self-portraits, true confrontations with the self in which Collazo appears bald-headed and naked, an existential nakedness intensified by the otherworldly, electric colours.

139

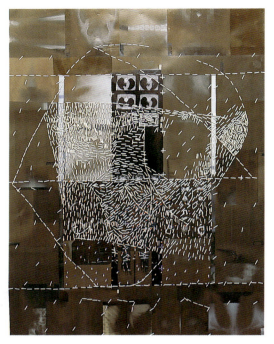

138 Ernest Breleur
Untitled from the *Suture*
series 1995

139 Carlos Collazo *Self-
Portrait I* 1989

140 Keith Morrison
Crabs in a Pot 1994

The Martiniquan Ernest Breleur (b. 1945) approaches the subject of death with emotional detachment, as a broader philosophical issue. Breleur was a founder of the indigenist Fwomajé group in Martinique but left the group in 1989 and rejected indigenism in favour of formal experimentation and universal subject matter such as the significance of religion and myth and the futility of human pursuits. After several series of paintings on death and the decomposition of the body, he turned in the mid-nineties to the symbolic reconstruction of the body in his *Suture* series of X-ray collages. While these recent works contain no anecdotic references to Martinique or the Caribbean, they are related to the intellectual and literary traditions of the Francophone Caribbean. The *Suture* series, more specifically, reminds of Aimé Césaire's collection of poems *Corps perdu (Lost Body)* (1950). In the last poem in that collection, *Dit d'errance (Song of Wandering)*, Césaire evoked the Ancient Egyptian myth of Osiris whose scattered body was reassembled by Isis.

Breleur's working method on his X-ray collages mimics that of a surgeon: the radiographies are carefully arranged on a horizontal surface reminiscent of an operating table and he wears a surgical mask and gloves to avoid infection, since some radiographies have been used during actual

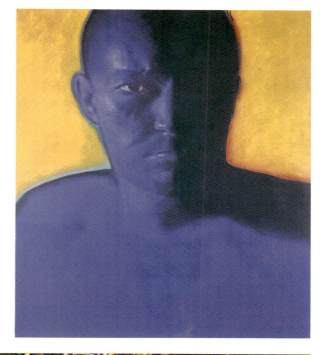

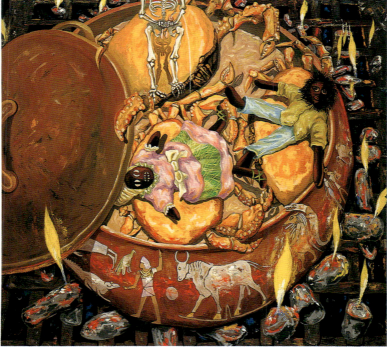

medical procedures. In spite of this clinical method, there is a singular poetry to the nocturnal, incorporeal X-ray images that appear to be 'sutured' together with white correction strips. These strips are also combined with red paper dots to form elaborate, abstract patterns that are sometimes cruciform, suggestive of tombs or the body. In the *Suture* series, Breleur also explores formal problems such as the representation of the body in space and the paradoxical effect of the opaque white strips that become highlights on the dark translucent surfaces.

Patrick Vilaire, the Haitian sculptor and ceramist, is interested in death, but based in Haitian culture – he has researched into the cosmogony and iconography of Vaudou. Vilaire's method of conceptualization and execution is slow and meticulous, devoid of the facile, highly commercialized exoticism that has plagued the Haitian art world. His recent work can be grouped chronologically into explorations of broad existential questions, all relevant to the Haitian situation, that are executed as monumental sculptures for which he uses various techniques, including the cut-metal techniques of the Haitian *feroniers*. So far, he has done a series on the subject of power, consisting of monumental thrones, one on death in Haiti and, most recently, one on the subject of memory. The latter includes *Le Carcan (The Collar)* (1996), a wood and metal sculpture of a shackled figure imprisoned in the solid block form of the wood. While the sculpture evokes the physical realities of slavery, particularly the iron collars and shackles that were routinely used to restrain rebellious slaves, it also refers to slavery as an existential state, a pessimistic image that seems to rule out the 'emancipation from mental slavery' the Jamaican reggae artist Bob Marley sang about in his *Redemption Song*.

Vilaire is an important representative of the recent revival of Caribbean sculpture, which is characterized by a shift of scale towards sober, monumental, mixed-media installations, often on subjects of identity and existential questions. Another exponent is the Jamaican sculptor Margaret Chen (b. 1951). Her *Steppe* series, a group of mural-size, mixed-media reliefs she produced in the early eighties while living in Canada, represents an exploration of her ancestral subconscious as a Jamaican of Chinese descent. She described her work on the series as: 'Assembling and gluing, building layer upon layer, scraping, scoring, carving to an inner compulsion that propelled me to work now furiously and spontaneously, at other times slowly and repetitively. That whole process became not only an exploration of the passage of time, but of my roots – an imaginary subterranean journey beneath the Steppes of Asia, of life that was no more and of what remained, accumulating, layer upon layer – vague shadows, nebulous shapes.' In spite of the word play on the stepped shape of the

142

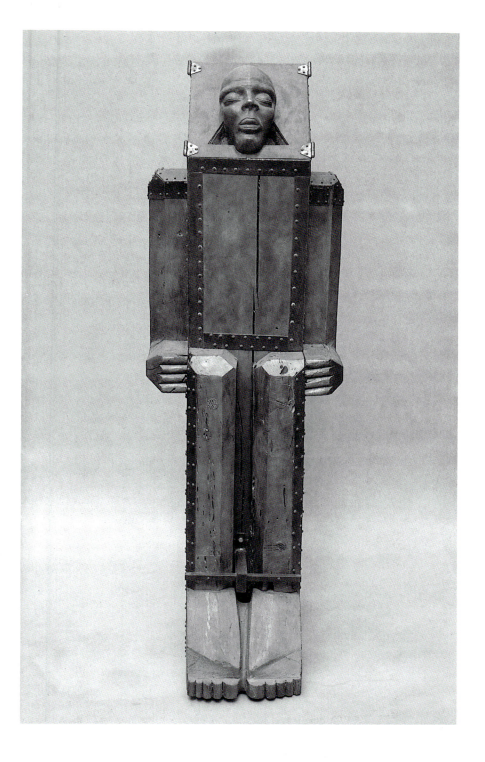

142 Margaret Chen *Steppe VII* 1982

reliefs and the calligraphic quality of the surfaces, her approach to this exploration of identity is entirely instinctive, without anecdotic references to China or Chinese art.

In contrast, cultural references are more specific in the work of Petrona Morrison (b. 1954), another Jamaican sculptor, who was profoundly influenced by her study of African art history and the year she spent in Kenya as a post-graduate exchange student, an exploration of her historic and symbolic 'roots' as a member of the African diaspora. Her monumental assemblages and installations have the verticality and frontality of Dogon art. Morrison's work deals with the general themes of transformation, renewal and healing, as autobiographic and socio-cultural issues. Most works evoke ritual structures, such as totems or altars, and she works primarily with impermanent, discarded materials – scrap wood and corroded metal – that support the symbolism of her work. In *Remembrance (124th Street)* (1995), an installation she produced as artist-in-residence at the Studio Museum in Harlem, she transformed fragments from a burnt-out derelict building behind the museum into a moving memorial to the woman who perished in the fire.

The Martiniquan writer Frantz Fanon, in *The Wretched of the Earth* (1961), spoke about the need to resurrect the pre-colonial past in order to address post-colonial existential questions. While this usually means

178

143 Petrona Morrison *Remembrance (124th Street)* 1995

the 'pre-diasporal' origins of Caribbean people, as in the work of Morrison and Chen, it also applies to the Prehispanic past. Although the Amerindians have virtually disappeared from the Island Caribbean, the Prehispanic past of the region has been granted considerable political and cultural significance as a symbolic ancestral culture that imparts an indigenous historical legitimacy to the current inhabitants of the region, regardless of their origin.

Artists of the nationalist schools occasionally referred to Prehispanic history, but it became a more important concern in the fifties and sixties, particularly in the work of Dominican and Puerto Rican artists. This is not surprising since the Amerindian heritage of these two countries is particularly well documented. It is surely no coincidence, however, that Puerto Rico and the Dominican Republic are the two Caribbean countries that have given least recognition to their African heritage.

Although he also used Afro-Dominican sources, the Dominican abstractionist Paul Giudicelli was, as we have seen, among the first artists in the region to use Amerindian symbols rather than anecdotic references. He influenced many younger Dominican artists, including Oviedo and Perdomo. In Puerto Rico, the Prehispanic past has particular political significance as a part of the defence mechanisms against Americanization. Even the name of the Young Lords party is derived from the Taíno word for Puerto Rico. The use of Amerindian symbols is therefore even more widespread in Puerto Rico than in the Dominican Republic, especially among US-based artists such as those associated with the Taller Alma Boricua.

In recent years, especially since 1992, the quincentenary of Columbus' landing, Prehispanic history and art have inspired artists throughout the Caribbean region. This is exemplified in the recent work of Roy Lawaetz (b. 1942), an artist from the US Virgin Islands, who, not unlike Perdomo, paints a fantastic, eclectic universe filled with references to Amerindian mythology, events in his own life and modern technology. The signs and symbols used in his semi-abstract compositions are heavily indebted to the Amerindian pictographs that are found in abundance in the Lesser Antilles and the *zemi* sculptures of the Taíno. Even the triangle and lozenge forms of his 'shaped canvases' are inspired by Amerindian art. Lawaetz' brilliantly coloured paintings are very appealing but also point towards the dangers of this 'neo-Amerindian' trend, which can easily deteriorate into empty decorative, formulaic work.

Amerindian culture is also an important source for the French artist Serge Goudin-Thébia (b. 1945), whose father was from French Guiana and of part Amerindian ancestry. He now lives in a secluded area of

144 Roy Lawaetz *Caribbean Myth* 1994

145 Serge Goudin-Thébia *Sawakou I, II, III* 1990

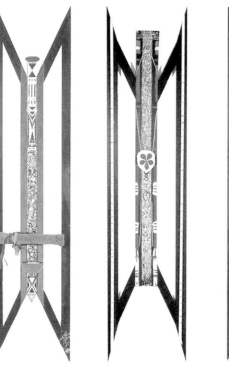

Martinique, near the sea, and strongly identifies with the nature philosophy of the Guianese and Caribbean Amerindians – the primary inspiration for his totemic assemblages. His interest in Amerindian
145 mythology is reflected in works such as the assemblage *Sawakou II* (1990), a highly stylized, anthropomorphic bird form inspired by the Sawakou bird deity of the Carib who, according to legend, became a star. Like most of his assemblages, it is made from wood, bamboo and found objects and painted in abstracted black-and-white patterns and flat blue areas, formal characteristics that are loosely inspired by Amerindian ritual art forms. While Goudin-Thébia could be criticized for 'new age' primitivism, his identification with Amerindian culture has additional personal significance as an exploration of his paternal heritage.

Whereas the Amerindian culture of the Island Caribbean is part of a semi-mythical past, it is a living culture in the Guianas where there is still a substantial Amerindian population. This has had a significant impact on the development of modern art in Guyana, Surinam and French Guiana.
116 As we have seen elsewhere, the Guyanese painter Aubrey Williams, himself an Afro-Amerindian, was a pioneer of this 'Amerindian Revival'. As a young agricultural officer, he lived with the Warau Amerindians in the interior of Guyana for two years, a decisive experience in the development of his work. Even after his move to Britain in 1952, Amerindian culture remained an important thematic and formal inspiration for his lyrical abstractions. Although he frequently referred to Guianese Amerindian culture, he was also fascinated by the lost civilizations of Mesoamerica, particularly the Olmec and the Maya, which he used as metaphors of the fragility of modern civilization.

Colonization and its aftermath had a devastating impact on the social and cultural life of the Guianese Amerindians, although they are now beginning to reclaim their space in the social and cultural mainstream of their respective countries. In recent years, several interesting Amerindian artists have appeared in the Guianas, including the painter and anthropologist George Simon (b. 1947) and his half-brother the woodcarver Oswald Hussein from Guyana. With the resurgence of Amerindian activism throughout the Americas, this revival will no doubt become more significant in the future.

CHAPTER SEVEN

Recent Developments

With the exception of the first two chapters of this book which deal specifically with artistic developments in the Caribbean area from the past, the other chapters include artists from roughly the last two decades such as Juan Francisco Elso, José Bedia, Arnaldo Roche Rabell, Edouard Duval-Carrié, José García Cordero and Petrona Morrison. And while their work underscores the continuities in twentieth-century Caribbean art, these artists belong to a new generation whose concerns differ, in some respects significantly, from those of their predecessors. Although painting is still the dominant medium, for instance, installation and multi-media art have also become prevalent, a departure from the traditional approach to form that dominated earlier modern Caribbean art. What is more important, however, is that this new generation has embarked on a reevaluation of Caribbean art in the rapidly changing social, political and cultural environment of the late twentieth century.

The Trinidadian artist and critic Christopher Cozier (b. 1959) has argued that the main difference between Trinidadian art of the sixties and seventies and his generation is the shift from 'representing culture' to 'creating culture', a polemical statement that is nonetheless applicable to contemporary Caribbean art as a whole. While Cozier may underestimate the contribution of the previous generation to the articulation of post-colonial culture, many established artists had lapsed into making highly marketable, formulaic representations of accepted 'culturally relevant' subjects, a tendency which was reinforced by the development of vigorous internal markets in countries such as Jamaica, Trinidad, the Dominican Republic and Puerto Rico. The work of the younger generation, therefore, also represents a challenge to what had become official post-colonial or revolutionary culture. In spite of this often contentious generation gap, several older artists have actively contributed to the recent developments. They include Ana Mendieta, Luis Cruz Azaceta, David Boxer, Milton George, Keith Morrison, Antonio Martorell and Ernest Breleur, who are also discussed in the previous chapters.

This new generation of Caribbean artists has come of age in an era characterized by disillusionment with the social and political ideals of the previous generation. The Cuban art critic Gerardo Mosquera, who has been closely associated with the development of contemporary Cuban art, has aptly termed the atmosphere in late twentieth-century Cuba as 'post-utopian', a description that can be extended to much of the region. This new uncertainty has been heightened by the effects of political instability, neo-colonial economic dependency, urbanization, modern technology, global communications and travel, tourism, migration and exile. Although this has fundamentally changed Caribbean culture and its relationship to the rest of the world, it has not come at the expense of the distinctiveness of contemporary Caribbean art, in contrast to the some-what naive universalism of the fifties and sixties. Instead, the present cul-tural climate has generated a new awareness of the political significance of culture and an even greater emphasis on interrogations of identity.

The cultural historian and theorist Stuart Hall, who lives in Britain, wrote in 1987 about his Caribbean background: 'What I have thought of as dispersed and fragmented comes, paradoxically, to be the representative modern experience.' Postmodernism, in this respect, seems to vindicate Caribbean cultural theory and ideas that have been central to Caribbean intellectual life since the twenties have now gained wider recognition. Writers such as Fernando Ortiz and Frantz Fanon have been rediscovered and several internationally noted contemporary cultural theoreticians, other than Stuart Hall himself, like Edouard Glissant and Antonio Benítez-Rojo, are of Caribbean descent. This has added to the self-consciousness of contemporary Caribbean art which is created with an awareness of its place in this postmodernist theoretical framework. This new theoretical awareness has been most pronounced in Cuban art and the work of artists of Caribbean descent in Europe and North America.

What is now often called New Cuban Art emerged in the early eighties in exhibitions such as *Volumen I* (1981) at the International Art Centre in Havana. The *Volumen I* exhibition included work by José Bedia, Juan Francisco Elso, José Manuel Fors (b. 1956), Israel León (b. 1957), Gustavo Pérez Monzón (b. 1956), Ricardo Rodríguez Brey (b. 1956), Leandro Soto (b. 1956) and Rubén Torres Llorca (b. 1957) and the photo-realists Tomás Sánchez, Rogelio López Marín 'Gory' (b. 1953) and Flavio Garciandía. Most of these artists were recent graduates of the ISA and several taught there as well, a testimony to the school's fundamental impact on Cuban artistic development. Although the work in *Volumen I* was embryonic, the exhibition helped to establish the main trends of the eighties and nineties. Garciandía, for example, was already moving towards conceptualism at the time and has contributed greatly to the self-referential character of New Cuban Art. Elso and Bedia have probably been even more influential with their highly individual syntheses of the personal, the mythical, the spiritual and the political.

It can be argued, however, that the Havana Biennial has played a much more significant role in the development of contemporary Cuban art than the ISA. The biennial was established in 1984 as an exhibition of Latin American art, but in 1986 was expanded to encompass 'Third World' art. The biennial has, among others, encouraged the development of process-oriented art forms such as installation and performance art, a trend reinforced by the scarcity of conventional art materials. It has also created a forum for artists and observers with related interests from all over the globe, resulting in a less insular critical context for Cuban art. By the late eighties, the Havana Biennial had become a much-noted event on the international art calendar, which has made the international exposure of Cuban art less dependent than before on the traditional power structures of the Western art world.

New Cuban Art emerged during a period of liberalization and greater openness and, for the first time since the revolution, young Cuban artists overtly challenged political and artistic dogma. This is exemplified in the work of Lázaro Saavedra (b. 1964), who started exhibiting in the mid-eighties. Saavedra has been a roving commentator on the idiosyncrasies of post-revolutionary Cuban life and art with subversive humour, but also with tenderness and compassion. His contribution to the Third Havana Biennial in 1989, for instance, consisted of an 'altar' to art and ideology, 146 under the mock political slogan 'Visual Artists of All Creeds, Unite'. The 'offerings' on the improvised altar included a 'device' to measure ideological deviations.

In the early eighties, Leandro Soto had already started incorporating official photographs of Ché Guevara and Fidel Castro in his collages and this trend of using revolutionary iconography and slogans for satirical purposes became more pronounced in the late eighties. While Soto and Saavedra tempered their political satire with playful humour, other artists were more aggressive. The painter Tomás Esson (b. 1963), for instance, combined images of Ché and Fidel with grotesque sexual and scatological imagery. In his notorious *My Homage to Ché* (1987), he portrayed Ché 147 Guevara as a black man, partly obscured by two copulating humanoids, an inflammatory mixture of sex, race and politics.

Predictably, this sort of work was not readily tolerated by the Cuban authorities, whose reactions ranged from unease to outright censorship. Even Elso's mystical portrayal of José Martí in *For América* (1986) had 71 caused some concern. One of the most publicized incidents was the closure of Esson's 1988 solo exhibition at a major Havana gallery, which

185

146 Lázaro Saavedra, installation, 1989

included *My Homage to Ché*. In the debates that followed, the Cuban Minister of Culture, Armando Hart, declared any disrespectful use of national symbols out of bounds for Cuban artists. It is surely no coincidence that this crisis took place during the so-called 'rectification' process of the late eighties, which marked the end of the period of political and economic liberalization.

While this ideological crisis was unfolding, the international fame of contemporary Cuban art was growing. The influential German collector Peter Ludwig acquired most of the *Kuba O.K.* (1990) exhibition, for instance, and established a representation of his foundation in Havana. With the growing commercial success of modern and contemporary Cuban art, the sale of art became an important part of the system of 'state capitalism' that has been in effect in Cuba since the fall of the Soviet Union. International sales are handled by the Fondo de Bienes Culturales (Cultural Property Fund) who until recently paid the artists in Cuban

186

147 Tomás Esson *My Homage to Ché* 1987

148 Tomás Esson *Portrait No. 10* 1995

pesos, at the very optimistic official exchange rate. Since Cuba was rapidly becoming a 'dollar economy', where many essential items can only be bought with US dollars, this arrangement added to the already mounting dissatisfaction among the artists. After much controversy, artists were eventually given access to their share of the hard currency earned by the sale of their work.

Prompted by these conflicts with the authorities and the severe economic crisis, many young Cuban artists left the country in the early nineties, in search of opportunities elsewhere. A few went to Europe, like Brey who settled in Gent, Belgium. Others, including Esson, applied for political asylum in the USA, although most moved to Mexico, where they can live in semi-exile without severing ties with Cuba. Since the Mexican economic crash, many have now moved on to the USA, however, including major figures such as José Bedia. Predictably, several of these 'defections' took place during overseas exhibitions and other cultural exchanges. Significantly, perhaps, Saavedra was one of the few of the eighties generation who stayed in Cuba.

Those who went to the USA were actually the second wave of Cuban 'refugee' artists to arrive there in recent years. The first group had come with the so-called Mariel Boat Lift of 1980, when about one hundred and twenty-five thousand dissatisfied Cubans were allowed to migrate to the USA. This included Carlos José Alfonso (1950–91) who had been involved in the events leading up to *Volumen I* and received some critical acclaim in the USA. Predictably, it has not been easy for the new 'refugees' to adjust to the market-driven art system of the USA and the dilemmas caused by Cuban–American politics. Controversy arose, for instance, when three of them, Arturo Cuenca (b. 1955), Florencio Gelabert (b. 1961) and Esson, participated in the 1992 *Absolut Freedom* advertising campaign for Absolut vodka, which sought to capitalize on their 'defector' status. Remarkably, however, most have refused to be typecast as dissidents in spite of the tempting commercial possibilities in anti-Castro Miami, where most have settled.

The response of the 'refugee' artists to their new environment has been highly individual. Although Bedia's work is closely linked to his 'Cubanness', for instance, Miami has an active Afro-Cuban culture and living in Mexico and the USA has allowed him to deepen his knowledge of Amerindian culture. His general outlook has therefore not changed dramatically, even though much of his recent work speaks of his migrant status, his being on the other side of the 'divide'. In contrast, the work of Brey has become less literally linked to his Cuban background, although the ideas that were current in Cuban art of the eighties continue to

149 Ricardo Rodríguez Brey, installation view of *Untitled* 1992

influence him. The ravaged interior space he constructed at *Documenta IX* in Kassel, Germany, in 1992, for instance, related to Western *arte povera* trends, but also suggested a decidedly 'post-utopian' metaphysical state. Similarly, his assemblages of incongruous materials such as fake pearls, animal skulls and horns and rubber tyres have ritualistic overtones that remind of his earlier interest in Santería. Esson now lives in New York and political allusions have disappeared from his work, although the themes of violence and sexuality have remained. His recent paintings show greater 148 formal refinement, due in part to his access to better art materials, which has somewhat tempered his hyperbolic expressionist style.

The artistic exodus from Cuba of the early nineties has largely been stemmed and younger artists have taken the place of those who left, although there are still occasional departures. More so than the eighties generation, these younger Cuban artists are conscious of their international visibility as the latest 'discoveries' from the new artistic 'Mecca' of the Caribbean. This has raised new critical questions such as whether concessions are made to the expectations of the metropolitan patrons, what role contemporary Cuban art plays in the promotion of Cuban

tourism and whether this international interest has changed their relationship with the Cuban public, important concerns in a cash-strapped,
post-colonial society. Although the adjustments to this new situation are
noticeable, they have been redeemed by the typical self-conscious irony
of much of contemporary Cuban art.

Whereas these younger artists have so far avoided any serious confrontations with the authorities, a rebellious spirit remains, as can be seen
in the provocative installations of Kcho (Alexis Leyva, b. 1970). He caused
controversy at the Fifth Havana Biennial with his installation *Regatta*
(1994) which referred to the rafters' crisis – then at its peak – and,
indirectly, to the flight of Cuban artists. The installation consisted of a
flotilla of miniature wooden and paper boats, egg trays and old shoes,
tragi-comical reminders of the improbable raft constructions many
Cubans have used in their attempts to flee to the USA. Kcho's use of
improvised, transitory materials also reflects the legacy of Elso, a persistent
influence on Cuban art, years after his death.

The satirical historicism of Pedro Alvarez, discussed in the introduction, represents another recent direction in Cuban art towards indirect

150 Kcho *Regatta* 1994

190

151 Fernando Rodríguez *At la Bodeguita* from the *Nuptial Dream* series 1994

commentary on social and political issues and a more traditional, self-referential *métier*. This strategy has been used very cleverly by the sculptor Fernando Rodríguez (b. 1970), who works through the fictional personality of Francisco de la Cal, a patriot and bona fide revolutionary who went blind during the early years of the Revolution. De la Cal's 'blindness' refers to naive dogmatism, but also to the loss of the original, more idealistic revolutionary values.

Rodríguez' series of polychromed relief carvings *Nuptial Dream* (1994) chronicles the 'nuptials' of Fidel Castro and the Cuban patron saint El Virgen del Cobre as a modern Cuban wedding, an opportunity for commentary on contemporary social issues. As part of their honeymoon, the 'newly weds' visit the tourist attractions of Old Havana which is fast becoming a colonial 'theme park' pointedly termed 'Havanaland' by the Cuban art historian Yolanda Wood. In one panel, they are seen at the famous café La Bodeguita which is too expensive for most Cubans and their 'chronicler' de la Cal is signing the wall, as celebrity visitors are traditionally asked to do. With its mock naive style, the series also reminds of the new wave of Cuban tourist kitsch that provides hard currency income for growing numbers of artisans and street-side vendors, who often have tertiary qualifications in fields such as economics or law. Some carvings of the *Nuptial Dream* series were censored, which shows that the relationship between the artists and the authorities is still strained.

This new conceptual sophistication and interest in craftsmanship are also evident in the work of Los Carpinteros (The Carpenters), a group consisting of the sculptors Alexandre Arrechea (b. 1970) and Dagoberto Rodríguez (b. 1969), and the painter Marco Castillo (b. 1971), one of several such Cuban artists' collectives of the eighties and nineties. They examine the ambivalent relationship with Cuba's pre-revolutionary past, with dead-pan formality in imagery and execution. In *Havana Country Club* (1994), for instance, the three artists are represented playing golf at the ISA campus, their alma mater, which was built on the grounds of the Havana Country Club, once a gathering place of the local and expatriate elite. While the knee-high grass is realistic (and a reflection of the neglect of the compound), other details, such as the 'home-made' golf clubs, are absurd reminders of the Cuban culture of 'bricolage', an amusing contrast with their own meticulous craftsmanship. The painting is mounted in an elaborately carved wooden picture frame like the frames often used for club memorabilia. Traditional woodcraft, from which the group takes its name, also reminds one of the once world-renowned Havana shipyards.

The city of Havana has been an important inspiration to modern Cuban artists. While René Portocarrero's 'cities' celebrated the baroque splendour of Old Havana, the conceptual artist Carlos Garaicoa (b. 1967) chronicles its slow decay. Garaicoa's Havana is a mythical, living place, where buildings bleed and invisible giants support the collapsing walls. His most striking installations juxtapose elevation drawings of bizarre utopian structures with nostalgic photographs of the disintegrating buildings, perhaps the most direct illustration in Cuban art of Gerardo Mosquera's notion of 'post-utopia'.

New Cuban Art is the most coherent contemporary school in the Caribbean and has received most international attention so far, but similar developments have occurred throughout the Caribbean, some of them triggered by the Cuban revival. The exposure to the Havana Biennial was crucial, for instance, to the development of contemporary art in the Dominican Republic, as is illustrated by the recent installations of Tony Capellán (b. 1955), Belkis Ramírez (b. 1957) and Marcos Lora Read (b. 1965). Since 1992, the Dominican Republic has held its own international biennial, the Santo Domingo Biennial of Caribbean and Central American Painting, which also promotes closer artistic contacts within the region.

Capellán is primarily a social commentator who has exposed rarely recognized Dominican problems such as the boat people who try to cross

152, 153 Carlos Garaicoa, installation view of *Rivoli, About the Place from Where the Blood Flows – Cruel Project* 1993–95

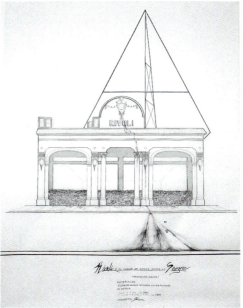

154 Los Carpinteros *Havana Country Club* 1994

the dangerous Mona Passage to Puerto Rico, child prostitution in the tourism sector and the rumours of kidnappings for the illicit human-organ trade. His subjects are not limited to the Dominican Republic, however, and he has also created works on subjects such as a news story about Brazilian Amerindians from a poor, remote settlement who had sold their testicles. Capellán's recent installations are deceptively simple and typically rely on the repetition of a single component, usually articles of clothing, arranged in a basic geometric pattern on the floor or wall or suspended in space. These generic, empty clothes symbolize the anonymous victims and their predicament is graphically represented by such attributes as plastic bags filled with animal organs.

While Capellán presents the perspective of the victim, Ramírez has pursued the perpetrators of a corrupt political and civic system with biting satire. This is obvious from her titles alone – *If Anything Happens, I Was Not Here* (1995) or, more subtly, *In a Plate of Salad* (1993). The public figures to which she alludes are often recognizably represented in her installations and are surrounded by menacing objects such as giant sling shots and heavy stones. Not all of her works are political, however, and some explore the pitfalls of interpersonal relationships. Ramírez is also an accomplished printmaker and often incorporates carved woodblocks in her installations, which adds to their solid monumentality.

155 Tony Capellán *Organ Theft* 1994
156 Belkis Ramírez *In a Plate of Salad* 1993

157 Marcos Lora Read *40 Metres of Schengen Space* 1995

Whereas Lora Read does not share the explicit socio-political concerns of Capellán and Ramírez, works such as *When the World is Getting Flat (Back Passage)* (1993) refer on a broader philosophical level to the history and present situation of the Caribbean and also allude to his own life (he lives between the Dominican Republic and the Netherlands). Like Capellán, however, Lora Read exploits the evocative power of the commonplace in his installations and manipulated objects which have a surreal poetic quality often reminiscent of the Belgian conceptual artist Marcel Broodthaers.

The work of these Dominican artists is representative of contemporary Caribbean art as a whole and, for the first time in modern Caribbean art history, regional similarities seem to outweigh national differences. Perhaps the most obvious common characteristic is a new, more reflective socio-political consciousness. This is exemplified in the satirical explorations of national and personal identity by Christopher Cozier. His installation *1962*, for instance, refers to the independence of Trinidad in 1962 when television broadcasting was introduced onto the island. The anachronistic little television set, with the Trinidadian national flag on screen, therefore embodies the utopian expectations associated with political independence and also parodies the Caribbean obsession with modernity and national symbols. Cozier's *1962* is also an example of the use of the metaphorical potential of everyday domestic objects, an interest he shares with many of his Caribbean contemporaries.

While Cozier is primarily concerned with local issues, other Caribbean artists have added a broader perspective to their social commentaries. For instance, in *Deforestation* (1992) by Hamid Moulferdi (b. 1961), who was 160 born in Morocco but has lived in Martinique since the mid-eighties, the point of departure was a toy belonging to his child and the association between children and the future led to a poetic statement on the world's ecological problems. Similarly, Elvis López (b. 1957) from Aruba also uses play, fragmentation and formal punning in his *Social Critic* series (1993) 159 to allude to serious socio-political and personal subjects, from AIDS to modern warfare. As we have seen before, punning is a distinctly Caribbean mode of expression. Concern with global issues is also manifest in *Nuclear Dogs* (1986), one of the spectacular, visionary 'chair sculptures' that brought the Trinidadian artist Francisco Cabral (b. 1949) to international attention in the mid-eighties.

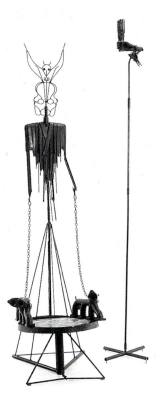

158 Francisco Cabral *Nuclear Dogs* 1986

159 Elvis López *The Six Proposals* from the *Social Critic* series 1993

160 Hamid Moulferdi *Deforestation* 1992

161 Ras Akyem Ramsay *Blakk King Ascending* 1994

162 Omari Ra 'African'
The Dick is Killed
(from the Opera
'Samedi's Mind Set') 1993

Examples mentioned above reflect cross-currents, but there are of course local differences. While race is only a marginal concern in contemporary art from the Hispanic Caribbean, for instance, it has remained important in the English- and French-speaking territories. Artists in the smaller, more conservative countries, where racial issues may have been viewed with unease in the past, now address the subject openly and sometimes provocatively. The Bahamian artist Stanley Burnside, for instance, explores racial identity in bold, exuberant images that trace their lineage to the local Junkanoo festival in which he is involved as a designer, but also to Raúl Martínez and pop art.

Rastafarianism has deeply influenced perceptions of race throughout the Caribbean, as can be seen in the work of the Barbadian painter
161 Ras Akyem Ramsay. His *Blakk King Ascending* (1994), a self-image as the black Christ, embodies the patriarchal, individualist philosophy of Rastafarianism and its politicized interpretations of biblical and historical imagery. With its enormous, erect penis, it is also an image of sexual and racial defiance. Ras Akyem's recent work has been heavily dependent on Jean-Michel Basquiat's, but he has recontextualized Basquiat's quintessentially urban imagery into one of the most orderly societies in the Caribbean where graffiti are virtually unknown. His work therefore also constitutes a challenge to Barbados' conservative social and cultural establishment, a concern he shares with several contemporary Barbadian artists.

The themes of race, politics and sexuality are also interwoven in the work of the Jamaican painter Omari Ra 'African' (Robert Cookhorne, b. 1960), who attended the Jamaica School of Art around the same time as Ras Akyem. As his complex, metaphorical imagery and theatrical titles suggest, Omari Ra samples a wide and disparate array of sources, ranging from Garveyism, Rastafarianism and Vaudou to Melville's *Moby Dick* and

200

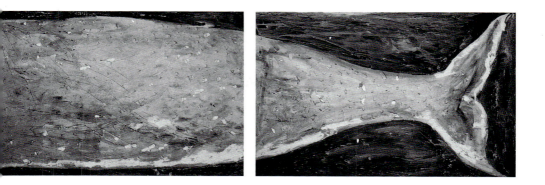

modern comic strips. In the triptych painting *The Dick is Killed (from the Opera 'Samedi's Mind Set')* (1993), the phallic white whale has ambiguous connotations of race, sexuality and death, another example of the use of punning in Caribbean art. Most of Omari Ra's works are on paper and although this was initially a matter of economic necessity, it has led to a recognizable style characterized by surface manipulations such as tearing, collage and encrustation, and a filmic fragmentation of the image when multiple panels are combined to achieve larger formats.

While graffiti are rare in the smaller islands, street art is becoming increasingly common in the more urbanized parts of the Caribbean, especially in Jamaica and Haiti. The Haitian street murals are of particular interest and appeared in the period following the deposition of the Duvalier regime in 1986. Although most of these murals were sponsored by political organizers, they depict the political ferment among the wider population. Some served an educational function, as the anonymous, undated mural captioned 'Don't Burn Them, Judge Them' in Port-au-Prince, an appeal to calm outbursts of popular anger against the Tonton Macoute militia and other Duvalier collaborators. These Haitian street murals combine realist depictions of contemporary events with traditional Vaudou iconography and Vaudou-inspired interpretations of North American pop icons, such as Rambo, another example of the Caribbean ability to absorb and transform foreign influences.

In spite of this popular political activism, it took until the 1996 elections for some semblance of stability to be restored to Haiti. The changing social and political climate has nonetheless contributed to a revival of mainstream Haitian art. As before, most of the younger mainstream artists come from the 'elite' and are well educated and well travelled, often dividing their time between Haiti and Europe or North

163

163 'Don't Burn Them, Judge Them', street mural, Port-au-Prince, Haiti

164 Mario Benjamin *Untitled c.* 1997

165 María de Mater O'Neill *Self-Portrait VIII* 1988

166 Annalee Davis *My Friend Said I Was Too White* 1989

91
164
America. They provide a newly critical perspective on Haitian issues, however, as in the work of Edouard Duval-Carrié, who lives in Miami, or younger artists such as Mario Benjamin (b. 1964) whose haunting paintings and installations deal with private existential questions, but also defy the conventions of the bourgeois Haitian art world.

This defiance of public expectations is also visible in the work of the Barbadian painter and printmaker Annalee Davis (b. 1963). Her early work represented an angry examination of her identity as a white Barbadian woman with family roots in the plantocracy, a painful subject very few Caribbean artists have tackled. More recently, her thematic emphasis has shifted to the land of Barbados that was once transformed from forest to sugar-cane fields and now in turn to tourist resorts and golf courses. Most of Davis' works contain a recognizable self-image, with provocative details such as ripped-out hearts and stylized genitalia, combined with schematic representations of the Barbados landscape, the national flag, the home, air planes, snarling dogs and, often, text. Her imagery is reminiscent of Frida Kahlo's whose troubling, autobiographical œuvre has influenced younger women artists in the Caribbean.

A similar, disconcerting combination of humour, anguish and stridency appears in the work of the Puerto Rican painter María de Mater

204

O'Neill (b. 1960), whose self-definition is also inextricably lin.
national identity. This is evident in her use of national icons, such ‹
Puerto Rican map, but perhaps most of all in her *Self-Portrait VIII* (19
a frenzied, iconoclastic interpretation of *Nude in Front of Mirror* (19‹
by Myrna Báez. Although she is not the only young Puerto Rican arti
to appropriate 'classic' Puerto Rican works of art, which have become
national icons in their own right, the choice of work and artist is significant since O'Neill's perspective is also distinctly female. O'Neill also
works in electronic media, such as video and the Internet, and edits 'El
Cuarto del Quenepón', an award-winning electronic journal on contemporary Puerto Rican culture.

Traditional photography is outside the scope of this book. However,
'constructed' photography has become very important in current
Caribbean art. One of the key artists to use the photographic medium is
the Cuban Marta María Pérez Bravo (b. 1959) – in some of her work
images of her body have been used, taken from carefully orchestrated
scenes photographed by her husband, Flavio Garciandía. Since 1986, her

167 Marta María Pérez Bravo *Parallel Cults* 1990

...es to Santería beliefs and mythology in addressing anxieties
...pregnancy and the birth of her twins, which are of special sig-
...n the Yoruba religion. In her more recent work, the rawness of
...photographs has been replaced by a more sensual, evocative
...t motherhood has remained her main subject. Thus, much of
...now deals with protection, a central notion in Santería. Her
...o frequently suggest self-sacrifice. It comes as no surprise that
...na Mendieta as a major influence.

...body-centred, ritualistic quality, in making use of constructed
...phy, is also present in the work of the Puerto Rican Víctor
...(b. 1950) and the Cuban Juan Carlos Alom (b. 1964), both of
...ork with models rather than with images of their own bodies.
...more of a purist photographer, his images resisting any literal
...iation with Afro-Cuban practices, but the cathartic effect of
...tualized violence is a persistent theme in his work. Vásquez incorporates
photographs of anonymous bodies and body parts in assemblages and
installations that are reminiscent of ex-votos. His images reflect his
interest in the iconography of Roman Catholicism and Santería and
allude to autobiographical issues and subjects such as AIDS, a recurrent
theme in contemporary Puerto Rican art.

As these examples show, constructed photography lends itself particularly well to represent the complex, syncretic nature of Caribbean identity
because of the possibilities it offers to transform images. The work of
Albert Chong (b. 1958), a Jamaican-born photographer who now lives in
the USA, shows this particularly in his extended series of *Ancestral Thrones*
(1990) which explore his identity as a Jamaican migrant of Afro-Chinese
descent. To create this series, he transformed common chairs into ancestral shrines by covering them with family photographs, personal documents, such as passports, and ritualistic items such as bones, his cut-off
'dreadlocks' and cowry shells. These 'thrones' have been used as installations in their own right or as the basis of photographic images that are
enhanced by overprinting, solarization, tinting and other manipulations.
The chair or throne is, as we have seen before, a recurrent motif in
Caribbean art, as in Wifredo Lam's *The Chair* (1943), and Chong's interpretation clearly relates to its ritual, ancestral significance. The chair is of
course also a proxy for the body, which is the main subject of Chong's
other photographic work.

Chong is one of an emerging generation of artists of Caribbean
descent in North America whose work parallels developments in
the Caribbean, but more specifically addresses the issues raised by
migration. The US-born artist Juan Sánchez (b. 1954), for instance, in

35

168 Juan Carlos Alom *Untitled* from the
Ablution for the Dark Book series 1995

169 Albert Chong *Throne for the Justice* from the
Ancestral Thrones series 1990

170 Víctor Vásquez *Prelude* 1994

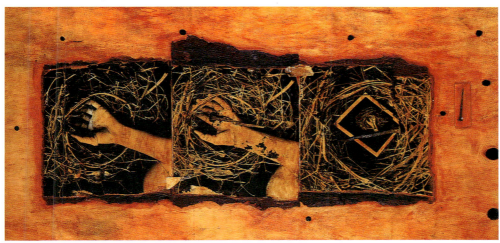

171 Juan Sánchez, installation view of *New Flag* from the *Rican/Structions* series 1994

his *Rican/Structions*, a title borrowed from the Salsa musician Ray Barretto, deals with the need of the Puerto Rican diaspora in the USA for personal, cultural and ideological self-definition. Like Chong's, his images are composed from symbols of identity such as the Puerto Rican flag, Taíno pictographs, palm trees, laser copies of Ramón Frade's famous
41   Jíbaro painting *Our Daily Bread* (c. 1905) and photographs. Some of these photographs are informal snapshots of the life of the Puerto Rican diaspora, while others are orchestrated, such as those of anonymous nude male and female figures, their faces obscured by the Puerto Rican flag, symbolic representatives of the Puerto Rican struggle. Sánchez also often uses text which adds a narrative element to his otherwise emblematic work.

Despite ritualist overtones in some of his works, Sánchez is in essence a political artist, perhaps most evident in the collage diptych *Nueva Bandera (New Flag)* (1994) made for El Museo del Barrio's twenty-fifth anniversary. The composition of this work was inspired by the cover of an issue of 'Pa'lante', the newsletter of the Young Lords Party, from the

172 Nari Ward *The Happy Smilers: Duty Free Shopping* 1996

year the museum was founded, which featured a group of activists in front of the Puerto Rican flag. Sánchez therefore decided to design a new 'flag', composed of references to the political struggles of the past that are an integral part of contemporary Puerto Rican identity.

This need to reconcile the ancestral past and the 'here and now' can also be seen in the work of Nari Ward (b. 1963) who, like Chong, left Jamaica at an early age and now lives in New York's Harlem district. His monumental installations typically consist of 'urban debris', such as children's strollers, electric fans or car tyres, which are methodically stacked, covered with grimy layers of caramelized sugar or 'tropical' soda, or neatly tied into package forms with fire hoses. While Ward's accumulations are indebted to mainstream Western artists like Arman or Christo, they also remind of the odd belongings many metropolitan street people carry with them and the African-American yard exhibitions, associations that add to the spiritually moving quality of his work.

Harlem is Ward's main inspiration, but some of his works refer to his Jamaican background, as in *The Happy Smilers: Duty Free Shopping* (1996), which was named after an album his uncle made when he sang with the band in a high-class Jamaican hotel. This installation alluded to cultural and racial stereotypes, economic exploitation and the alienating effect of migration, but also spoke of the resilience of the migrant, alluded to by the almost incidental detail of the potted aloe vera plant in the main room of the installation.

Similar questions arise in the work of Felix de Rooy (b. 1952), a film-maker, theatre director and visual artist from Curaçao who has lived in Amsterdam since the mid-seventies. He is the curator of the Negrophilia Collection in Amsterdam, which contains artefacts and images of blacks in popular Western culture that document racism and racial stereo-typing in all its forms. Such 'negrophilia' elements are included in surreal assemblages such as *Cry Surinam* (1992), which he has described as a state-ment on the desperation of the Surinamese migrants who have to endure the 'artificial' heat of the Netherlands as a substitute for the tropical heat at home.

Artists of Caribbean descent have played a prominent role in the new wave of black British art that emerged from the racial unrest in Britain of the late seventies and early eighties. They include Keith Piper (b. 1960), Eddie Chambers and Sonia Boyce (b. 1962), all born in Britain, who define themselves as black artists and members of the African diaspora rather than as Caribbean artists. Not surprisingly, therefore, these artists have focused on the politics of race and 'otherness', in contrast to the 'recon-structions' of cultural identity of their North American counterparts.

Chambers' early work is perhaps most directly linked to its political context. What started out as angry rebuttals of the racist propaganda of the National Front, however, led to a more thoughtful exploration of the rhetoric and visual language of racism and black nationalism, including the iconography of Garveyism and Rastafarianism which relates indirectly to his Jamaican background. Chambers is also one of several black artists in Britain to take matters into their own hands in response to the lack of opportunities for black artists, and is an influential curator, critic and pub-lisher of black British art.

Like Chambers, Piper's work at the beginning of his career commented directly on the British political situation of the early eighties, particularly the racial policies of the Thatcher government. He gradually abandoned direct political comment and turned towards the closely related subjects of black masculinity and the relationship between the transatlantic passage and twentieth-century migration. These themes are explored in works like *Go West Young Man* (1988), an installation of photo-panels with text which includes statements such as 'We had been reduced to

173 Felix de Rooy *Cry Surinam* 1992

objects of fantasy and fear.... The practice came first, the theory was soon to follow', statements directly indebted to the writings of Frantz Fanon, in particular his *Black Skin, White Masks* (1952). Piper's interest in graphic techniques has recently led him to video and interactive computer graphics.

Boyce, on the other hand, came to note in the mid-eighties with her powerful, autobiographical pastel drawings that commented candidly on the social and personal issues facing black British women. These were followed by a series of surreal collages that juxtaposed photographic self-portraits with caricatural racial images. In her most recent work, she has abandoned traditional formats in favour of photographic installations and ready-made objects. These include a series of objects made from artificial 'Afro' hair that address the fetishist fascination with hair and 'otherness', but also relate to the 'hair culture' in London's black neighbourhoods, like Brixton, where flamboyant artificial hairstyles are often to be seen. Such works bring to mind the 'hair pieces' by the African-American artist David Hammons whose provocative explorations of race have noticeably influenced contemporary black British artists.

212

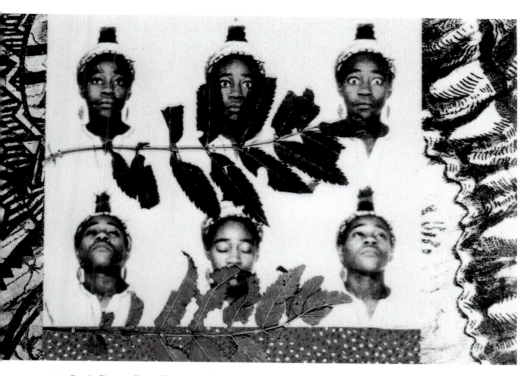

174 Sonia Boyce *From Tarzan to Rambo: English Born 'Native' Considers Her Relationship to the Constructed/Self Image and Her Roots in Reconstruction* 1987

175 Keith Piper *Go West Young Man* 1988 (detail)

In contrast to the more politicized aspects in the art of Chambers, Piper and Boyce, the Jamaican-born painter Eugene Palmer (b. 1955) offers a more contemplative perspective on the subject of race and displacement. His most striking recent works represent black persons in poses reminiscent of formal studio photographs, set in English landscapes or interiors, painted in an anachronistic, romantic style. The dark moodiness of these images, the uneasy tilts and angles of the composition and the compressed sense of space add to the surreal atmosphere of alienation.

Despite many similarities between the artistic interests of the 'Caribbean diaspora' and contemporary art in the Caribbean, the two have until recently developed in relative isolation from each other. Many artists of the 'Caribbean diaspora' had never previously exhibited or worked in the Caribbean, but this is now changing. Boyce, Chong, Piper and Sánchez, for instance, have all exhibited in Havana Biennials. Chong also started exhibiting in Jamaica in the early nineties and has since been included in several overseas exhibitions of Jamaican art. Some have also returned to the Caribbean. The Dominican artist Bismarck Victoria moved to the Dominican Republic in 1988 to direct the restoration of the Cathedral of Santiago and lived there permanently until 1992. His recent conceptual work makes subtle reference to the country's troubled social history and political culture.

Such interactions are particularly significant in the case of Cuba and the USA because of political barriers. Although Cubans who live elsewhere, such as Garciandía and Brey, regularly exhibit in Cuba, this is not yet possible for the recent 'defectors' to the USA and art is more than ever caught up in the politics of the region. Recently, for instance, the Cuban authorities limited their support to a major Spanish-organized survey exhibition of modern Cuban art because several of these 'defectors' had been included. A major American travelling exhibition of contemporary Caribbean art, on the other hand, did not include artists living in Cuba, an incomprehensible omission given the importance of contemporary Cuban art. There have been some hopeful signs, however, such as the case of the Brooklyn-based artist Ernesto Pujol (b. 1957) who had his first exhibition in Havana in 1995, the first Cuban-American to do so since Ana Mendieta.

Recent artistic interaction between the Caribbean and the 'Caribbean diaspora' also reminds us that modern Caribbean culture generally has been crucially shaped by continuous diverse exchanges, perhaps more so than any other culture in world history. It therefore seems appropriate to close this book with Marc Latamie (b. 1952), a New York-based Martiniquan artist. In his work, Latamie, like Wifredo Lam before him,

176 Eugene Palmer *Duppy Shadow* 1993

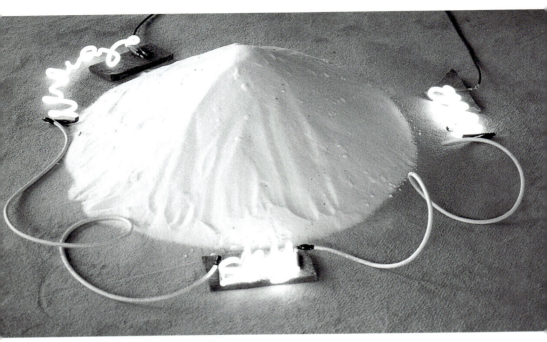

177 Marc Latamie *Caldera* 1995

uses sugar as a metaphor, sugar being powerfully associated with the Caribbean. Since the start of European colonization, sugar has been the local product and vehicle of exchange between the Caribbean and the rest of the world. It is now traded electronically on the metropolitan commodity markets. Sugar is thus associated with transatlantic trade, the Plantation experience and the current economic dependency of the Caribbean. Latamie's sugar installations are deceptively simple, but teeming with allusions. *Caldera* (1995), for instance, is a conical mound of refined sugar, surrounded by the neon words 'sky', 'terre' (earth) and 'indigo', which evokes the volcanic nature of Martinique. Indigo is itself an Antillean commodity, but also alludes to the sea, another vehicle of exchange. And since the accompanying text is in English and French, *Caldera* refers to bilinguality as well as to the identity shifts that accompany migration. Latamie's metaphor therefore hints at the Caribbean condition of always being in transit, but also at the complexity, as well as the continuity, of its experience.

216

Bibliography

General: Art

Acha, Juan, et al., *Plastica del Caribe*, Havana: Letras Cubanas, 1989; Ades, Dawn, ed., *Art in Latin America: The Modern Era, 1820–1980*, exh. cat., London: Hayward Gallery, 1989; Araeen, Rasheed, *The Other Story: Afro-Asian Artists in Post-War Britain*, exh. cat., London: South Bank Centre, 1989; Archer-Straw, Petrine, and Kim Robinson, *Jamaican Art*, Kingston: Kingston Publishers, 1989; Binnendijk, Chandra van, and Peter Faber, *Twintig jaar beeldende kunst in Suriname/Twenty Years of Visual Art in Suriname*, exh. cat., Paramaribo: Stichting Surinaams Instituut, 1995; Bocquet, Pierre, ed., *1492/1992 Un Nouveau regard sur les Caraibes*, exh. cat., Paris: Creolarts, 1992; Borras, Maria Lluïsa, et al., *Cuba Siglo XX: Modernidad y Sincretismo*, exh. cat., Las Palmas de Gran Canaria: Centro atlántico de arte moderno, 1996; Boxer, David, *Jamaican Art 1922–1982*, exh. cat., Washington: S.I.T.E.S. and National Gallery of Jamaica, 1982; Boxer, David, and Veerle Poupeye, *Modern Jamaican Art*, Kingston: Ian Randle and UWI Development and Endowment Fund, 1997; Cancel, Luis, et al., *The Latin American Spirit: Art and Artists in the United States 1920–1970*, exh. cat., New York: The Bronx Museum of the Arts and Harry N. Abrams, 1988; *Caribart: Contemporary Art of the Caribbean*, exh. cat., Curaçao: UNESCO, 1993; *Caribbean Art Now*, exh. cat., London: Commonwealth Institute, 1986; Cervantes, Miguel, ed., *Myth and Magic in America: The Eighties*, exh. cat., Monterrey, Mexico: Museo de Arte Contempóranea de Monterrey, 1991; Christensen, Eleanor Ingalls, *The Art of Haiti*, New York: S. A. Barnes, 1971; Delgado Mercado, Osiris, *Artes plasticas: Historia de la Pintura in Puerto Rico*, in *La Gran Enciclopedia de Puerto Rico*, vol. 8, Madrid: Forma Gráfica, 1976; Glinton, Patricia, et al., *Bahamian Art 1492–1992*, Nassau: The Counsellors,1992; Juan, Adelaida de, *Pintura Cubana: Temas y Variaciones*, Havana: Letras Cubanas, 1978; Juan, Adelaida de, *Mas allá de la Pintura*, Havana: Letras Cubanas, 1993; *Karaibische Kunst Heute*, exh. cat., Kassel: Projektgruppe Stoffwechsel, 1994; *La Habana: Salas del Museo Nacional de Cuba – Palacio de Bellas Artes*, catalogue, Havana: Letras Cubanas, 1990; Lerebours, Michel Philippe, *Haiti et Ses Peintres – de 1804 à 1980*, 2 vols, Port-au-Prince, Haiti: L'Imprimeur II, 1989; Lewis, Samella, et al., *Caribbean Visions*, exh. cat., Alexandria, Virginia: Art Services International, 1995; Lucie-Smith, Edward, *Latin American Art of the 20th Century*, London and New York: Thames and Hudson, 1993; MacLean, Geoffrey, *Contemporary Painting – Trinidad and Tobago: Leroy Clarke, Isaiah James Boodhoo, Kenwyn Crichlow, Emheyo Bahabha*, exh. cat., London: October Gallery, 1992; Miller, Jeannette, *Historia de la Pintura Dominicana*, Santo Domingo: Amigos del Hogar, 1979; Mosquera, Gerardo, *Exploraciones en la Plástica Cubana*, Havana: Letras Cubanas, 1989; Mosquera, Gerardo, *Africa in the Art of Latin America*, in *Art Journal*, # 51, Winter 1992, pp. 30–38; Nadal-Gardère, Marie-José, and Gérald Bloncourt, *La Peinture Haïtienne/Haitian Arts*, Paris:

Editions Nathan, 1986; Nunley, John, and Judith Bettelheim, *Caribbean Festival Arts*, Seattle: University of Washington Press, 1988; Powell, Richard, *Black Art and Culture of the 20th Century*, London and New York: Thames and Hudson, 1997; Ramírez, Mari Carmen, *Puerto Rican Painting Between Past and Present*, exh. cat., Princeton: The Squibb Gallery, 1987; Rasmussen, Waldo, ed., *Latin American Artists of the Twentieth Century*, exh. cat., New York: The Museum of Modern Art, 1993; Santos, Danilo de los, *La Pintura en la Sociedad Dominicana*, Santiago, Dominican Republic: Universidad Católica Madre y Maestra, 1978; Stratton, Suzanne, ed., Elizabeth Ferrer and Edward Sullivan, *Modern and Contemporary Art of the Dominican Republic*, exh. cat., New York: Americas Society and The Spanish Institute, 1996; Sullivan, Edward, ed., *Latin American Art of the Twentieth Century*, London: Phaidon, 1997; Taylor, René, et al., *Colección de Arte Latinoamericano/Latinamerican Art Collection*, catalogue, Museo de Arte de Ponce, Fundación Luis A. Ferré; Wood, Yolanda, *De la Plastica Cubana y Caribeña*, Havana: Letras Cubanas, 1990

Note: A survey of modern Barbadian art entitled 'Sixty Years of Barbadian Art' will be published by Ian Randle, Kingston, in 1998

The following specialized journals frequently contain articles on Caribbean art and related subjects: *Anales del Caribe* (Cuba), *Art Nexus* (Colombia, published in Spanish and English), *Conjonction* (Haiti), *Jamaica Journal* (Jamaica), *Revolución y Cultura* (Cuba), *Revue Noire* (France), *Ten.8* (Britain), *Third Text* (Britain). The in-flight magazine of the Trinidadian airline BWIA, *Caribbean Beat*, frequently contains useful articles on art from the English-speaking Caribbean.

General: History, Culture, Ideas

Benítez-Rojo, Antonio, *The Repeating Island: The Caribbean and the Postmodern Perspective*, Durham and London: Duke University, 1992; Bernabe, Jean, Patrick Chamoiseau and Raphaël Confiant, *Eloge de la Créolité*, Paris: Gallimard/Presses Universitaires Créoles, 1989; Brathwaite, Edward, *The Development of Creole Society in Jamaica 1770–1820*, Oxford: Clarendon Press, 1971; Brathwaite, Edward, *Contradictory Omens: Cultural Diversity and Integration in the Caribbean*, Mona, Jamaica: Savacou Publications, 1974; Césaire, Aimé, *Discourse on Colonialism*, New York: Monthly Review Press, 1972 (originally published in 1955); Clarke, John Henrik, ed., *Marcus Garvey and the Vision of Africa*, New York: Vintage Books, 1974; Clifford, James, *The Predicament of Culture, Twentieth Century Ethnography, Literature and Art*, Cambridge, Massachusetts: Harvard University Press, 1988; Dabydeen, David, and B. Samaroo, eds, *India in the Caribbean*, London: Hansib, 1987; Fanon, Frantz, *Black Skin, White Masks*, New York: Grove Weidenfeld, 1967, 1st published 1952; Fanon, Frantz, *The Wretched of the Earth*, Harmondsworth: Penguin, 1970, 1st published 1961; Glissant, Edouard, *Caribbean Discourse*, Charlottesville: University of Virginia Press, 1989, 1st published 1981; Hall, Stuart, *Pluralism, Race and Class in Caribbean Society*, in J. Rex, ed., *Race and Class in Post-

Colonial Society*, Paris: UNESCO, 1975, pp. 98–106; Hall, Stuart, *Minimal Selves*, in *ICA Documents 6: Identity*, London: Institute of Contemporary Art, 1987; Harris, Wilson, *History, Fable & Myth in the Caribbean and Guianas*, Wellesley, Massachusetts: Calaloux Publications, 1995, 1st published 1970; Horowitz, Michael, ed., *Peoples and Cultures of the Caribbean: An Anthropological Reader*, Garden City, New York: Natural History Press, 1971; James, C. L. R., *The Future in the Present: Selected Writings*, London: Allison & Busby, 1977; James, C. L. R., *The Black Jacobins: Toussaint L'Ouverture and the San Domingo Revolution*, London: Allison & Busby, 1980, 1st published 1938; Lewis, Gordon, *Main Currents in Caribbean Thought*, Baltimore: Johns Hopkins University Press, 1983; Métraux, Alfred, *Le Vaudou Haitien*, Paris: Gallimard, 1958; Nettleford, Rex, *Mirror, Mirror: Indentity, Race and Protest in Jamaica*, New York: William Morrow, 1972, 1st published 1970; Nettleford, Rex, *Caribbean Cultural Identity – The Case of Jamaica: An Essay in Cultural Dynamics*, Kingston: Institute of Jamaica Publications, 1978; Nettleford, Rex, *Inward Stretch, Outward Reach: A Voice from the Caribbean*, Basingstoke: Macmillan, 1993; Simpson, George Eaton, *Religions, Cults of the Caribbean: Trinidad, Jamaica and Haiti*, San Juan: Institute of Caribbean Studies, University of Puerto Rico, 1970; Smith, M. G., *Plural Society in the British West Indies*, Berkeley: University of California Press, 1965; Thompson, Robert Farris, *Flash of the Spirit: African & Afro-American Art & Philosophy*, New York: Vintage Books, 1983; Williams, Eric, *Capitalism and Slavery*, London: André Deutsch, 1964; Williams, Eric, *From Columbus to Castro: The History of the Caribbean 1492–1969*, New York: Vintage Books, 1984, 1st published 1970

Introduction

Fouchet, Max-Pol, *Wifredo Lam*, Barcelona: Polígrafa, 1976; Levall, Susana Torruella, *25th Anniversary Exhibition: Part I Reclaiming History*, New York: El Museo del Barrio, 1994; Ortiz, Fernando, *La Cubanidad y los Negros, Estudios Afrobubanos # 3*, 1939, pp. 3–15; Walcott, Derek, *The Caribbean: Culture or Mimicry?*, in *Journal of Interamerican Studies and World Affairs*, vol. 16, # 1, February 1974; Marshall, Richard, *Jean-Michel Basquiat*, exh. cat., New York: Whitney Museum of American Art, 1993; Thompson, Robert Farris, *Royalty, Heroism and the Streets: the Art of Jean-Michel Basquiat*, in the exh. cat. of the XXIII Bienal Internacional de São Paulo, Brazil, 1997; Hervé Télémaque, in the catalogue of the permanent collection of the Fonds Régional d'Art Contemporain de Martinique, Fort de France; Alvarez, Lupe, *Flavio Garciandia: Una visita al museo de Arte Tropical*, exh. cat., Havana: Museo Nacional, Palacio de Bellas Artes, 1995; Boxer, David, and Rex Nettleford, *The Intuitive Eye*, exh. cat., Kingston: National Gallery of Jamaica, 1979

Chapter 1: Prehispanic and Colonial Art

Rouse, Irving, *The Tainos: The Rise and Decline of the People Who Greeted Columbus*, New Haven and London: Yale University Press, 1992; Fagg, William, *The Tribal Image*, London: Trustees of the British Museum, 1970; Kerchache, Jacques, ed., *L'Art Taino*,

exh. cat., Paris: Musée du Petit Palais, 1994;
Rigol, Jorge, *Apuntes Sobre la Pintura y el
Grabado en Cuba*, Havana: Letras Cubanas,
1982; Lewis, Lesley, *English Commemorative
Sculpture in Jamaica*, monograph edition of
Jamaica Historical Review, Kingston, vol. 9,
1972; Barrenechea, Francisco, et al., *Campeche
– Oller – Rodón: Tres Siglos de Pintura
Puertorriqueña*, San Juan: Instituto
de Cultura Puertorriqueña, 1992; *Paintings
and Prints of Barbados in the Barbados Museum*,
catalogue, St Ann: The Barbados Museum
and Historical Society, 1981; Boxer, David,
Five Centuries of Jamaican Art, exh. cat.,
Kingston: National Gallery of Jamaica, 1976;
Colón Camacho, Doreen, *La Iconografía de
los Santos de Puerto Rico: Colección de Eduardo
Fernández Cerra*, exh. cat., Santurce: Galería
de Arte, Universidad del Sagrado Corazón,
1995; MacLean, Geoffrey, *Cazabon: An
Illustrated Biography of Trinidad's Nineteenth
Century Painter*, Port-of-Spain: Aquarela
Galleries, 1986

Chapter 2: Modernism and Cultural
Nationalism

Césaire, Aimé, *Return to My Native Land*,
Paris: Presence Africaine, 1968, 1st published
1939; Martínez, Juan, *Cuban Art and National
Identity*, Gainesville: University of Florida
Press, 1994; Hurston, Zora Neale, *Tell My
Horse: Voodoo and Life in Haiti and Jamaica*,
New York: Harper and Row, 1990, 1st
published 1938; Alonso, Alejandro, *Amelia
Peláez*, Havana: Letras Cubanas, 1988; Rigol,
Jorge, *Víctor Manuel*, Havana: Letras Cubanas,
1990; Fernández Retamar, Roberto, *Marcelo
Pogolotti*, exh. cat., Havana: Museo Nacional,
Palacio de Bellas Artes, 1986; Sánchez, Juan,
Fidelio Ponce, Havana: Letras Cubanas, 1985;
Carpentier, Alejo, *La Ciudad de las Columnas*,
in *Tientos y Diferencias*, Montevideo: ARCA,
1967; Lezama Lima, José, *La Visualidad
Infinita*, Havana: Letras Cubanas, 1994;
Alonso, Alejandro, *Amelia Peláez*, Havana:
Letras Cubanas, 1988; Pogolotti, Graziella,
and Ramón Vásquez Díaz, *René Portocarrero*,
Havana: Letras Cubanas and Berlin: Henschel,
1987; Balderrama, Maria, ed., *Wifredo Lam and
His Contemporaries 1938–1952*, New York:
Studio Museum, Harlem, 1992; Pogolotti,
Graziella, et al., *Sobre Wifredo Lam*, Havana:
Letras Cubanas, 1986; Cabrera, Lydia, *El
Monte*, Miami: Colección del Chicherekú,
1983, 1st published 1954; Ortiz, Fernando,
Contrapunteo Cubano del Tabaco y el Azúcar,
Caracas, Venezuela: Biblioteca Ayacucho,
1978, 1st published 1940; Gómez Sicre, José,
Pintura Cubana de Hoy, Havana: Maria Luisa
Gómez Mena, 1944; Alexis, Gerald, et al., *50
Années de peinture en Haiti 1930–1950, Tome
I: 1930–1959*, Port-au-Prince: Fondation
culture création, 1995; Price-Mars, Jean, *Ainsi
Parla l'Oncle*, New York: Parapsychology
Foundation, 1970, 1st published 1928; Savain,
Pétion, *La Case de Damballah*, Nendeln:
Kraus, 1970, 1st published 1939; Rodman,
Selden, *Renaissance in Haiti: Popular Painters in
the Black Republic*, New York: Pellegrini and
Cudahy, 1948; Colson, Jaime, *Memorias de un
Pintor Trashumante: Paris 1924 – Santo Domingo
1968*, Santo Domingo: Fundación Colson,
1978; Boxer, David, *Edna Manley: Sculptor*,
Kingston: Edna Manley Foundation and
National Gallery of Jamaica, 1990; Poupeye-
Rammelaere, Veerle, *Garveyism and Garvey

Iconography in the Visual Arts of Jamaica, in
Jamaica Journal, Part I: 24/1, 1991, pp. 9–21;
Part II: 24/2, 1992, pp. 24–33; Moody,
Cynthia, *Ronald Moody: A Man True to His
Vision*, in *Third Text*, 8/9, 1989; MacLean,
Geoffrey, *Boscoe Holder*, Port of Spain:
MacLean Publishing, 1994

Chapter 3: Popular Religion, the Festival
Arts and the Visionary

Rodman, Selden, *Where Art is Joy, Haitain Art:
The First Forty Years*, New York: Ruggles de
Latour, 1988; Stebich, Ute, *Haitian Art*, exh.
cat., New York: Brooklyn Museum and
Harry N. Abrams, 1978; Williams, Sheldon,
Voodoo and the Art of Haiti, Nottingham:
Morland Lee; *The Sacred Arts of Haitian Vodou*,
exh. cat., Los Angeles: Fowler Museum
of Cultural History, 1995; Malraux, André,
La Métamorphose des Dieux. L'Intemporel,
Paris: Gallimard, 1976; Boxer, David, *Fifteen
Intuitives*, exh. cat., Kingston: National
Gallery of Jamaica, 1989; Seaga, Edward,
Revival Cults in Jamaica, in *Jamaica Journal*, 3/2,
June 1969; Boxer, David, ed., *Kapo: The Larry
Wirth Collection*, catalogue, Kingston: National
Gallery of Jamaica, 1982; Barrett, Leonard,
The Rastafarians: The Dreadlocks of Jamaica,
Kingston: Sangster's and Heinemann, 1977;
Poupeye-Rammelaere, Veerle, *The Rainbow
Valley: The Life and Work of Brother Everald
Brown*, in *Jamaica Journal*, 21/1, pp. 2–14;
Bender, Wolfgang, et al., *Rastafari Kunst aus
Jamaika*, Berlin: Haus der Kulturen der Welt,
1992; Vandenbroeck, Paul, et al., *America:
Bride of the Sun*, exh. cat., Antwerpen:
Koninklijk Museum voor Schone Kunsten,
1992; Feldman, Melissa, and Gustavo Pérez
Firmat, *José Bedia: De donde Vengo*, exh. cat.,
Philadelphia: Institute of Contemporary Art,
University of Pennsylvania, 1994; Hernandez,
Orlando, et al., *José Bedia, Carlos Capelan,
Saint Clair Cemin*, Bogotá: Galeria; Fernando
Quintana, 1995; Hill, Errol, *Trinidad Carnival:
Mandate for a National Theatre*, Austin:
University of Texas Press, 1972; Rozelle,
Robert, ed., et al., *Black Art: Ancestral Legacy.
The African Impulse in African-American Art*,
exh. cat., Dallas: Dallas Museum of Art,
1989; Chambers, Eddie, et al., *The Artpack:
A History of Black Artists in Britain*, Bristol:
Eddie Chambers and Tam Joseph, 1988

Chapter 4: Revolution, Anti-Imperialism
and Race Consciousness

Bowling, Frank, *Postscript*, in *The Dub Factor*,
exh. cat., Bristol: Eddie Chambers, 1992;
Tió, Teresa, *El Portafolios en la Gráfica
Puertorriqueña*, exh. cat., San Juan: Museo de
las Américas, 1996; Traba, Marta, *Propuesta
Polémica sobre Arte Puertorriqueño*, San Juan:
Ediciones Librería Internacional, 1971; Darié,
Sandú, *El Mundo Nuevo de los Cuadros de
Carreño*, exh. cat., Havana: Instituto Nacional
de Cultura, Palacio de Bellas Artes, 1957;
López Oliva, Manuel, et al., *Luis Martínez
Pedro: Exposición Retrospectiva*, exh. cat.,
Havana: Museo Nacional, Palacio de Bellas
Artes, 1987; Goldman, Shifra, *Dimensions
of the Americas: Art and Social Change in
Latin America and the United States*, Chicago:
University of Chicago Press, 1994; *Congreso
de Artistas Abstractos de Puerto Rico*, exh. cat.,
San Juan: Instituto de Cultura Puertorriqueña,
1984; Tolentino, Marianne de, *Luis Hernandez
Cruz: Tiempos y Formas de un Itinerario*

Artístico, San Juan: Publicaciones
Puertorriqueñas, 1989; *Frente: Movimiento
de Renovación Social de Arte*, exh. cat., San
Juan: Instituto de Cultura Puertorriqueña,
1978; Rivera Rosario, Nelson, et al., *Antonio
Martorell: Obra Gráfica 1963–1986*, exh. cat.,
San Juan: Museo de Arte de Puerto Rico,
La Casa del Libro and Instituto de Cultura
Puertorriqueña, 1986; Tió, Teresa, *El cartel en
Puerto Rico: 1946–1985*, exh. cat., Río Piedras:
Museo de la Universidad de Puerto Rico,
1985; Juan, Adelaida de, *Pintura Cubana:
Temas y Variaciones*, Havana: Letras Cubanas,
1978; Stermer, Dugald, and Susan Sontag, *The
Art of Revolution: Castro's Cuba: 1959–1970*,
New York: McGraw-Hill, 1970; Mosquera,
Gerardo, et al., *Nosotros: Exposición Antológica
Raúl Martínez*, exh. cat., Havana: Museo
Nacional, Palacio de Bellas Artes, 1988;
Fernández Retamar, Roberto, *Raúl Martínez:
El Desafío de los Sesenta*, exh. cat., Havana:
Museo Nacional, Palacio de Bellas Artes,
1995; Castillo, Efraím, *Oviedo 25 Años:
Trascendencia Visual de Una Historia*, Santo
Domingo: Galería de Arte Moderno, 1988;
Merewether, Charles, *Edouard Duval-Carrié*,
exh. cat., Monterrey, Mexico: Ediciones
MARCO, 1992; Smith-McCrea, Rosalie,
Eugene Hyde: A Retrospective, exh. cat.,
Kingston: National Gallery of Jamaica,
1984; Roopnaraine, Rupert, et al., *Caribbean
Metaphysic: Another Reality. An Exhibition
of Mini Paintings of Stanley Greaves*, exh. cat.,
Bridgetown: Queen's Park Gallery, 1993;
Lee, Simon, *Warrior Art*, in *Caribbean Beat*,
Autumn 1995, pp. 50–56; Barreros del Rio,
Petra, et al., *Taller Alma Boricua: Reflecting on
Twenty Years of the Puerto Rican Workshop
1969–1989*, exh. cat., New York: El Museo del
Barrio, 1990; Walmsley, Anne, *The Caribbean
Artists Movement 1966–1972: A Literary and
Cultural History*, London and Port of Spain:
New Beacon Books, 1992; Mennekes,
Friedhelm, *Luis Cruz Azaceta*, exh. cat.,
Köln: Kunst-Station Sankt Peter, 1988

Chapter 5: Nature in Caribbean Art

Césaire, Aimé, *Corps Perdu*, in *Œuvres
complètes*, vol. 1 *Poèmes*, Fort-de-France:
Désormeaux, 1976, p. 278, 1st published
1950; Walmsley, Anne, ed., *Guyana Dreaming:
The Art of Aubrey Williams*, Aarhus, Denmark:
Dangaroo Press, 1990; Gooding, Mel, *Grace
Abounding: Bowling's Progress*, in *Third Text*, #
31, Summer 1995, pp. 37–46; Gayford,
Martin, et al., *Frank Bowling on through the
Century*, exh. cat., Bristol: Eddie Chambers,
1996; Perreault, John, and Petra Barreras del
Rio, *Ana Mendieta Sculpture*, exh. cat., New
York: New Museum of Contemporary Art,
1987; Moreno, Maria Luisa, and Marimar
Benítez, *Jaime Suarez: Ceramica 1975–1985*,
exh. cat., Ponce: Museo de Arte de Ponce,
1985

Chapter 6: The Self and the Other

Pogolotti, Graziella, *Angel Acosta León*, exh.
cat., Havana: Museo Nacional, Palacio de
Bellas Artes, 1991; Traba, Marta, and Marimar
Benítez, *Myrna Báez: Diez Años de Gráfica y
Pintura 1971–1981*, exh. cat., New York: El
Museo del Barrio, 1984; Tibol, Raquel, et al.,
Tres Decadas Gráficas de Myrna Báez 1958–1988,
exh. cat., San Juan: Museo de Arte de Puerto
Rico and Instituto de Cultura Puertorriqueña,
1988; Perodin Jérôme, Mireille, et al., *Jean-

René Jérôme Rétrospective II, exh. cat., Port-au-Prince: Musée d'Art Haitien, 1992; García Gutiérrez, Enrique, *Arnaldo Roche Rabell: Fuegos*, exh. cat., Santurce, Puerto Rico: Museo de Arte Contemporáneo, 1993; Frerot, Christine, *José Garcia Cordero: Gardens of Delirium*, exh. cat., Coral Gables: Lumbreras-Fisher Fine Art, 1994; Powell, Richard, et al., *Keith Morrison: Recent Paintings*, exh. cat., New York: Alternative Museum, 1990; Benítez, Marimar, et al., *Carlos Collazo Mattei: Whatever*, exh. cat., San Juan: Liga de Arte de San Juan; Césaire, Aimé, *Dit d'Errance*, in *Œuvres complètes*, vol. 1 *Poèmes*, Fort-de-France, Martinique: Désormeaux, 1976, p. 278, 1st published 1950; Daguillard, Fritz, et al., *Patrick Vilaire: Réflexion sur la Mort*, Port-au-Prince: Fondation Afrique en Créations, 1994

Chapter 7: Recent Developments

Cozier, Christopher, and Ulrich Fiedler, *Four Contemporary Artists from Trinidad*, Port of Spain: Christopher Cozier and Ulrich Fiedler, 1996; Camnitzer, Luis, *New Art of Cuba*, Austin Texas University Press, 1994; *Bienal de la Habana* catalogues, Havana: Centro Wifredo Lam, 1986, 1989, 1991, 1994, 1997; Weiss, Rachel, et al., *The Nearest Edge of the World: Art and Cuba Now*, exh. cat., Brookline, Massachusetts: Polarities Inc., 1990; Mosquera, Gerardo, *Los Hijos de Guillermo Tell*, exh. cat., Caracas: Museo de Artes Visuales Alejandro Otero, 1991; Sullivan, Edward, *Tomás Esson: Chá-Chá-Chá*, exh. cat., Monterrey, Mexico: Galería Ramis Barquet, 1993; Mosquera, Gerardo, et al., *Kuba OK*, exh. cat., Düsseldorf, Germany: Städtische Kunsthalle, 1990; Blanc, Giulio, *Miami: Little Havana*, in *Poliester*, Mexico City, # 4, 1993, pp. 42–52; Guadagnini, Walter, and Jan Hoet, *Ricardo Brey*, exh. cat., Milan: Mazzotta, 1996; Fernandez, Antonio Eligio, et al., *New Art from Cuba*, exh. cat., London: Whitechapel Gallery, 1995; Blanco, Delia, et al., *Otras Visiones: Cuarto Artistas Dominicanos Contemporaneos*, exh. cat., Santo Domingo: Casa de Francia, 1994; Pellegrini, Elena, *Tony Capellan: Campo Minado*, exh. cat., Santo Domingo: Casa de Francia, 1996; Lenz, Iris, *Marcos Lora Read*, exh. cat., Bonn: Institut für Auslandsbeziehungen, 1995; Noceda Fernández, José, *Elvis Lopez*, exh. cat., Oranjestad: Instituto di Cultura Aruba, 1994; Roopnaraine, Rupert, and Alison Thompson, *Retentions and Redemptions: Recent Paintings of Ras Akyem-I Ramsay*, exh. cat., Bridgetown: Mervyn Awon, 1995; Archer-Straw, Petrine, et al., *New World Imagery: Contemporary Jamaican Art*, exh. cat., London: The South Bank Centre, 1995; Butcher, Pablo, *Invoking the Spirits: Haiti's Charged Murals*, exh. cat., Miami: The Haitian Cultural Arts Alliance, 1996; Damian, Carol, *Contemporary Expressions of Haitian Art*, exh. cat., Miami: Haitian Cultural Arts Alliance, 1996; Njami, Simon, et al., *Otro país: Escalas Africanas*, exh. cat., Centro Atlantico de Arte Moderno, Las Palmas de Gran Canaria, 1994; 'El Cuarto del Quenepón' [electronic journal on Puerto Rican art and culture], http://cuarto. quenepon.org/cuarto.htmi; Mosquera, Gerardo, *Marta María Perez: Autoretratos del Cosmos*, in *Art Nexus*, Bogota, # 17, July–September 1995, pp. 84–87; Monograph

issue on contemporary Cuban photography of *Aperture*, USA, # 141, Fall 1995; Ríos Avila, Rubén, *Victor Vasquez: El Cuerpo y El Autoretrato Extendido*, exh. cat., San Juan: Galería Botello, 1994; Reid, Michael, ed., *Ancestral Dialogues: The Photographs of Albert Chong*, San Francisco: The Friends of Photography, 1994; Jimenez-Muñoz, Gladys, *Rican/Structed Realities: Confronted Evidence. New Paintings and Prints by Juan Sanchez*, exh. cat., Binghamton, New York: University Art Museum, 1991; Mercer, Valerie, *From the Studio: Artists-in-Residence 1992–1993*, Bob Rivera, Michelle Talibah, Nari Ward, exh. cat., New York: The Studio Museum in Harlem, 1993; Malbert, Roger, et al., *In Fusion: New European Art*, exh. cat., London: The South Bank Centre, 1993; Bailey, David A., et al., *Mirage: Enigmas of Race, Difference and Desire*, exh. cat., London: Institute of Contemporary Arts and Institute of International Visual Arts, 1995; Tawadros, Gilane, *Black Women in Britain: A Personal and Intellectual Journey*, in *Third Text*, # 15, Summer 1991, pp. 71–76; Hall, Stuart, *Reconstruction Work*, in *Ten.8*, 2/3, Spring 1992, pp. 106–113; Shelton, Anthony, ed., *Fetishism: Visualising Power and Desire*, exh. cat., London: South Bank Centre and Lund Humphries, 1995; Norrie, Jean, and Petrine Archer Straw, *Eugene Palmer*, exh. cat., Bristol: Eddie Chambers, 1993; Brebion, Dominique and Octavio Zaya, *XXIIIè Biennale de Sao Paulo Bresil: Marc Latamie*, exh. cat., Fort-de-France: DRAC, 1996

Glossary

An asterisk ★ *refers to another entry*

Abakuá: All-male secret society in Western Cuba of West African Ejagham origin

Afrocubanismo: The nationalist use of Afro-Cuban subjects in Cuban art and literature

Bembé: ★Santería dance ritual

Boriquen, Boricua: Ancient ★Taíno name for Puerto Rico, Boricua hence means Puerto Rican

Cacique: Amerindian chieftain

Cacos: The peasant rebels in northern Haiti during the early years of the US occupation (1915–34). The revolt ended in 1919 when one of their leaders, Charlemagne Péralte, was killed

Costumbrismo: Artistic genre of depicting local 'customs and manners'. It originated in the colonial period, but became a major nationalist genre in Latin American and Caribbean art in the early 1900s

Creole: Initially meant 'locally born' and was used to refer to the white colonial elite and locally born slaves. The term is now used to describe the dialects and syncretic languages of the Caribbean and the syncretic nature of Caribbean culture

Feronier: French for iron worker, used here to refer to the Haitian school of iron sculptors, which is centered in the town of Croix-des-Bouquets

Ganja: Jamaican patois term for marihuana

Grand Maître: Literally 'the Great Master', used to refer to the chief god of the ★Vaudou pantheon

Guajiros: Cuban peasants

Guanin: A gold-copper alloy used by the Caribbean Amerindians, probably imported from South America

Hosay: Festival of Muslim origin practised in the areas of the Caribbean with a strong East Indian presence, particularly Trinidad and Guyana. Takes the form of a procession in which the 'tadjah', an elaborately decorated wood and paper model tomb, is carried around and then cast into the sea at the end of the ceremony

Hounfort: ★Vaudou sanctuary

Houngan: Male ★Vaudou priest

Indigenism: Expression of cultural nationalism whereby indigenous cultural traditions are celebrated and foreign or colonial influences rejected

Ireme: The masqueraders of the ★Abakuá secret society. They wear a costume decorated with fibres, mirrors and cow bells and a pointed hood headdress. Also called Diablito or Little Devil

Island Carib: The Amerindians who lived in the Eastern Caribbean at the time of Columbus' arrival. They resisted European colonization until the end of the 18th century. Small groups survive in Dominica and St Vincent

Jíbaro: Spanish for peasant

Jonkonnu: Jamaican Christmas time masquerade, derived from West African and European masquerade traditions. Similar masquerades exist elsewhere in the Caribbean, primarily in the Bahamas where it is know as ★Junkanoo

Jordanites: Guyanese popular religion, originated in the late 19th century and named after the visionary leader Nathaniel Jordan. Although the Jordanites believe in Jesus Christ, the Old Testament is their main source. They also promote community values and are primarily from the Afro-Guyanese working class

Junkanoo: Major Boxing Day masquerade from the Bahamas. Related to Jamaican ★Jonkonnu

Loa: ★Vaudou divinity or spirit

Lucayans: Bahamian branch of the ★Taíno who greeted Columbus in 1492

Mambises: The peasant rebels in the Cuban Independence Wars of the 19th century

Marielitos: Cubans who came to the USA during the so-called Mariel Boatlift from Cuba in 1980

Maroons: Runaway slaves and their descendants who settled in remote areas of the Caribbean, the Guianas and Brazil. Because of their autonomy, they have contributed greatly to the preservation of African and Amerindian traditions in the Caribbean

Mas: Preferred term for Trinidad carnival, derived from 'masquerade'

Nañigo: A member of the ★Abakuá secret society

Necklacing: Mob execution whereby a car tyre is put around the neck of the victim who is then doused with fuel and burnt. Many ★Tonton Macoutes and other Duvalier collaborators were killed in this manner after the deposition of the Duvalier regime in 1986

Nuyorican: Neologism used to describe a Puerto Rican living in New York

Obeah: Afro-Caribbean sorcery, used for healing and for causing harm

Orisha: *Santería divinity or spirit
Palero: Practitioner of *Palo Monte
Palo Monte: Afro-Cuban religion, predominantly of Kongo origin. Also known as 'regla de Congo'
Papiamentu: The *Creole language of Curaçao and Aruba, combines Spanish, Portuguese, Dutch and West African elements
Phegua: East Indian spring festival, known as Holi in India, when colourful dyes are thrown on participants
Plenas: Puerto Rican popular satirical songs on topical subjects
Poto-Mitan: Centre pole in the main room of the *hounfort, represents the link between the spiritual and the temporal world. Also the name of the art centre established in 1968 by the Haitian artists Tiga (Jean Claude Garoute), Patrick Vilaire and Frido (Wilfrid Austin)
Rara: Haitian carnival, practised throughout Lent and closely associated with *Vaudou
Rastafarianism: Black nationalist religion, emerged in the 1930s in the economically depressed urban and rural areas of Jamaica. Rastafarians regard the Emperor of Ethiopia Haile Selassie I as the black messiah and Ethiopia as the legitimate home of the 'African Diaspora'. Rites and beliefs derive from multiple influences such as Garveyism, the Ethiopian Orthodox Church, Revivalism, Judaism and Hinduism. Characterized by a militant anti-establishment stance, reinforced by the sacramental use of *ganja and the wearing of long matted 'dread locks'
Reggae: Jamaican popular music genre. Originated in the late 1960s, combined *Revivalist and *Rastafarian music traditions with jazz and blues influences. Characterized by heavy four-beat bass rhythm. Brought to international attention in the mid 1970s by Bob Marley, whose work embodies the genre's characteristic socio-political consciousness
Revivalism: Used here as a generic term for the Afro-Jamaican religions that originated in the mid 1800s. Similar to *Vaudou and *Santería, although the Christian elements stem from the non-conformist Christian churches that contributed to the abolition of slavery rather than Roman Catholicism
Santería: Afro-Cuban religion, primarily of Yoruba origin, which has assimilated elements of Roman Catholicism, particularly the cult of the saints. Also known as 'Regla de Ocha'. Similar practices exist in Puerto Rico and the Dominican Republic
Santos: Spanish for 'saints', primarily used to describe the Puerto Rican popular carvings of Roman Catholic saints
Taíno: Preferred term for the Amerindian people, probably of Orinoco origin, who dominated the Greater Antilles at the start of European colonization. Also known as the Island Arawak
Taller: Spanish for workshop or studio
Tassa: Small, portable drum of East Indian origin
Tonton Macoute: The Haitian creole name for the militia established by the dictator François Duvalier, deliberately made to look like the *guédés*, the unruly death spirits of the *Vaudou pantheon
Vaudou: Haitian religion, closely related to Dahomean Vodun and other West African religious practices, combined with elements of Roman Catholicism and, possibly, Amerindian religions. Spirit possession and healing practices are central to the Vaudou rites. Also spelled as 'Vodou', 'Vodun', 'Voudun', 'Vodoun' or 'Voodoo'
Vejigante: Puerto Rican masqueraders, mainly from the city of Ponce, characterized by colourful costumes and horned masks made from coconut shell and papier mâché. The name refers to the water-filled animal bladders carried by the masqueraders. A related tradition exists in the Dominican Republic, primarily in the city of Santiago
Vèvè: Intricate ritual ground drawings of *Vaudou, representing the attributes of a *loa, made from substances such as corn flour or ashes
La Zafra: Spanish for the sugar harvest. 'La Zafra' was a major political rallying cry during the early years of the Cuban Revolution, culminating in 1970 when the Cuban government attempted to produce ten million tons of sugar on the nationalized sugar estates
Zemi: *Taíno divinity or representation of such a divinity

List of Illustrations

Measurements are given in centimetres and inches, height before width

1 Wifredo Lam *The Jungle* 1943. Gouache on paper mounted on canvas 239.4 × 229.9 (94½ × 90½). The Museum of Modern Art, New York. Inter-American Fund. Photograph © 1997 The Museum of Modern Art, New York. © S.D.O. Wifredo Lam, Paris; **2** Bismarck Victoria *Avis Rara* 1981. Tone-coated aluminium, multi-electrode flow unit with neon and mercury, electrified, H 168 (66⅛). Private collection; **3** Rafael Ferrer, a lithograph from the *Island's Tale* series 1974. Lithograph, one in a series of five, 50.8 × 68.6 (20 × 27). Collection El Museo del Barrio, New York. Photo Ken Showell; **4** Eddie Chambers *Untitled* 1994. Courtesy the artist; **5** Isaac M. Belisario *Koo-Koo or Actor Boy* from the *Sketches of Character* series 1837. Lithograph 21.5 × 31 (8½ × 12¼). Courtesy of the National Library of Jamaica, Kingston. Photo NLJ; **6** Jean-Michel Basquiat *Six Crimee* 1982. Acrylic and mixed media on wood, 3 panels, each 182.9 × 121.9 (72 × 48). Museum of Contemporary Art, Los Angeles. The Scott D. F. Spiegel Collection. Photo Paula Goldman. © ADAGP, Paris and DACS, London 1998; **7** Hervé Télémaque *Currents No. 2* 1985. Acrylic on canvas 200 × 310 (78¾ × 122). Collection du FRAC, Martinique. © ADAGP, Paris and DACS, London 1998; **8** Flavio Garciandía, a work from *A Visit to the Tropical Art Museum* series 1994. Installation of paintings of various sizes and objects. Photo Galeria Ramis Barquet, Mexico; **9** Pedro Alvarez *The End of History* from the *Variations on the End of History* series 1994. Oil on canvas, triptych total size 408 × 378 (160⅝ × 148⅞). Private collection; **10** 'Bird Man', found at Carpenter's Mountain, Vere, Jamaica, in 1792. Wood H 89 (35). Copyright British Museum, London; **11** Cotton reliquary *zemi*, Taíno Dominican Republic. Cotton, shell and human skull H 75 (29½). Museo di Antropologia ed Etnografia, Turin; **12** José Nicholás de Escalera *The Holy Trinity* second half of the eighteenth century. Oil on canvas 180 × 203 (70⅞ × 79⅞). Museo Nacional, Havana, Cuba; **13** José Campeche *Portrait of Governor Ustariz c.* 1792. Oil on canvas 62 × 43 (24⅛ × 16⅞). Instituto de Cultura Puertoriqueña, San Juan, Puerto Rico. Courtesy Galeria Botello, Hato Rey, Puerto Rico. Photo John Betancourt; **14** Agostino Brunias *Chatoyer, the Chief of the Black Charaibes, in St Vincent with his Five Wives c.* 1770–80. Engraving 28 × 21.5 (11 × 8½). From the Collection of the Barbados Museum and Historical Society, St Michael; **15** George Robertson *Rio Cobre c.* 1773. Oil on canvas 45.7 × 61 (18 × 24). Institute of Jamaica, Kingston; **16** Numa Desroches *The Palace of Sans Souci* n.d. Gouache on paper 58.5 × 84 (23 × 33⅛). Private collection; **17** Photograph of a 'voodoo shrine' by Sir Harry Johnston, Haiti *c.* 1900. © Royal Geographical Society, London; **18** Anonymous La Mano Poderosa *c.* 1900. Wood H 25.5 (10). Collection Myrna Baéz. Courtesy Galeria Botello, Hato Rey, Puerto Rico. Photo John Betancourt; **19** Víctor Patricio de Landaluze *Epiphany Day in Havana* second half of nineteenth century. Oil on canvas 51 × 61 (20⅛ × 24). Museo Nacional, Havana, Cuba; **20** Víctor Patricio de Landaluze *The Cane Harvest* 1874. Oil on canvas 51 × 61 (20⅛ × 24). Museo Nacional, Havana, Cuba; **21** Paul Gauguin *Fruit Gatherers* 1887. Oil on canvas 89 × 116 (33⅞ × 45⅝). Stedelijk Museum, Amsterdam; **22** Winslow Homer *The Gulf Stream* 1899. Oil on canvas 71.5 × 125 (28⅛ × 49¼). The Metropolitan Museum of Art, New York; **23** Michel-Jean Cazabon *View of Immortelle Tree on Belmont Hill c.* 1850. Watercolour on paper. National Museum and Art Gallery of Trinidad, Port-of-Spain; **24** Henri Cleenewerck *The Yumuri Valley at Dawn* 1865. Oil on canvas 95 × 136.5 (37⅜ × 53¾). Museo Nacional, Havana, Cuba; **25** Guillermo Collazo *The Siesta* 1886. Oil on canvas 65.5 × 83.5 (25¾ × 32⅞). Museo Nacional, Havana, Cuba; **26** Francisco Oller *The Wake* 1893. Oil on canvas 243.8 × 397.5 (96 × 156½). Museo de Historia, Antropología y Arte, Universidad de Puerto Rico, Rio Pedras. Courtesy Galeria Botello, Hato Rey, Puerto Rico. Photo John Betancourt; **27** Víctor Manuel *Gitana Tropical* 1929. Oil on wood 46 × 38 (18⅛ × 15). Museo Nacional, Havana, Cuba; **28** Eduardo Abela *The Triumph of the Rumba c.* 1928. Oil on canvas 65 × 54 (25⅝ × 21¼). Museo Nacional, Havana, Cuba; **29** Antonio Gattorno *Women by the River* 1927. Oil on canvas 193 × 117 (76 × 46⅛). Museo Nacional, Havana, Cuba; **30** Carlos Enríquez *The Abduction of the Mulatas* 1938. Oil on canvas 162.5 × 114.5 (64 × 45). Museo Nacional, Havana, Cuba; **31** Marcelo Pogolotti *Cuban Landscape* 1933. Oil on canvas 73 × 92.5 (28¾ × 36½). Museo Nacional, Havana, Cuba; **32** Fidelio Ponce de León *Tuberculosis* 1934. Oil on canvas 91 × 122 (35⅞ × 48). Museo Nacional, Havana, Cuba; **33** Amelia Peláez *Still Life* 1942. Oil on canvas 75.7 × 72 (29⅞ × 28⅜). Photo courtesy Christie's, New York; **34** René

Portocarrero, a work from the *Interiors from El Cerro* series 1943. Oil on canvas 71 × 57 (28 × 22½). Museo Nacional, Havana, Cuba; **35** Wifredo Lam *The Chair* 1943. Oil on canvas 115 × 81 (45¼ × 31⅞). Museo Nacional, Havana, Cuba. © S.D.O. Wifredo Lam, Paris; **36** Mario Carreño *Afro-Cuban Dance* 1944. Gouache on paper 59.5 × 48.5 (23½ × 19). The Art Museum of the Americas, Washington D.C.; **37** Philomé Obin *Toussaint L'Ouverture in his Camp c.* 1945. Musée d'Art Haitien, Port-au-Prince. © Photo Pablo Butcher; **38** Yoryi Morel *At the Fiesta* 1948. Oil on canvas 82 × 105 (32¼ × 41⅜). Museo Juan José Bellapart, Santo Domingo, Dominican Republic; **39** Jaime Colson *Merengue* 1937. Tempera on board 51 × 67 (20⅛ × 26⅜). Museo Juan José Bellapart, Santo Domingo, Dominican Republic; **40** Eugenio Fernández Granell *Nostalgia of an Indian in Love* 1946. Oil on canvas 40.6 × 33 (16 × 13). Museo Juan José Bellapart, Santo Domingo, Dominican Republic; **41** Ramón Frade *Our Daily Bread c.* 1905. Oil on canvas 127 × 81.5 (50 × 32). Instituto de Cultura Puertoriqueña, San Juan, Puerto Rico. Courtesy Galeria Botello, Hato Rey, Puerto Rico. Photo John Betancourt; **42** Miguel Pou *A Race of Dreamers: Portrait of Ciquí* 1938. Oil on canvas 87 × 71 (34¼ × 28). Museo de Arte de Ponce, Fundación Luis A. Ferre, Ponce, Puerto Rico. Courtesy Galeria Botello, Hato Rey, Puerto Rico. Photo John Betancourt; **43** Edna Manley *Negro Aroused* 1935. Mahogany H 51 (20⅛). National Gallery of Jamaica, Kingston. Photo Maria La Yacona; **44** Edna Manley *Horse of the Morning* 1943. Guatemalan redwood H 129.5 (51). National Gallery of Jamaica, Kingston. Photo Maria La Yacona; **45** Alvin Marriott *Banana Man* 1955. Acrylic on board 81 × 113 (31⅞ × 44½). National Gallery of Jamaica, Kingston. Photo Maria La Yacona; **46** John Dunkley *Banana Plantation c.* 1945. Mixed media on board 89 × 60 (35 × 23⅝). National Gallery of Jamaica, Kingston; **47** Albert Huie *Crop Time* 1955. Acrylic on board 81 × 113 (31⅞ × 44½). National Gallery of Jamaica, Kingston; **48** David Pottinger *Nine Night* 1949. Oil on canvas 75 × 94 (29½ × 37). National Gallery of Jamaica, Kingston; **49** Ronald Moody *Johanaan (Peace)* 1936. Elm H 155 (61). Photo Copyright Tate Gallery, London; **50** Boscoe Holder *Portrait of Louise de Frense Holder* 1938. Oil on board 35.5 × 28 (14 × 11). Collection the artist; **51** Sybil Atteck, a work, *c.* 1950s. Watercolour. National Museum and Art Gallery of Trinidad, Port-of-Spain; **52** Robert Saint-Brice *The Queen Erzulie* 1957. Oil on masonite 76.5 × 61 (30⅛ × 24). Musée d'Art Haitien, Port-au-Prince. © Photo Pablo Butcher; **53** Hector Hyppolite *The Great Master* 1946–48. Oil on cardboard 96 × 65 (37¾ × 25⅝). Musée d'Art Haitien, Port-au-Prince. © Photo Pablo Butcher; **54** Georges Liautaud *Sirène Diamant* n.d. H 45.5 (18). Musée d'Art Haitien, Port-au-Prince. © Photo Pablo Butcher; **55** Préfète Duffaut *Heaven and Earth* 1959. Oil on masonite 90 × 61 (35⅜ × 24). Musée d'Art Haitien, Port-au-Prince; **56** Rigaud Benoit, Philomé Obin and Castera Bazile, *The Nativity*, *The Crucifixion* and *The Ascension*, Cathedral of the Holy Trinity, Port-au-Prince, 1950–51 (detail). Mural in the lower part of the apse; **57, 58** Philomé Obin *Last Supper*, Cathedral of the Holy Trinity, Port-au-Prince, 1950–51 (details). Mural. © Photo Pablo Butcher; **59** Mallica 'Kapo' Reynolds *Revival Goddess Dina* 1968. Lignumvitae wood H 86.5 (34½). National Gallery of Jamaica, Kingston. Photo Jacqueline Gannie; **60** Prospère Pierre-Louis *Spirit* n.d. Oil on canvas 146 × 117 (57½ × 46⅛). Musée d'Art Haitien, Port-au-Prince. © Photo Pablo Butcher; **61** Everald Brown *Ethiopian Apple* 1970. Oil on canvas 65 × 90 (25⅝ × 35⅜). National Gallery of Jamaica, Kingston; **62** Albert Artwell *Judgment Day* 1979. Oil on board 63.5 × 119.5 (25 × 47). Private collection, Kingston. Photo National Gallery of Jamaica, Kingston; **63** Gladwyn Bush *The Judge of Nations* 1989. Oil on canvas 89 × 120 (35 × 47¼). Courtesy the artist and the Cayman National Cultural Foundation. Photo Carib Art Management, Curaçao; **64** Osmond Watson *Peace and Love* 1969. Oil on hardboard 43.2 × 29.2 (17 × 11½). National Gallery of Jamaica, Kingston; **65** Leonard Daley *The Pickpocket* 1984. Mixed media on plywood 99 × 118 (39 × 46½). Private collection, Kingston, Jamaica; **66** Philip Moore *The Cultural Centre* 1996. Acrylic on canvas 117 × 175 (46⅛ × 68⅞). Mervyn Awon Collection, St Michael, Barbados; **67** Gilberto de la Nuez *Memory of the Colonial Past* 1989. Mixed media on linen 40 × 36 (15¾ × 14⅛). Mervyn Awon Collection, St Michael, Barbados; **68** Manuel Mendive *Slave Ship* 1976. Casein and carving on wood 102.5 × 126 (40⅜ × 49⅝). Museo Nacional, Havana, Cuba; **69** Manuel Mendive, live performance at the Havana Biennial, 1997. Photo Pan American Gallery, Dallas; **70** Gaspar Mario Cruz, a mahogany carving, *c.* 1950s. Museo Juan José Bellapart, Santo Domingo, Dominican Republic; **71** Juan Francisco Elso *For América* 1986. Mixed media 150 × 100 × 100 (59 × 39⅜ × 39⅜). Private collection, Mexico; **72** José Bedia *Island Playing at War* 1992. Acrylic on canvas with found objects, diam. 300 (118⅛). Phoenix Art Museum, Arizona. Courtesy of George Adams Gallery, New York; **73** Wendy Nanan, a work from the *Idyllic Marriage* series 1989. National Museum and Art Gallery of Trinidad, Port-of-Spain; **74** René Portocarrero *Little Devil No. 3* from the *Colour of Cuba* series 1962. Oil on canvas 51 × 41 (20⅛ × 16⅛). Museo Nacional, Havana, Cuba; **75** Peter Minshall *ManCrab* from the Trinidad Carnival *The River* 1983. Mobile mixed-media sculpture animated by Peter Samuel and an electric compressor. Photo Noel Norton; **76** Gaston Tabois *John Canoe in Guanaboa Vale* 1962. Oil on hardboard 61 × 76 (24 × 29⅞). National Gallery of Jamaica, Kingston; **77** Brent Malone *Junkanoo Ribbons* 1984. Oil on canvas 84 × 76 (33⅛ × 29⅞). National Gallery of Jamaica, Kingston; **78** Amos Ferguson *Junkanoo Cow Face: Match Me If You Can* 1990. Enamel paint on card 96.3 × 81.8 (38 × 32¼). National Gallery of Art, The Bahamas. Photo courtesy The Pompey Museum of Slavery & Emancipation, The Bahamas; **79** Tam Joseph *Spirit of the Carnival* 1983. Acrylic, gouache and glue on brown paper 182.9 × 162.6 (72 × 64). Collection the artist; **80** Lorenzo Homar, poster for the *5ta Feria de Artesanías de Barranquitas* 1966. Silkscreen 71 × 47 (28 × 18½). Courtesy Galeria Botello, Hato Rey, Puerto Rico. Photo John Betancourt; **81** Rafael Tufiño *Storm* from *Portafolio de Plenas* 1953–55. Linocut 27 × 45.7 (11 × 18). Museo de Arte de Ponce, Fundación Luis A. Ferre, Ponce, Puerto Rico. Courtesy Galeria Botello, Hato Rey, Puerto Rico. Photo John Betancourt; **82** Julio Rosado del Valle *Vejigantes (Carnival Devil)* 1955. Oil on masonite 80.5 × 81 (31¾ × 32). Collection Dr Armaury Rosa. Courtesy Galeria Botello, Hato Rey, Puerto Rico. Photo John Betancourt; **83** Paul Giudicelli *Untitled* 1963. Oil on canvas 98 × 67.5 (38½ × 26½). Museo Juan José Bellapart, Santo Domingo, Dominican Republic; **84** Sandú Darié *Spatial Multivision* 1955. Oil on canvas 136 × 102 (53½ × 40⅛). Museo Nacional, Havana, Cuba; **85** Soucy de Pellerano *Machine Lever Structure* 1990. Iron, aluminium and rubber 225 × 450 × 200 (88⅝ × 177⅛ × 78¾). Museo del Hombre Dominicano, Santo Domingo, Dominican Republic; **86** Luis Martínez Pedro *Territorial Waters No. 14* 1964. Oil on canvas 206 × 190.5 (81 × 75). Museo Nacional, Havana, Cuba; **87** Luis Hernández Cruz *Composition with Ochre Shape* 1976. Acrylic on canvas 127 × 152.5 (50 × 60). Collection the artist; **88** Lope Max Díaz *Ancestral Penetrations* 1982. Acrylic on canvas on wood 121.9 × 182.9 (48 × 72). Collection José Enrique Jimenez. Courtesy Galeria Botello, Hato Rey, Puerto Rico. Photo John Betancourt; **89** Antonio Martorell *Joker* from *The Alacrán Cards Deck* 1968. Silkscreen 6.5 × 8.8 (2½ × 3½). Courtesy the artist; **90** Raúl Martínez *Island 70* 1970. Oil on canvas 200 × 451.5 (78¾ × 177½). Museo Nacional, Havana, Cuba; **91** Edouard Duval-Carrié *J.C. Duvalier as Mad Bride* 1979. Oil on canvas 244 × 107 (96⅛ × 42⅛). Private collection. © Photo Pablo Butcher. © ADAGP, Paris and DACS, London 1998; **92** Raúl Martínez, poster for *Lucia* 1968. Silkscreen 45.5 × 30.5 (18 × 12); **93** Alfredo González Rostgaard, poster for Canción Protesta 1967. Silkscreen 112 × 75.5 (44⅛ × 29¾); **94** Wifredo Lam *The Third World* 1966. Oil on canvas 251 × 300 (98⅞ × 118⅛). Museo Nacional, Havana, Cuba. © S.D.O. Wifredo Lam, Paris; **95** Adigio Benítez *Welders* 1963. Oil on canvas 118 × 80.5 (46½ × 31¾). Museo Nacional, Havana, Cuba; **96** Jasmin Joseph, title unknown, *c.* 1980 (detail). Museé d'Art Haitien, Port-au-Prince. © Photo Pablo Butcher; **97** Bernadette Persaud *A Gentleman at the Gate* 1987. Oil on canvas 165 × 76.2 (65 × 30). Collection the artist; **98** Carl Abrahams *Christ in Rema* 1977. Acrylic on canvas 50 × 37.5 (19⅝ × 14¾). Private collection, Kingston. Photo National Gallery of Jamaica, Kingston/Maria La Yacona; **99** Eugene Hyde *Good Friday* from the *Casualties* series 1978. Mixed media on canvas, 6 panels, each 49.5 × 34 (19½ × 13⅜). National Gallery of Jamaica, Kingston; **100** Isaiah James Boodhoo *Breakdown in Communications* 1970. Oil on canvas 112 × 102 (44⅛ × 40⅛). Mervyn Awon Collection, St Michael, Barbados; **101** Stanley Greaves *The Annunciation* from *There is a Meeting Here Tonight* series 1993. 122 × 108 (48 × 42½). Mervyn Awon Collection, St Michael, Barbados; **102** Louis Laouchez *Free Brothers and Sisters* 1986. Oil on canvas 140 × 160 (55⅛ × 63). Collection du FRAC, Martinique; **103** Serge Hélénon *Sun Inside* 1990. Painted wood 120 × 100 (47¼ × 39⅜). Collection du FRAC, Martinique; **104** LeRoy

Clarke, a work, *c.* 1980. National Museum and Art Gallery of Trinidad, Port-of-Spain; **105** Namba Roy *Jesus and his Mammie* 1956. Ivory H 35.5 (14). Private collection. Photo National Gallery of Jamaica, Kingston; **106** Martín 'Tito' Pérez *Untitled* 1972–74. Acrylic on canvas 91.4 × 61 (36 × 24). El Museo del Barrio, New York. Photo Ken Showell; **107** Luis Cruz Azaceta *Ark* 1994. Acrylic, polaroids, charcoal, shellac on canvas 280.7 × 303.5 (110½ × 119½). Courtesy of George Adams Gallery, New York; **108** Justo Susana, a landscape, *c.* 1970s. Gouache on cardboard. Museo Juan José Bellapart, Santo Domingo, Dominican Republic; **109** Alison Chapman-Andrews *A Last Day in the Country* 1987. Acrylic on canvas 122 × 160 (48 × 63). Courtesy of the Barbados Gallery of Art; **110** Llewellyn Xavier *Red Vermillion* from *Global Council for the Restoration of the Earth's Environment* series 1992. Hand-made paper, nineteenth-century original print, silk-screen printing, collectible card, postage stamp, marbling, ribbons and embossing on paper 76.2 × 56.5 (30 × 22¼). Private collection. Courtesy the artist; **111** Colin Garland *In the Beautiful Caribbean* 1974. Oil on canvas, triptych, each panel 122 × 76 (48 × 29⅞). National Gallery of Jamaica, Kingston; **112** Gesner Armand *Cemetery* n.d. Oil on canvas 104 × 85 (41 × 33½). Musée d'Art Haitien, Port-au-Prince. © Photo Pablo Butcher; **113** Tomás Sánchez *Relations* 1986. Acrylic on canvas 200 × 350 (78¾ × 137¾). Museo Nacional, Havana, Cuba; **114** Winston Patrick *Mahogany Form* 1974. Mahogany H 137 (53⅞). National Gallery of Jamaica, Kingston; **115** Hope Brooks *Nightfall – The City* from *The Nocturne* series No. II 1991. Gouache and modelling paste on canvas, 20 panels, each 40.5 × 45.5 (16 × 18). Collection Bank of Jamaica, Kingston. Photo Kent Reid; **116** Aubrey Williams *Olmec Maya – Night and the Olmec* 1983. Oil on canvas 119 × 178 (46⅞ × 70⅛). Courtesy Eve Williams; **117** Kenwyn Crichlow *Whispers in the Rainforest* 1985. Oil on paint on cotton canvas 121.9 × 101.6 (48 × 40). Collection Mervyn Crichlow; **118** Frank Bowling *Chaguaramusbay* 1989. Acrylic on canvas 182 × 348 (71⅝ × 137). Courtesy the artist; **119** Bendel Hydes *Roncador Cay* 1995. Oil on canvas 188 × 167.6 (74 × 66). Clive and Elaine Harris Collection, Cayman Islands; **120, 121** Ana Mendieta *Guanaroca (First Woman)* and *Guanbancex (Goddess of the Wind)* from the *Rupestrian Sculptures* series 1981. Carved cave walls Jaruco Park, Cuba. Photos by Ana Mendieta, Courtesy of the Estate of Ana Mendieta and Galerie Lelong, New York; **122** Jaime Suárez *The Hour of the Rites* 1992. Ceramic and wood installation 122 × 183 (48 × 72). Courtesy Galeria Botello, Hato Rey, Puerto Rico. Photo John Betancourt; **123** Angel Acosta León *Metamorphosis* 1960. Oil on masonite 193 × 118.7 (76 × 46¾). Photo courtesy Christie's Images, London; **124** Antonia Eiriz *Death at the Ball Game* 1966. Oil on canvas 206 × 342.5 (81⅛ × 134⅞). Museo Nacional, Havana, Cuba; **125** Luce Turnier *Little Girl* 1974. Acrylic on hardboard 97 × 61 (38⅛ × 24). Musée d'Art Haitien, Port-au-Prince. © Photo Pablo Butcher; **126** Barrington Watson *Mother and Child* 1958. Oil on canvas 100.5 × 127 (39½ × 50). National Gallery of Jamaica, Kingston; **127** Myrna Báez *Nude in Front of Mirror* 1980. Acrylic on canvas 83 × 163 (32⅝ × 64⅛). Collection Rosario Ferré. Courtesy Galeria Botello, Hato Rey, Puerto Rico. Photo John Betancourt; **128** Erwin de Vries *Dancing Woman* 1994. Acrylic on canvas 135 × 105 (53⅛ × 41⅜). Collection of the artist. Photo courtesy KIT Press, Amsterdam; **129** Jean-René Jérôme *Woman with Pigeon* 1973. Oil on canvas. Musée d'Art Haitien, Port-au-Prince. © Photo Pablo Butcher; **130** Milton George *The Ascension* 1993. Oil on canvas 178 × 180 (70⅛ × 70⅞). Private collection, Jamaica; **131** José Perdomo *The Magical World of JOP* 1994. Oil, paintstick and wood on canvas 147 × 178 (57⅞ × 70⅛). Courtesy the artist; **132** Ramón Oviedo *Sterile Echo* 1975. Oil on canvas 147.3 × 147.3 (58 × 58). Collection of the Art Museum of the Americas, Washington D.C.; **133** David Boxer, installation view of *The Passage*, 1997. Exhibited at the 6th Havana Biennial. Photo José Figueroa, Vedado, Havana, Cuba; **134** David Boxer *Self-Portrait with Four Brain Patterns* 1988. Mixed media on canvas. Private collection, Kingston. Photo National Gallery of Jamaica, Kingston; **135** Arnaldo Roche Rabell *You Have to Dream in Blue* 1986. Oil on canvas 213 × 152 (83⅞ × 59⅞). Collection John Belk, San Juan, Fundación Luis A. Ferre, Ponce, Puerto Rico. Courtesy Galeria Botello, Hato Rey, Puerto Rico. Photo John Betancourt; **136** José García Cordero *Bilingual Dog* 1993. Acrylic on canvas 80 × 80 (31½ × 31½). Courtesy the artist; **137** Antonio Martorell *Pasaporte Portacasa* 1993. Mixed-media installation. Exhibited at the 5th Havana Biennial, 1994. Courtesy the artist; **138** Ernest Breleur *Untitled* from the *Suture* series 1995. Radiography collage 237 × 190 (93¼ × 74¾). Collection the artist; **139** Carlos Collazo *Self-Portrait I* 1989. Oil and acrylic on linen 127 × 117 (50 × 46⅛). Collection Maud Duquella. Courtesy Galeria Botello, Hato Rey, Puerto Rico. Photo John Betancourt; **140** Keith Morrison *Crabs in a Pot* 1994. Oil on canvas 152.4 × 162.6 (60 × 64). Courtesy the artist; **141** Patrick Vilaire *The Collar* 1996. Wood, iron and bronze. Collection the artist. Photo Jean Guèry; **142** Margaret Chen *Steppe VII* 1982. Mixed media on plywood, triptych 213.5 × 305 (84 × 120). Wallace Campbell Collection, Kingston, Jamaica; **143** Petrona Morrison *Remembrance (124th Street)* 1995. Mixed-media assemblage, H 256.5 (101). Photo Beckit Logan; **144** Roy Lawaetz *Caribbean Myth* 1994. Acrylic and lava sand on canvas 198.1 × 127 (78 × 50). Private collection, Copenhagen. Courtesy the artist; **145** Serge Goudin-Thébia *Sawakou I, II, III* 1990. Mixed-media assemblage 190 × 42 (74¾ × 16½). Collection du FRAC, Martinique; **146** Lázaro Saavedra, installation, 1989. Photo courtesy of Ludwig Forum für Internationale Kunst, Aachen; **147** Tomás Esson *My Homage to Ché* 1987. Oil on canvas 160 × 198 (63 × 78). Collection the artist; **148** Tomás Esson *Portrait No. 10* 1995. Oil on linen 173 × 173 (68 × 68). Collection the artist; **149** Ricardo Rodríguez Brey, installation view of *Untitled* 1992. Exhibited at Document IX, Kassel. Glass, ventilator, blanket, pillow, turkey legs, curtains, wood, pigment, coca-cola, dimensions variable. Collection Museum van Hedenaagse Kunst, Gent. Courtesy Documenta IX, Kassel. Photo Dirk Pauwels, Gent; **150** Kcho *Regatta* 1994. Mixed media, dimensions variable. Photo courtesy Barbara Gladstone Gallery, New York; **151** Fernando Rodríguez *At la Bodeguita* from the *Nuptial Dream* series 1994. Mixed media 85 × 135 × 15 (33½ × 53⅛ × 5⅞). Private collection; **152, 153** Carlos Garaicoa *Rivoli, About the Place from Where the Blood Flows – Cruel Project* 1993–95. Installation consisting of cibachrome colour photograph 48 × 48 (19 × 19) and acrylic watercolour and ink drawing 200 × 154 (78¾ × 60⅝). Courtesy the artist; **154** Los Carpinteros *Havana Country Club* 1994. Oil on canvas on wooden frame 140 × 140 (55⅛ × 55⅛). Collection the artists; **155** Tony Capellán *Organ Theft* 1994. Mixed-media installation 400 × 400 × 200 (157½ × 157½ × 78¾). Courtesy the artist; **156** Belkis Ramírez *In a Plate of Salad* 1993. Mixed-media installation, dimensions variable. Courtesy the artist; **157** Marcos Lora Read *40 Metres of Schengen Space* 1995. Oil drums and salt 0.5 × 1 × 40 m (1'8" × 3'3" × 131'3"). Courtesy the artist. Photo Carlos Rodés; **158** Francisco Cabral *Nuclear Dogs* 1986. Wood, steel, acrylic on wood 244 × 92 × 92 (96⅛ × 36¼ × 36¼). Courtesy the artist; **159** Elvis López *The Six Proposals* from the *Social Critic* series 1993. Acrylic and conté on paper 25 × 30 (9⅞ × 11¾). Courtesy the artist; **160** Hamid Moulferdi *Deforestation* 1992. Mixed media objects on canvas and wood 120 × 120 (47¼ × 47¼). Courtesy the artist; **161** Ras Akyem Ramsay *Blakk King Ascending* 1994. Acrylic on canvas 213 × 137 (84 × 54). Mervyn Awon Collection, St Michael, Barbados; **162** Omari Ra 'African' *The Dick is Killed (from the Opera 'Samedi's Mind Set')* 1993. Mixed media on paper, triptych, left panel 110 × 185 (43⅜ × 72⅞), centre panel 110 × 155 (43⅜ × 61), right panel 110 × 138 (43⅜ × 54⅜). Collection Annemie Maes, Belgium. Photo courtesy Randall Morris; **163** 'Don't Burn Them, Judge Them', street mural, Port-au-Prince, Haiti. © Photo Pablo Butcher; **164** Mario Benjamin *Untitled c.* 1997. Oil on canvas. Musée d'Art Haitien, Port-au-Prince. © Photo Pablo Butcher; **165** María de Mater O'Neill *Self-Portrait VIII* 1988. Mixed media 76 × 62 (30 × 24½). Museo de Arte Contemporaneo de Puerto Rico, Santurce. Courtesy Galeria Botello, Hato Rey, Puerto Rico. Photo John Betancourt; **166** Annalee Davis *My Friend Said I Was Too White* 1989. Linoleum print 71 × 48.5 (28 × 19). Courtesy the artist; **167** Marta María Pérez Bravo *Parallel Cults* 1990. Photograph. Photo Galeria Ramis Barquet, Mexico; **168** Juan Carlos Alom *Untitled* from the *Ablution for the Dark Book* series 1995. Silver gelatin print. Courtesy the artist; **169** Albert Chong *Throne for the Justice* from the *Ancestral Thrones* series 1990. Photograph 94 × 61 (37 × 24). Courtesy the artist; **170** Víctor Vásquez *Prelude* 1994. Photograph and mixed media 122 × 244 (48 × 96⅛). Courtesy the artist; **171** Juan Sánchez, installation view of *New Flag* from the *Rican/Structions* series 1994. El Museo del Barrio, New York, 1994. Photo laser print with collage diptych, total size 231 × 272 (91 × 107⅛). Courtesy the artist. Photo Charles Erikson; **172** Nari Ward *The Happy Smilers: Duty Free Shopping* 1996. Mixed-media installation including firescape, firehose, household objects, salt, speakers, audio recording, aloe vera plant, variable dimensions. Courtesy the artist; **173** Felix de Rooy *Cry Surinam* 1992. Mixed-media sculpture H 110 (43¼). Courtesy the artist; **174** Sonia Boyce *From Tarzan to Rambo: English Born 'Native' Considers Her Relationship to the Constructed/Self Image and Her Roots in Reconstruction* 1987. Photograph and mixed media 124 × 359 (48¼ × 141⅓). Photo Copyright Tate Gallery, London; **175** Keith Piper *Go West Young Man* 1988 (detail). Photo panel 35.5 × 63.5 (14 × 25). Courtesy the artist; **176** Eugene Palmer *Duppy Shadow* 1993. Oil on canvas 213 × 152 (83¾ × 59¾). Wolverhampton Museum and Art Gallery. Courtesy the artist; **177** Marc Latamie *Caldera* 1995. Installation sugar and neon, dimensions variable. Courtesy the artist

Index

Italic numerals refer to plate numbers